He took out his gu[...]d his back against the[...]

No answer.

He waited and pushed the door all the way open.

He waited some more.

No sounds. No movement. Nothing.

Bronson stuck his head in. The first thing he noticed was the overturned lamp, then the pool of blood that had already started to congeal on the floor.

The body lay on the floor, a spilled can of Sprite beside it. The victim's throat had been so severely cut that he'd almost been decapitated. The note rested on top of his stomach.

Bronson bent down and read it:

Harry, Harry, Harry,

Round Three is over and I won again. I can't believe you let another innocent person die.

What's wrong, hot shot? You're beginning to bore me.

--- ★ ---

Previously published Worldwide Mystery title by
L. C. HAYDEN

WHY CASEY HAD TO DIE

WHEN DEATH INTERVENES

L. C. HAYDEN

W🌐RLDWIDE.

TORONTO • NEW YORK • LONDON
AMSTERDAM • PARIS • SYDNEY • HAMBURG
STOCKHOLM • ATHENS • TOKYO • MILAN
MADRID • WARSAW • BUDAPEST • AUCKLAND

F
HAY

To my brother and his wife, Joe "Pete" Amaro and Sarah Amaro, with lots and lots of love.

Recycling programs for this product may not exist in your area.

MW ET

WHEN DEATH INTERVENES

A Worldwide Mystery/January 2012

First published by Five Star

ISBN-13: 978-0-373-26783-5

Printed in U.S.A.

While the authoring process is often a lonely road, the editing process is filled with many off-stage folks. I am forever indebted to all of the Five Star personnel, but especially to Roz Greenberg, Tiffany Schofield, and my editor, Diane Piron-Gelman. A person couldn't possibly have a better editor. This book is a thousand times better because of Diane's dedication. Also a big thanks to Tracey Matthews, who did a tremendous job on my manuscript during the production process.

I'd also like to salute all of the fine folks who allowed me to use their names: Linda Randig, Ellen Biebesheimer, Mike Hoover, Paul McKenzie, Roy E. Kasdorf, Carol Babel, and Belen Oaxaca. Thanks for honoring me. Any similarities between the real person and the character are strictly coincidental.

I would also like to thank my husband, Richard Hayden, for all of his support and encouragement and for doing such a great job at creating and maintaining my website.

I couldn't do it without you, hon.

A huge salute goes to Dick Schwein, retired FBI Special Agent in Charge. Thanks for keeping me straight on all of the police procedures and for answering my many questions. His and Don Moss's critique and comments helped to shape this novel. Thanks, I appreciate you both.

And finally, an extra big hug and kudos goes to all of my readers. Your support and dedication humble me. For your convenience, book club leaders, my website includes a set of questions you can use for your discussion of *When Death Intervenes*.

If you'd like to learn more about me, please visit my website at www.lchayden.com and don't forget to sign my guestbook. I love hearing from you.

ONE

LINDA RANDIG SAT, STARING at the half-empty cup of hot apple cider. She hadn't moved for the last five minutes. She had tried calling her parents, again, and again, but the calls went unanswered. Something had to be wrong.

She took a sip of cider and tried to let her mind relax, tried to stop the worry from eating at her gut. She reached for the telephone handset that had become her constant companion. She punched in the numbers for the hundredth time.

Pick up. Pick up.

Her parents loved their hometown of Two Forks, Wyoming, but they also loved to travel. Had they left town and forgotten to tell her? Even so, that didn't explain why they wouldn't answer the cell. Linda slammed the phone back into its cradle.

She looked up at her husband. "I can't stand this. I'm going over there."

Mitch set down the newspaper and stood up. "I'll go with you." He grabbed the keys to the Mercedes.

As Mitch drove, Linda embraced the silence that surrounded them. His forced smile told her he, too, feared the worst. Linda stared out the side window until Mitch pulled into her parents' sprawling driveway.

The Hummingses lived in a nice, comfortable house, but it didn't match the glamour of Mitch and Linda's luxurious home. "You wait here." Mitch turned off the engine and pocketed the keys. "I'll go in and check."

Linda shook her head. "I'm going with you."

"Linda, please." Mitch reached for her hand.

She opened the car door, pushing back his touch. The walk between the driveway and the door seemed to stretch for miles. Linda handed Mitch her parents' key.

He unlocked the door and looked at his wife. She nodded. He took a deep breath and swung the door open.

"Mom? Dad?" Linda's voice quivered. She worried her lip and listened to the silence. Now she reached for Mitch's hand, it felt good, and together they headed past the living room on toward the dining room, the kitchen, and the utility room. Each place stood neat and empty. The bedroom, she had to check the bedroom.

Linda held her breath as she opened the bedroom door. The king-size bed had been made and only a comb and brush rested on top of the dresser. She moved on to the spare bedroom, the sewing room, and the library. Somewhere around then she noticed that Mitch was no longer following her.

As she stepped into the hallway, she saw her husband approach. The deep crease lines she had noticed in his forehead and around his eyes seemed to have evaporated. "I checked the garage. Their car is gone." He smiled.

Tears danced in Linda's eyes. "They're on vacation, then? They'll remember to call, won't they?"

Mitch nodded and hugged her.

FIVE DAYS LATER, THE RINGING of the doorbell woke Linda from a much-needed nap. She opened the door and when she saw a Wyoming trooper, she knew. She could read it on the young man's face. "Mitch! Get over here. Now." She opened the door wider and the trooper stepped in.

He remained standing, removed his hat, and played with its rim. "David and Irene Hummings—they're your parents?"

Linda nodded and reached for Mitch's hand.

"They were driving up Highway 85, heading away from town. Mr. Hummings…" The trooper cleared his throat. "We believe he fell asleep at the wheel. They went off the road. We estimate—based on the bodies' appearance—the car had been down there for maybe a week."

A week. A fog of sheer, hopeless misery enveloped Linda.

AT THE FUNERAL, LINDA'S thoughts focused on her parents' last days. Had the car trapped them, their injuries, thirst, and hunger being their only constant companions? Had they suffered or had their deaths been instantaneous? The police had conducted a routine investigation, but other than ruling it an accident, they couldn't answer the questions Linda needed to know. The thought tore at her heart.

She looked at her husband, who sat next to her. He provided the strength she lacked and for that, she felt thankful. She took a moment to glance around the funeral home. So many people had attended. Linda's next-door neighbors, Russ and Belen Oaxaca, smiled and waved at her, trying to give her courage. Behind them, Eric stood. His blue eyes had lost their vibrant color, like jars filled with sorrow.

Eric. Linda had thought he wouldn't show up, but he had. She wanted to reach out to him, hold him like she had when he loved her, when he was young. She could almost see him as a child doing what he enjoyed most, swimming in the family pool, splashing and laughing. Linda stood up and he walked away.

Eric. He hadn't spoken to her for six long months. Half a year of silence, and she didn't understand why. What had she done wrong? What had she said that angered him so?

Linda didn't know she was going to cry until she felt the tears gushing down her cheeks. She held her hands over her mouth, trying to stifle racking sobs.

Eric.

A WEEK AGO, LINDA HAD BURIED her parents and today she didn't feel any better than she had back then. She poured herself a cup of hot apple cider and sat in the dining room staring at the cup, letting the drink grow cold.

The doorbell rang. She reached for her cider and took a sip. Its cold taste left a bitter sting in her mouth. She set the cup down and looked at her watch. Mitch had been gone for over two hours.

At first, he hadn't wanted to leave her alone, but she'd insisted he go. She needed time by herself, and she wasn't ready to face her parents' empty home. "My dad has all those ham antennas all over the roof. The house will never sell that way. You've got to go and take them down."

"You're sure?"

Without looking up, she nodded.

He bent down, kissed her forehead, and walked out.

Since then, she'd been sitting, staring at the cider, or standing, looking out the window at the empty pool.

The doorbell rang again.

She looked up toward the front door. The wall between the vestibule and the living room prevented her from seeing outside. Who would be so persistent? What did he want?

He? Eric? Oh, my God, had Eric come to see her? Did he want to talk to her now? Did he love her again? She bolted up, knocking the chair down in her haste to answer the doorbell. She went into the black-and-white-tiled foyer, with its huge chandelier that rained down hundreds of crystal lights. All this beauty—this glamour—surrounded her and she'd give it all away if she could see Eric, or her parents, one more time.

She swung the door open and her heart did a flip-flop. Not Eric. Never Eric and not anyone else. She looked up and down the street. She'd call Eric and leave a voice message telling him if he had come, she had answered the door too late.

She started to close the door, thinking how Eric wouldn't

return this call either, when she caught a glimpse of something that didn't belong. Someone had delivered a large manila envelope to her door. Why did people assume she wanted sympathy cards filled with pictures of her dad and mom—pictures that would only bring her pain?

She set the envelope down on the entryway table and walked back toward the dining room where her cold cider awaited her.

The phone rang. Without thinking, she picked it up. "Hello?"

"The envelope, Mrs. Randig. You need to open it."

A chill went through her body. "What?"

"The envelope. The one you set down on the entry table. You need to open it."

Linda dropped the phone and stifled a scream. She felt as if an entire drum line pounded inside her chest. Someone was watching her. She glanced at the caller I.D. screen—nothing. She dialed star sixty-nine. The call had been blocked.

Her gaze searched every corner of the room. She couldn't see anyone, but that didn't mean she wasn't alone. She ran outside and her cell phone rang. She unhooked it from her belt and looked at the caller I.D. The display read *Unknown Caller*. She flipped the cell open.

"Mrs. Randig, don't be ridiculous." The same voice. "You don't want to attract attention. Get back inside."

Linda gasped.

The caller continued, "Yes, I can see you, but I'm not inside your house. You're perfectly safe there. You need to open that envelope. It'll explain a lot."

Linda stood, trembling, cold in spite of the warm breeze blowing. She stared at the cell. *Call ended,* the digital screen read. Feeling like a zombie, she dragged herself back inside and grabbed the envelope. Her name was printed on it in large, block letters. No other marks offered any hint as to its source. She ripped it open.

It contained three smaller envelopes. One was marked *Open Me First*, another one *Open Me Second*, and the final one *Open Me Last*. She thought about going out of order but decided to follow the sender's instructions.

The first envelope contained a five-by-eight picture. Linda recognized her parents' car. The photographer had snapped the picture after the car had gone off the road and before it hit the bottom. Linda could see her mother's face plastered against the window. Her wide-open eyes revealed the terror she felt. Her mouth gaped grotesquely in a scream that only Linda's father would hear.

"Oh, my God! Oh, my God!" Linda couldn't stop shaking. She unfolded the piece of paper attached to the picture. The laser-printed message on it read:

I pushed your parents' car off the road. It was not an accident.
Don't do anything stupid like going to the police. Take a look at the second envelope.

Trembling hands reached for and opened the second envelope. More pictures. This time, one of Eric as he made his way toward his car. The next one showed one-and-a-half-year-old Brad. How big he'd gotten since she'd last seen him. He stood at the daycare, clutching a ball.

The note read:

Self-explanatory. Cute grandson. You go to the police, they die.
Remember, I'm watching you, and don't try to contact your son again.
Start packing. Two weeks from now, you're going on a trip.
That'll give you plenty of time to take care of matters

*here at home. Take the camper. I'll get back to you with
more instructions before the time is up.
You're now ready to open the last envelope.*

Linda felt as if every nerve in her body would pop. Her
hands shook so much, she dropped the envelope. She retrieved it. She wanted to open it. She didn't want to open it.

What else could this monster do? Who was he? Was it
money he wanted? If so, she gladly would have given it to
him. He didn't have to kill her parents—but he hadn't even
asked.

She drew a deep breath and forced herself to open the last
envelope. No note this time, just a picture.

Mitch. Over two hours ago, he had kissed her and gone to
her parents' house to take down the antennas. He had been
on the roof, but now he lay on the ground, a pool of blood by
his side.

Linda dropped the picture. Her world turned gray, then
pitch-black.

TWO

ONE GOOD THING ABOUT campgrounds, folks always seemed friendly and tended to enjoy shooting the bull with a stranger. While Carol bathed, napped, and read, Harry Bronson decided to see if he could find someone for some stimulating conversation. He stepped out of his motor home and looked around.

He had to admit, South Dakota housed its share of beauty—or at least this part of the state, the area surrounding Custer State Park, did. But beauty didn't captivate him. Work did, but he no longer had that. He'd been given the option to retire or be fired. Bronson felt that hadn't left him with a hell of a lot of choices.

He had put in twenty-eight years as a detective with the Dallas Police Department, and his willingness to sometimes bend the rules had led to his forced retirement, something he couldn't face at the moment.

Best to keep busy. Talk to fellow motor-home owners. Find out how they kept their sanity. Bronson enjoyed traveling, but not the way Carol did.

He stood by his doorway, scoping The Roost Resort campground. No one in sight. Damn. Just his luck. He would at least walk around the campground. As he headed back toward his camper, he spotted a woman sitting on the step of her motor home. Her bent back and her lowered head gave her a look of desperation or loneliness. Bronson would do the neighborly thing.

He got within five feet from her before she noticed him.

"Evenin', ma'am." He offered her his usual warm smile and stood back, giving her space.

She looked up, and Bronson realized she'd been crying. *Tears. I hate tears.* He wished he hadn't approached her, but what could he do now? He took a step forward.

She bolted to her feet. "What do you want?"

Bronson raised his hands as though surrendering. "Whoa. Sorry. I didn't mean to scare you."

"What do you want?" The venom in her voice sent Bronson a warning signal.

"Nothin'. Nothin' at all. I just stopped to introduce myself. Me and the Mrs.—that's Carol—we're right next door. Sorry to have bothered you. I'll leave you alone." He stepped away, aware of her watchful eyes.

Bronson went inside the camper and flopped down on the couch.

Carol set her book down. "What's wrong?"

Bronson told her about their next-door neighbor. Carol got up. "I'll go talk to her. Sounds like she needs some cheering up."

"Don't bother. She's going to bite your head off."

"Maybe not." She bagged some homemade cookies, kissed his lips, and walked out.

Bronson flipped on the TV. *Cops* was on. Great.

FORTY-FIVE MINUTES LATER, Carol returned. "Can you flip three hamburgers?"

Bronson turned the TV off and set the remote down. "Three?"

"We're having company."

"Don't tell me. Not Ms. Grouch next door."

Carol frowned and placed her hands on her hips. "She's not a grouch. She's just a very sad woman. Didn't tell me why and I didn't ask. I sensed she could use a friend and that's all I offered."

Bronson's heart swelled with pride. Carol was definitely a keeper. "I'll go get the grill ready." He stepped out, opened the outside storage, retrieved the barbeque grill, and began to clean it.

"Damn it!" Bronson heard the Grouch say. He snuck a look over. She was attempting to take out the awning, but wasn't having much success. Bronson continued to wipe the grill.

"Damn it!" she repeated.

As he turned on the grill to warm it up, he thought about ignoring her plight, but the gentleman part of him won. "Need some help?" He deliberately stayed still, not yet crossing into her campground area.

She jerked as she turned to stare at Bronson. Her glance slipped away from him and searched the campground. "I could use it."

Bronson ambled over, wondering why she seemed so paranoid. "May I?" He pointed to the awning.

She nodded and stepped away from him.

He loosened the brackets on each pole and flipped the small lever on top of the awning's front. He grabbed the loop and pulled the awning out. "There you are," he said as he raised and locked the poles in place.

She continued to look around the campground. Bronson followed her gaze, but saw nothing out of the ordinary. "They're watching, you know. I'm sure they're watching."

Oh, oh. "Who's watching?"

She turned to face him. She opened her mouth, but nothing came out. Her gaze shifted from motor home to motor home. She bit her lip.

Years of experience had taught Bronson to recognize the warning signals of a person on the run. This lady needed help. His police instincts piqued like a hound on a trail.

"Maybe we should begin by introducing ourselves. My name is Bronson—Harry Bronson, from Texas."

She studied him, as though debating if she could trust him. He smiled and nodded once. She took a deep breath. "I'm Linda Randig from Two Forks, Wyoming. Thanks for your help."

"You're welcome." Good, she'd taken one step toward opening up. A small step, but still a step. Bronson would have to rely on every questioning technique he'd ever learned in his twenty-eight-year career. "So tell me, Linda, who's watchin' you?" He swallowed the urge to ask if she was a certified lunatic.

Her eyes danced with fear as she stifled a cry.

"It's okay. I'm not one of them."

"How do I know that?"

Good question. "The police are usually the good guys."

Linda gasped and took a step back. "You're a policeman?"

"Not anymore. I'm a retired detective from the Dallas Police Department."

"Retired?"

He nodded. "My wife, Carol, I believe she invited you to dine with us. So if you'll excuse me, ma'am, I've got some grillin' to do." He turned and walked away.

"Detective."

Bronson stopped and pivoted.

"I need…" She shrugged. Her eyes narrowed, and Bronson felt his soul scrutinized.

"I feel like drinkin' a good cup of coffee," he said. "You know of a place where we could get one? We'll sit down and talk."

Slowly, she nodded. "I make a great cup of coffee."

Home-brewed coffee, something Carol—an otherwise perfect woman—had never learned to make. Bronson could

almost taste the brew. Like a dog, he felt he would start sali-
vating at any moment. "I accept."

"You wait here." She pointed to the lawn chair by her front
door. "I'll bring the coffee out."

He watched as she stepped into her motor home and closed
the door. He wondered if she would come out again. Bronson
walked to his own site, lowered the heat on the grill, grabbed
a lawn chair and the newspaper, and returned to his neighbor's front door.

He set the chair down, opened the newspaper, and read.
Fifteen minutes later, he folded it and placed it under his
chair. By now other campers had begun to gather in groups
of twos or threes and exchange friendly chatter. Bronson
watched them.

Ten minutes later, he reopened the newspaper and read the
articles that hadn't originally interested him. He read every
headline and skimmed over the comics one more time. He
put the paper away.

Some of the other campers busied themselves by barbe-
quing. He should be doing the same. He picked up the paper
again, sighed, and set it down. He waited some more and
almost fell asleep—or he might have napped, he couldn't tell.
He considered walking away, but Linda seemed so desperate.

The door behind him opened. "You're still here."

"Yes, ma'am." He spoke without turning around. "I'd wait
an eternity for a good cup of coffee."

Linda stepped out, leaving the front door open. Bronson
noticed she hadn't brought the coffee. Damn.

She sat beside him, stared ahead, and remained quiet. So
did Bronson.

Time marched on. The seconds extended into minutes.

"Two Forks, Wyoming—that's where it happened?" Bronson spoke without looking at her.

She nodded.

He focused his attention on the white-to-purple bed of pasqueflowers. He'd read somewhere that South Dakota had adopted this tuliplike blossom as their state flower. "How long ago?"

"A bit over a month."

"Ah." Bronson paused. "What was the first indication you had that something was happenin'?"

"My parents died in a car…accident."

"I'm sorry."

She nodded.

Bronson glanced her way and knew it'd be hard to get her engaged in a conversation again. "Those flowers there." He pointed to the pasqueflowers. "The Indians called them the navel flowers because when they bloom, spring is born."

Linda looked at the flowers. "That's nice."

"Yes, ma'am, it is. Spring is a time of hope and this is spring. Maybe you can tell me about the accident."

Linda's gaze quickly returned to the flowers.

Bronson leaned forward and watched for her reaction. "It wasn't an accident, was it?"

She gasped. "How…how did you know?"

"You paused between *car* and *accident*. That indicates you question it."

She nodded. Then she got up and went back into her camper.

Bronson stood up, folded the paper and his chair, and returned to his own campsite. He got busy grilling three burgers, his mind focused on Linda. He couldn't wait to resume their conversation.

IT BEING NEITHER HOT NOR COLD, Carol chose to eat outside on the camp's picnic table. Bronson covered it with a white-and-red-checkerboard tablecloth.

Throughout the meal, Linda remained quiet and withdrawn. Not that Carol noticed. She chatted away, causing even Linda to smile every so often.

After they finished eating, Carol gathered the paper plates and stood up. "I made a cake for dessert. Lemon—Harry's favorite, but I still have to put on the frosting. You two wait here while I get it ready." Carol hummed as she went back inside.

Bronson leaned back in his seat. "Tell me about the accident."

She looked at him, her eyes piercing his soul. "You know, you remind me of my father."

Great. Linda was older than him. "Your father?"

"Yes. He had a quality about him that made people want to trust him. You have that same characteristic."

"Huh. Thanks, I guess."

Linda's lips barely formed a smile. "Maybe it's not that. Maybe I just desperately need to unload and you're it." She cleared her throat. "You probably think I'm looney tunes."

That thought had entered his mind. He shrugged.

"I brought evidence."

Bronson sat up straighter as she reached into her purse and handed him three pictures. The one of the man lying in a pool of blood captured his interest the most. He looked at her. "Tell me about these pictures."

At first, Linda hesitated and spoke slowly, but the deeper she got into the story, the more she crowded her words. Somewhere during her narration, Bronson retrieved his spiral pocket notebook and jotted down the pertinent information. When she finished, she said, "Please tell me what to do."

"The most obvious thing is to go to the police. I'll go with you."

"No. No police. The man who contacted me, he said…he explicitly said—"

"I know what he said." Bronson had heard it before.

"That's the first thing they always tell you. No police. Of course they don't want you callin' the police. It's to their advantage if you don't call, but years of experience tell me it's the best thing to do."

"No, absolutely not. Promise me you won't contact them."

"They can help."

"No! This is my son's life—my grandson's life—we're talking about." She wagged her index finger in Bronson's face to emphasize the points she made. "I'll do anything to protect them."

Her steady, almost threatening tone told Bronson not to push it. "Anything," she repeated.

Bronson raised his arms as though surrendering. "I understand, and I will abide by your wishes, but if things get out of hand, or if I feel we have no choice but to notify the police, I'll do so. But, if at all possible, I'll let you know ahead of time. Fair enough?"

She frowned. "I still don't like the idea."

"Think about it. If savin' your son's and grandson's lives means police involvement, then that's the way to go. What do you say?"

Linda nodded reluctantly. "Maybe. If it gets to that point, we can talk about it. Right now, I'm so worried about the kids and I can't even warn them."

"I could do that for you."

Linda's eyes lit up. "You will?" She bit her lip. "What if they find out?"

"They?"

"The people watching me."

Oh, that *they*. "They won't. I'll be careful."

"But they're watching me."

"That's right, they're watchin' you, not me. I have more freedom to move around, at least for a little while."

Linda raked her hair with her fingers. "How do I know they're not watching me right now, and they've seen you?"

Bronson scanned the area. Everyone seemed to be minding his own business. "They probably bugged your home. That's how they're able to keep up with you." He pointed to her motor home. "You said they insisted you drive that?"

Her eyes narrowed. She nodded.

"That means it's probably bugged. They didn't want you stayin' at motels where they can't keep track of you. They probably can't see you or hear you right now."

Linda bolted to her feet, her hands folded against her chest. She breathed hard through her mouth. "Oh, God. Oh, God." She stepped away from the camper as though it had the power to attack her. "My camper is bugged?"

Bronson stood up. "I'm assumin' it is. If it's okay with you, ma'am, I'll go and check."

Linda's forehead formed deep furrows. "Yes, of course."

"But first, tell me about the voice on the phone."

She looked at her motor home. "What about the bugs?"

"That's next. First the voice." Bronson retrieved his notebook and pen. "Is it the same one all the time?"

"I think so."

"But you're not sure?"

She shrugged. "It sounds the same, I guess. Only one."

"Anythin' unusual about the voice? High-pitched? Low-pitched? Raspy?"

Linda considered his questions. She shook her head in frustration. "Sorry."

"No problem. Next time he calls, pay close attention. How does he phrase his words? Is there any background noise you can identify? Does he have an accent? Maybe you can leave your cell on speaker mode, and I'll be able to listen."

"I can do that. I'm so damn frightened, I know I won't be able to pay attention to the details you ask for."

"You will, once you're aware of what you're supposed to be listenin' for. I have no doubt in my mind." He smiled.

She almost returned the smile. Bronson felt he'd made progress. "I'm ninety-nine percent sure they placed a bug in your camper. I'm hopin' it's nothin' more than a listenin' device. If they have visual, things will be trickier. Either way, we'll have to explain my presence. After I search the place, I want you to go in there and pretend you're talkin' on the cell. You're going to tell me, your cousin, that you're having problems with the motor home. Maybe the sink isn't drainin' or the stove won't turn on. Somethin'—anythin'. Pause while I supposedly tell you that I'm comin' over. You're goin' to insist that I don't need to come over, just tell you what to do. But of course, I'm goin' to insist on comin' over. Maybe after you 'hang up,' you can cuss and say you hope I don't blow everythin' for you. Think you can do that?" He stood up, headed for her camper, and studied it.

She followed his glance. "Yeah, I've done a bit of acting in my life. I can handle that. Are you searching for a transmitter?"

"Sort of. I'm really lookin' for a trackin' device."

"A what?"

"It's a little piece of equipment that enables them to track you." He pointed to the black Mercedes that Linda towed behind her camper. "Is that your car?"

She nodded.

He headed toward it. She followed him. "Chances are they're using a trackin' device on the car. If you were to bolt in a hurry, you'd take the car and ditch the camper." Bronson ran his hand under the car's front wheel well. Nothing. He moved to the back, did the same, and stopped.

"You found it." Her tone implied a statement, not a question.

Bronson nodded.

"Aren't you going to take it off?"

"And let them know we're on to them? We'll leave it there until we need to remove it." He signaled for her to join him.

"Feel here for the small-type box thing."

She reached under the car and felt around. "I feel it."

"Good. Now you know where it is. It's magnetic. All you'll have to do is pull it out."

"I don't like having it on my car."

"Not much we can do about that. Once it's gone, they'll know we're on to them. We don't want that. Let them think we're oblivious."

She frowned but agreed.

Bronson looked at his own campsite and spotted Carol coming out. "Let's have some dessert, then I'll search the camper."

THREE

BRONSON ENTERED LINDA'S CAMPER and stood perfectly still staring at each item, corner, nook, and shelf. He studied the curtains, the driving compartment, the TV, and the DVD player. His mind told him no good hiding places existed for a camera, but still he checked once again.

Finally convinced that no one watched him, he felt free to move around and check for the audio bug. If he were to plant one, he'd want it centrally located in an area that would pick up a conversation from either end of the camper. That meant it would have to be placed on the dinette, the refrigerator, or the range areas. The dinette offered greater possibilities. He bent down and looked under the table. Nothing. He felt around. His fingers found a bump that shouldn't have been there. The device had been attached to the underside of the table, next to the wall. The bug had been painted to match the wallpaper and blend with the table, a professional job. No wonder he hadn't seen it at first.

Bronson spent a few more minutes looking for a backup, but just as he expected, he came up empty-handed. He stepped outside and joined Linda.

She looked up at him. "Well?"

"Under the dinette, there's a listenin' bug." He didn't tell her that listening devices similar to hers had a range of no more than one or two miles. If they were listening, as he suspected they were, they couldn't be more than two miles away from her at all times. He pulled up the lawn chair and sat down.

"The bug, it's still there?"

Bronson nodded.

"I hate that."

Bronson couldn't blame her. He hated it, too. "I realize that, but there's not much we can do."

Linda nodded and frowned. "What now?"

Bronson pointed to her car. "Let's go for a ride."

"A ride? Why? Where to?"

"It doesn't matter. The neighborhood store would be fine. We're almost out of milk, but the main reason we're going is to see if we're followed."

Linda gasped and placed her hands on her chest. "Do you think they're watching us now?"

"There's only one way to tell. Let's go for a spin."

Linda stood up, went inside the camper, retrieved her purse, and closed the door behind her. "Ready."

Bronson nodded and followed her to the Mercedes. "Mind if I drive? This way I'll be able to use all the mirrors to make any pursuer." He failed to mention that he'd never driven such a fancy car and wondered what it would feel like.

She handed him the keys and Bronson beamed. As they headed toward the car, he memorized all the vehicles at The Roost Resort. He drove slowly out of the campground. His gaze focused, not on the road, but on any movement behind him. He didn't see anyone jump into a car. He made a right turn onto the main street and kept the needle of the speedometer steady at thirty-five, not so fast that he wouldn't be able to spot anyone following them, but not so slow as to arouse their suspicions.

He drove for over a mile, and all the drivers who surrounded him seemed to have their own agenda. Bronson made a right turn. Not a single car behind them turned. He slowed down, giving any pursuer a chance to catch up. No one did.

Bronson made another turn, this time to his left. Still, no one followed. "Where's the store?"

Linda looked at him.

"I wasn't kiddin' about needin' milk."

"It's about four blocks from here, I think. Just keep heading straight."

They took a couple of wrong turns, found it, and Bronson parked at the back of the lot. He looked around as he walked in, and realized that this store, like all other grocery chains, kept the milk on the back wall so that customers had to walk through the store in order to purchase the milk. Bronson wandered around the front shelves pretending to look for something. No one seemed to pay him any attention. He headed toward the back, got a gallon of low-fat milk, paid for it, and headed back to the car.

No one followed them out. This time, Bronson headed directly back to The Roost Resort. Once there, Linda turned to look at him. "Satisfied?"

Bronson nodded. "Unless they're exceptionally good, no one's following us."

"That's always good to know." Linda locked the car and headed for the camper. "What happens next?"

"I want you to go in and make that call I told you about. In about half an hour, I'll knock on your door. You'll greet me as though it's the first time you've seen me since the funeral. At this point, we're assumin' we're not being watched."

"Is that safe?"

"I reckon so."

She stood up and made a movement toward the motor home, but stopped. "What should I call you?"

"Bronson. Better stick to my real name so as not to cause any slip-ups later."

Linda nodded. "I insist on paying you for your help."

"Fine. We can discuss the details later."

"Whatever you ask for, I'll double it as long as neither Eric nor Brad gets hurt. That's the only way I'll accept your help."

No problem with that. Bronson liked money. He nodded.

Linda mouthed a "thank you," turned, and went inside, closing the door behind her.

Bronson headed back to his own camper, his mind focused on a slice of cake. Maybe he could talk Carol into also letting him drink a cup of coffee. He felt snack pangs stir within him.

Much to his surprise, he found the camper full of women. Soon as Carol spotted him, she made her way toward him. "There you are. Come in and say hi to my friends. These are the ladies from the Badger Society. Badger Clark was South Dakota's first poet laureate, and he lived right here in the park. Ladies, you remember my husband, Harry Bronson."

"Ladies." Bronson tilted his head as though saluting them.

A murmur of "hi's" followed.

Carol wrapped her hands around her husband's arm and leaned toward him. "They're taking some of his poems and dramatizing them."

"I remember. That's the reason we came here."

Carol nodded. "But they're a little bit behind schedule, and we'll have to extend our time here. You don't mind, do you?"

"How much longer are we going to be stayin' here?"

"Just two more days, so we'll be here a total of ten days."

"How about Little Carol? We told her we'd visit her as soon as this was over."

"And we will, just two days later. That's okay, isn't it?" She looked at him through wide-open eyes, reminding Bronson of the child still in her.

When she did that, Bronson couldn't resist. He'd lasso the moon and hand it to her if at all possible. "Sure, why not? We're not in a hurry. I'll call Little Carol and let her know not to expect us for at least ten more days. We'll stay here until you're finished."

The ladies clapped and cheered.

"Told you I had the best husband in the world." She leaned and kissed his lips.

More clapping and cheering—and perhaps some off-color remarks—followed that episode. At least Bronson assumed that, based on the giggles that escaped some of the ladies.

He took a step backward. "I'll leave you to your preparations. I saw a couple of guys out there. I think I'll go introduce myself." His lips brushed Carol's forehead. He winked at her and stepped out.

So much for that slice of cake. On the other hand, he'd be able to enjoy a cup of coffee without Carol constantly reminding him that drinking so much coffee would harm him.

FOUR

AT THE ROOST RESORT's office, Bronson headed straight for the coffee urn and poured himself a cup. He added two spoonfuls of sugar and lots of cream. He paid, stepped outside, found a picnic bench that faced the campground, sat down, and enjoyed his drink. As he did, he took careful note of each camper and its tow vehicle. He studied the people around him and wrote in his notebook, *Campground made up of mostly elderly people. None look particularly threatening.* He returned the notebook to his shirt pocket and called his daughter. They talked for over half an hour and Bronson savored each second. Afterward, he knocked on Linda's door.

She swung the door open. "Hi. Thank you for coming on such short notice. It's good to see you. It's been a long time. Come in, come in."

Bronson retrieved his notepad and wrote, *Don't talk so loud. Use natural voice. Don't want to rouse their suspicions.*

She nodded.

"It's good to see you, too. You're lookin' well. I'm so sorry about Uncle Dave's and Aunt Irene's accident. Then your husband. Poor Mitch. I'm so sorry. Are you doin' okay?"

"I'm hanging in there, best I can. That's why I left town. Had to get away."

"I understand."

Linda looked toward the dinette. She opened her mouth to say something, but Bronson waved his hands and shook his head. "You said you were havin' problems with the camper. What can I do for you?"

"It's the toilet. It's not flushing properly."

He looked at her.

She shrugged.

"Let's go take a look." Bronson wrote down, *Do you have the note with the instructions that you're supposed to follow?*

She shook her head and made the symbol for a phone.

Bronson banged on the toilet. "Nothin' wrong at this end. Must be your connection outside. Let's take a look."

They stepped outside and walked over to the sewer connection. "So what did the instructions tell you?"

"No police. No contacting Eric."

Bronson leaned on the camper, scanning the area. "Besides that?"

"I'm supposed to drive the camper to Minneapolis. I'll receive further instructions prior to reaching there."

"Why Minneapolis?"

Linda shrugged. "I've asked myself the same question. All I can think of is that I have an uncle there, my father's brother, Uncle Phillip."

"Why would they want you to go see him?"

"I didn't say I was supposed to go see him. All I said is that I'm supposed to go to Minneapolis and I don't know why. It doesn't make any sense."

"Tell me about this Uncle Phillip."

"He's the most loving, generous man who's ever walked this earth. We were just there, Mitch and me, a few weeks before my parents' accident."

"Anything unusual happen while you were there? Anybody make any remarks that raised an eyebrow or sent a warnin' signal?"

"No, nothing like that. We had a very nice visit. We always do."

From where he stood, Bronson hadn't spotted anything

unusual. He moved so he could scan the area behind him. "Have you seen your uncle since then?"

"Yes, he came to my parents' funeral. He stayed with us and left two days later. Then he returned for Mitch's funeral. Only stayed a day, though."

"He lives alone, does he?"

Linda nodded. "His wife—Aunt Brenda—died about two years ago."

"He's still workin'?"

A cool breeze blew and Linda wrapped her arms around herself. "Yeah."

Lucky dog.

"If you can call what he does work." Linda smiled.

"Meanin'?"

"He creates computer games. He sits in front of a computer all day long and creates all these games."

By now Bronson had reassured himself that no one watched them. He relaxed. "Interestin'."

"Yes, he is. He's fascinating, he's kind, he's still a child, he's…he's exactly what every kid dreams of having when they're told they have an uncle."

"Makes me wish I had an uncle like that." Bronson looked down at the sewer connection. "I think we've been here long enough to fix the problem. Once we're back inside, I want you to thank me for helpin' you."

Linda nodded.

"Anythin' else you can tell me about the instructions?"

"Nothing I can think of."

"In that case, let's head inside."

Once inside, Linda said, "Thank you very much for your help. I don't know what I would have done if you hadn't come over. Do I owe you anything?"

Bronson sat down on the couch. "Depends."

"On what?" She sat across from him in the single recliner.

"Which way you're headed."

Linda's eyes widened in amazement. Bronson mouthed the word *Minneapolis*. She said, "I'm heading to Minneapolis."

"Yeah? I need to go to St. Paul. Maybe we can hook up over there and have dinner."

Again, she looked at Bronson as though asking, *What are you doing?*

"So can we?" he repeated.

"I...I don't know."

"It's not that hard. A simple yes or no. We're both goin' to be there. Maybe I can even save on motel bills. I can stay here in your camper. You've got plenty of room. We can have our meals together—my treat. Won't that be fun?"

"I suppose so, maybe."

"Good. When I get there, I'll contact you." He stood up. "First thing tomorrow, I'll go to the hardware store and get the part I need to finish fixin' your sewer connection. If that's not done, it's going to need fixin' again. I'll come in sometime tomorrow to finish the job. Then you'll be set to go."

"I'll wait for you to tell me when it's safe to leave."

"Sounds like a plan." He signaled for her to follow him outside. "Now me and my couch got a date with the TV. See you tomorrow."

"I'll walk you to your car," she said. Once outside, she added, "What was all that about?"

"Not too sure I want you in Minneapolis by yourself, and I just bought us an extra day. Tomorrow, I plan to visit your son and warn him. Maybe set up some security around him. They'll need to be paid, though."

"Money is the only thing I don't have to worry about."

They walked toward the side of the camper and Bronson glanced at his own. He could hear laughter all the way out here. Shiiit. All the women were still there. "Would you mind tellin' me what Mitch did for a livin'?"

"We each have—had—" she paused, closed her eyes, and swallowed hard "—family money, but he also earned quite a bit. For over thirty years he worked at McGory and Stein Pharmaceutical Research Center and Lab. He invested most of his salary. He knew a lot about bonds, stocks, and those kinds of things."

"Did he talk about his job?"

"I know that sometime close to retirement, my husband and a couple of other researchers were working on some kind of wonder cream. Supposedly, this was the real thing. Guaranteed to make your skin young again—that sort of thing."

Bronson retrieved his notebook and jotted down the information. "What happened to this cream?"

"Nothing that I know of. Mitch retired and the others continued with the research. They've been working on that for about three, four years. Will probably work on it for that many more years before the company comes out with their new product. And then it'll compete with all the other ones already out there." She folded her arms and leaned against the camper.

"The stock and bonds—they're still there?"

Linda flashed him a quizzical look. "The money is intact. Why do you ask?"

"I'm just tryin' to get familiar with the case. If you think of anythin' you think I should know, please get in touch right away."

She nodded and headed back inside.

Bronson drew in a deep breath as he worked his way toward his motor home. Laughter still rang in the air. Damn. He braced himself and stepped inside. His gaze automatically focused on the two untouched pies, the tray partially filled with fresh vegetables and a dip, a half-eaten chocolate cake, a basket filled with a variety of cookies, cans of soda, and—bless them—a large coffee urn.

"Where have you been?" Carol asked. "We saved you some snacks." She pointed to the food. "Eat."

First thing he did was reach for the coffee. Carol flashed him a disapproving frown.

Bronson ignored it.

FIVE

BRONSON LEANED BACK on the dinette bench and sipped his coffee. Seven minutes past seven and Carol had not yet awakened. No wonder. She had stayed up with her friends until past midnight. Bad thing about that was that he had also been forced to stay up.

He picked up the newspaper and read the leading paragraph—for the third time. Still didn't make any sense. Not the paper's fault, but his. Soon as Carol got up, he'd have to tell her about Linda. Carol would be furious that he had gotten involved, but it hadn't been his fault. Not that it mattered. Carol would be disappointed, and that was the part that bothered him.

Behind him, he heard Carol stir. He braced himself. How could he tell her that today he planned to drive to Rapid City and talk to Linda's son, and provide protection for him and his kid? Bronson could have called the police or simply walked away. But that went against his nature. Would Carol understand that?

"Why the big frown?"

Bronson looked up to see Carol looking down at him and smiling. He opened his arms and drew her in. God, he never wanted to hurt this woman.

"I'm meeting the girls at eight." Carol drew away from her husband's embrace. "Have you called Little Carol to let her know we'll be arriving later than expected?"

He nodded.

Carol wrapped her hands around her husband's. "This

is something I really want to do. It's silly, I know, but I've always had this childhood dream of being onstage. This is my one and only chance. Silly, huh?" She looked away.

Bronson's heart swelled with love. Carol looked so vulnerable, so embarrassed. "Sweetheart, we all have secret dreams. I'm glad you're able to live yours."

Carol's eyebrows arched. "Really? You don't mind?"

Bronson smiled and shook his head. "Go for it."

She threw her arms around his neck and gave him a big kiss, then stepped back. "I'm running late. We're going to be busy all day today and tomorrow. I probably won't be home until nine or ten o'clock tonight. That's okay, right?"

You betcha. "I don't mind at all. You go on and have a good time."

She kissed him. "That's why I love you so much."

He patted her behind. "Go take your shower before you're late."

She headed toward the bathroom, but stopped. "What will you do all day long?"

"Don't worry about me. I'll find something to do. I hear there's a pretty good geology museum in Rapid City. I like that stuff. You don't. Think I'll drive up there."

"Go for it."

You bet I will. He sipped his coffee and smiled.

As BRONSON DROVE UP Highway 16 heading toward Rapid City, he reached for his cell and dialed Michael Hoover's number. Back in Dallas when they were both detectives, Hoover's desk had been two away from Bronson's. Hoover still carried the detective title. The sting pierced Bronson's heart.

Bronson expected to hear *Homicide, Hoover speaking.* Instead, Hoover said, "Bronson, don't tell me you've got yourself involved in someone else's problem again."

"Hi to you, too."

"You're doing it again."

"Doing what?"

"Avoiding answering my question."

"Can't a guy call just to say hi to his buddy?"

"Not if that guy is named Bronson. What's up?"

Bronson drove past Crazy Horse Monument, a carving-in-progress similar to Mount Rushmore. Some individual had taken upon himself to carve the mountain into a giant statue of Crazy Horse riding his horse and pointing. Bronson made a mental note to bring Carol to this monument honoring the Indians. That'd be something she'd enjoy. Besides, its snack bar served buffalo burgers, something both of them wanted to try.

"Bronson? You there?"

That brought his mind back to the reason he had called his once-upon-a-time partner. "I need a contact in Rapid City, South Dakota."

"What kind of contact?"

"There's two people in Rapid City whose lives may be in danger—and one is still an infant."

"Geesh, Bronson. What have you got yourself into now?"

Bronson briefly explained. When he'd finished, Hoover said, "Talk about a cross to bear. That poor lady. Her entire world has either collapsed on top of her, or she's created some kind of soap opera world to live in."

"I thought so, too, at the beginning. Then she showed me those photos, and I found her place and car had been bugged. Turned me into a believer. Think you can help?"

"Depends. What do you want?"

"I'm looking for someone who can provide protection. Bodyguards for Eric and his son."

"Geesh, Bronson. What do you think I am? Do you think I can just push a button and get you connected to anybody in the world?"

"Exactly."

A small pause followed. Bronson could almost see Hoover thumbing through his index file, searching for a contact. "This'll take longer than I thought. Give me a few minutes. I need to make a couple of calls before I get back to you. I assume this is a paying job?"

"You assume right. Talked to Linda last night. Seems she's loaded. Money is no object to her. They'll be paid and paid well."

"Good. That'll make it easier to find someone."

"Thanks, buddy. I owe you."

"Exactly," Hoover said, and hung up.

Bronson smiled and put the phone away. He turned his attention to his driving and the surrounding scenery. The vast number of ponderosa pines that surrounded him made him suspect that this was the dominant tree in the Black Hills area. He liked ponderosa pines.

FINDING ERIC RANDIG PROVED to be a snap. Linda had given him excellent directions. A long, sweeping driveway led to the old, wooden house. Bronson pulled in, parked, got out, and rang the doorbell.

A tall, lean man in his mid-to-late twenties opened the door.

Bronson recognized him from Linda's picture. "Yeah?"

"Eric Randig?"

"What if I am?"

"I'd like to talk to you."

"About?"

"It's a delicate matter. Is there someplace we can talk in private?"

Eric looked around. "Looks pretty private to me."

He had a point. Bronson gestured toward the porch swing. "Mind if we sit down? Out here would be fine."

Eric stared at him through inquisitive, blue eyes. He stepped out and closed the door behind him. He walked quietly to the swing, thrusting his head up as though stalking prey. Bronson followed him and they both sat.

"What's this about?"

"My name is Harry Bronson and your mom sent me."

Eric bolted up. "I want nothing to do with her."

"Wait! This involves your son—and you."

"I don't need or want her money." He started to walk away.

"This has nothin' to do with money." Or at least he assumed so.

Eric stopped but did not sit.

Bronson stood up. "Someone wants somethin' from your mom and is willin' to kill to get it."

Something flashed through Eric's eyes, but before Bronson could pinpoint it, it vanished. "That's not my problem, is it?"

"It is, because the ones who were threatened were you and your son." Bronson paused. "What about Brad's mother?"

Eric cast him a long, hard look. "If it's any of your business, Nancy walked out on me and Brad shortly after giving birth. I don't know where she is and I don't care. Anything else you need to tell me?"

"Right now your mother is followin' this man's instructions to the letter in order to protect you and your son."

Eric's eyes hardened. He looked like a demolition expert eyeing a deserted building. "My mother is a liar and likes to exaggerate. She's a drama queen and like I told you before, I want nothing to do with her or her money."

"Would you have any objections if I provided you with protection—just in case?"

Eric's expression didn't change, but his eyebrows twitched. "You're a cop?"

"Retired, detective."

"So she called the police even though...?" He wet his lips.

"Does that bother you? Is there somethin' you don't want the police to know?"

Eric attempted a smile, but it came out as trembling lips. "I couldn't care less." He turned and walked away.

Bronson said, "About the protection..."

Eric paused and faced him. "If any of your men come near me, I'll sue your ass off. Leave us alone." He walked to the door, reached for the doorknob, and paused. "Wait. On second thought... They'll know what's... I mean, they could tell me... Do as you please."

Bronson watched Eric open the door and close it behind him. The sense of hardness about him bothered Bronson. He recorded Eric's reaction in his notebook and wondered what game he had chosen to play.

SIX

BRONSON SPENT THE NEXT two hours at the Museum of Geology. He had told Carol he'd be going there, and he wasn't about to lie to her. As he admired the astonishing array of fossils, minerals, and rocks, he wished Carol was with him, but this, she wouldn't have enjoyed.

He concentrated on the two spectacular marine reptiles that dominated the central exhibit hall and for the moment, his thoughts wandered away from Linda Randig and her problems. When he finished with the museum, he strolled toward the car. He sat behind the wheel, tapped it, and looked at his watch. He considered eating, or better yet, drinking a cup of coffee. After all, he had plenty of time.

His cell rang. He glanced at the caller I.D. Hoover had come through. The contacts turned out to be two retired policemen, both in good shape and eager to work again.

Bronson called them and arranged to meet them at a local diner. Thirty minutes later, he sat staring at the two men he was about to hire, and savoring the aroma of the warm cup of coffee in front of him. "I'm assumin' both of you have surveillance experience."

The taller of the two, a sixty-year-old with bushy white hair who'd introduced himself as Jay Pilot, nodded. "Yeah, we both do, and it's boring as hell."

Bronson smiled. He had used the dead hours of surveillance to write a book. During twenty-eight years on the police force, he had managed to write a bit over one chapter—a darn good chapter even if it was only four pages long. He looked at both men and said, "Then you know I'm not offering you a picnic."

Pilot raked his white hair with his fingers and looked at his friend, Pete Acevedo. They exchanged amused looks. "Oh, yeah, but you know how that goes," Pete said. "Living on a retirement income is for the birds. I hate it. I need the money. What are the specifics?"

Bronson briefed them on the few skimpy details he had. When he finished, he said, "The main thing to remember is to keep your eyes peeled for any suspicious characters." He cringed inwardly as the words left his mouth. He sounded like a cliché. He needed to get in with some hip people. Yeah, fat chance. He cleared his throat. "Call the police if you get the smallest inclination that someone plans to harm either the baby or his dad." He sipped his coffee. He could almost hear Carol's warning reproach. He hated that. He set the cup down. This would have to be a one-cup-of-coffee meeting. "One more thing, I've got the feelin' Eric knows somethin' or is involved somehow. If he does anythin' suspicious, give me a call."

Pete leaned forward, paying close attention. "Wait. I'm confused. Is this the same Eric we're supposed to be protecting?"

Bronson nodded.

"And he's the old lady's son."

"He is."

Pete frowned and shook his head. "Is this a messed-up family?"

"Most of them are." Bronson drank the last of his coffee and longingly looked at the waitress for some more.

IF BRONSON DROVE TWENTY-TWO miles farther, he'd reach Sturgis, Little Carol's hometown. He smiled at the name. "Little" Carol had turned twenty-five this past month—not so little anymore. He had to acknowledge her as a married, full-grown woman. That image conflicted with his memories of her as Daddy's little girl. Not that he'd been there all the time while those memories should have been created. He had tried. He had wanted to be the ideal dad, but his job had often interfered, keeping him away for days at a time.

Now Little Carol had become Mrs. Carol Babel, wife to Jim Babel—the Slug with a capital S. All he cared about were his motorcycles, his friends, and partying all the time. He had even dragged her to live in the God-forsaken town of Sturgis, home of the famous Sturgis Motorcycle Rally. This Jim Babel—definitely not family material, not someone Bronson would have chosen for his little girl. Worst of all, the blame fell on Bronson's shoulders. He hadn't been there to advise her.

But now he had time. He'd drop in unexpectedly—sort of. She knew her mom and he were in the area and would be stopping by for a visit, but she wouldn't be expecting him today, and especially him alone. He'd pick her up and take her out to a movie, dinner, and ice cream afterward. Something he should have done a long time ago.

Half an hour later, he pulled into the Babels' driveway. Pretty little house, he had to admit. Nestled in a neighborhood lined with ponderosa pines, the house seemed to come out of a picture postcard depicting an older time when life and laughter thrived—a simpler time, a better time.

Not what Bronson had expected. He rang the doorbell.

"Daddy!" Little Carol's voice vibrated with enthusiasm even before she opened the door all the way.

Daddy. She had called him *daddy,* not *dad*. Bronson's heart melted. He could make up for lost time. He embraced her and felt the years fade away. Little Carol, Daddy's girl. She pulled away.

"I thought you said you wouldn't be here for several days." She looked around. "Where's Mom?"

"She's back at The Roost Resort, still involved with that show."

"I'm glad she's doing something she enjoys." She looked around her father's massive body. "But she will be joining us, right?"

Bronson detected the edge of panic in his daughter's voice. "Of course, but not today." He stepped inside. "Thought maybe you and I—we could go out. How about it?" He stopped.

"Go out, Dad? What are you talking…about?" She followed his gaze.

The opened closet door revealed stacked suitcases. "Somebody goin' somewhere?"

"Me, Dad. I knew you and Mom were coming over one of these days. So I packed. I thought maybe as soon as you all got here, I'd jump in the camper and you'd take me away."

"Take you away? Where?"

"Anywhere. I don't care. I need to get away."

"What about—?"

"He's a slug—as you so appropriately call him."

Her words startled him. He had thought it, but he had never voiced his opinion. "I—"

"It's okay. I know how you feel. Now let's get out of here before he returns."

Bronson reached down for a suitcase and stopped. "Why are you leavin' him? Is he abusin' you? Doing drugs? Alcohol?"

"No, Dad. We just don't get along anymore. His interests are different than mine. Now let's go before he comes home."

Bronson grabbed two suitcases and headed for the car.

"Wait. I've changed my mind."

Bronson stopped. Did this mean she'd give the Slug a

second chance? If she wasn't leaving, maybe they could still do dinner and a movie. That'd be good.

"Put the suitcases in my car. I'll follow you back to The Roost Resort. I'm not going to leave him my car. Can't wait to see Mom and talk to her."

"Oh." Not only were they not going to spend some quality time together, they wouldn't be driving back together. Bronson put the suitcases in her car, jumped into his own, and drove off. He checked his rearview mirror to be sure Little Carol followed him.

SEVEN

DOC PONCE STARED AT THE phone and bit his lip. He had to make the call, but the rising bile in his esophagus prevented him from doing much of anything. He should have never gotten involved, but the medical bills gnawed at him, a little at a time until there was nothing left.

It had been such a simple plan. He had never meant for anyone to get hurt and especially poor Mitch and his parents-in-law. Innocent bystanders. All dead and their blood stained his hands. Doc Ponce plastered his hands to his face and cried.

After a few moments he got hold of himself. He walked to the bathroom, splashed cold water on his face, and stared at the image in the mirror. These past few days, he had aged. He looked worn out and fragile, but at least he was alive. He had learned the game and knew how to play it well.

The phone in his office beckoned him. Reluctantly, he picked up the receiver and punched the appropriate numbers.

"This better be damn important," said the voice at the other end. "I told you not to call me."

"I know, but I felt you'd want to know what I have to tell you."

The silence between them lingered, smothering Doc Ponce. He cleared his throat and continued. "There's been a small delay."

"There's no such thing as a small delay. Time is of the essence here. I thought you understood that."

"I do, but it couldn't be helped."

"Everything can be helped. That's why I hired you. Explain yourself."

"Something went wrong with the camper. Linda called her cousin, Harry Bronson, to fix it. He's in the process of doing that."

"When do they expect the camper to be ready?"

"They're talking about maybe tomorrow." He paused. "There's more." He waited for a response. None came. He wondered why he should have expected one. This man reminded him of a mighty chief who crossed his arms and listened, but never commented. Maybe he should start calling him Chief. Doc Ponce smiled at that, and then realized Chief was still waiting. Doc Ponce quickly added, "Seems Bronson is also heading for the Twin Cities. To save money, he suggested staying with Linda in her camper."

"That won't do."

"I figured as much.'

"Then take care of it."

The line went dead.

Doc Ponce didn't like too many people, but he especially disliked Benjamin Carrier. Today, unfortunately, he'd have to deal with him. He didn't have a choice. He flipped open his cell and punched in the numbers.

"Yes?"

"There's a man by the name of Harry Bronson. He might show up at Linda's camper in Minneapolis. The Chief doesn't want him there."

"The Chief?"

Doc Ponce gave a nervous smile. "Yeah. That's my name for—"

"I know. It's very appropriate."

"I thought so, too."

"This Bronson—kill him or just make sure he doesn't show up?"

"A serious enough accident to keep him from traveling would suffice."

"That's too bad. I would've preferred to kill him."

"Do as you please, just don't leave a trail."

"I never do."

Doc Ponce hung up.

EIGHT

As soon as LITTLE CAROL pulled into her parents' assigned camping space, she brought her car to a screeching halt, bolted out, and ran inside the camper. "Mom! Mom!"

Carol disengaged herself from the group of ladies. Wide-eyed and with eyebrows raised, she ran to hug her daughter. "What are you doing here?"

"Oh, Mom."

Carol pulled away from her and studied her eyes. She turned to the ladies. "Excuse me for a while. My daughter and I—we need to talk." She wrapped her arm around Little Carol, led her toward the bedroom, and closed the door.

BRONSON STOOD IN THE camper's doorway watching the interaction between mother and daughter. No matter how busy or how important Carol thought her projects were, she always made time for their girl.

Bronson's heart swelled with pride as he watched Carol, but at the same time, a little bit of envy crept in. Little Carol—Daddy's girl—why hadn't she turned to him?

He walked out.

LINDA OPENED HER DOOR. "Bronson, I was thinking about you. Come in." She stepped aside.

"I've got bad news for you," he said once he had entered and sat on the dinette couch.

Linda stiffened.

"Oh, no. Sorry," Bronson quickly said. "Not that kind o

bad news. It's about your camper. The part didn't arrive, and it won't for a couple of days." He stood up. "Come with me outside, and I'll show you what the problem is."

Linda stood up and followed him out. "What's going on?"

"I need a couple of days to do some research, and I don't want you alone in Minnesota. The part not arrivin' story is good reason for you to stay put."

"What kind of research do you plan to do?"

"I'm not sure. I need to familiarize myself with all the facts. What did the police tell you? How's the investigation into Mitch's death comin' along?"

"I didn't tell them about the pictures or the notes, so it was ruled an accident. There's no investigation going on."

Bronson wrote that down in his spiral notebook. "Then I'll start one. I'll begin with your house in Two Forks. Did Mitch have an office at home?"

Linda nodded.

"That'll make a good startin' place. Would you mind givin' me the keys to your house? I also need the address. I'd like to go through his desk. Maybe talk to some of his co-workers. Any suggestions?"

"I guess Henry Clark would be good. Mitch worked pretty closely with him. Other than that, I'm not sure. Mitch didn't like to talk about his work with me."

Bronson added that piece of information to his notes. "So it's okay with you if I go through your husband's stuff?"

Linda frowned, shifted position, and glanced down.

Bronson continued. "I know I'm askin' a lot. I wouldn't particularly want a complete stranger going though my house either, but I'm askin' you to trust me."

Linda's gaze traveled up to meet Bronson's. She crossed her arms and stared at him.

"Going cold to Minnesota isn't a good idea. We need to know what we're up against. Checkin' your husband's past—

maybe even your parents' past—might provide the answer. What do you say?"

She shrugged.

Bronson continued, "Right now I'd say you have no one you can depend on, except me." He captured her gaze and held it. "Will you trust me?"

She looked away, sighed, and nodded. "The key's inside the camper. I'll go get it and write down the address and directions."

"Thank you. While I'm gone, I want you to stay put. Do not go to Minnesota, especially alone. If you get in trouble, go to the front office. Have them contact the police. Promise me you'll do that."

"I promise."

"Good. My wife and daughter will be here, right next door. You've met Carol. I'll introduce you to my daughter."

BRONSON WAITED UNTIL ALL the ladies from the poetry guild left before he approached Carol. "Remember when Little Carol was growin' up and she'd get in trouble and she'd say we needed to have a family pow-wow?"

Carol's eyes narrowed. "What are you getting at, Harry Bronson?"

"We need a family pow-wow."

She set down the manuscript she had been studying and stood up. "You've been spending a lot of time with the lady next door. Is this what it's all about?"

Little Carol sat upright on the dinette couch, hastily shutting the book she had been reading. It dropped to the floor. She ignored it. "Mom! Dad!" She glared at Bronson.

Carol smiled. "No, honey, it's not what you're thinking. When your dad spends extra time with a woman, it's because he's working."

Dammit. How did she know? Here he thought she'd been

too preoccupied to pay any attention to him. He should have known better. He flashed his daughter a disapproving glance, before turning his attention to his wife. "Now, sweetheart—"

"Don't you *sweetheart* me. You've been working, haven't you?"

"I wouldn't say workin'. All we've been doin' is talkin'—sort of."

"Work's work, Harry Bronson, no matter what you call it. This is our vacation."

"I know that. But you've been busy with that reading group of yours, and now with Little Carol here, you've got your hands full."

"True, but I'll never be too busy to spend time with you."

Ouch, that hurt. If only he could reciprocate. He remembered broken dates, uneaten dinners, missed family gatherings. Carol might have groaned in private, but she never complained. "I need to take off. I'll be gone two, three days at the most. When I get back, you'll still be involved with the production. I'll be here for openin' night." He smiled and winked. "Going to Two Forks, Wyoming, will keep me busy while you're busy. I'll be earning some darn good money, which we will use to expand our vacation time. You'll like that, won't you?"

Carol placed her hands on her hips. "Harry Bronson, don't you try that rationalization crap with me. Work's work, no matter what pretty bow you tie it up with." She frowned. "But you're right. A little extra income sure would come in handy. Besides, there's nothing I can say to keep you here. You stay safe, and I swear, Harry Bronson, if you get involved in something else after this, I'll be working with you, side by side."

Bronson gathered her in his arms. "Sweetheart, I will never allow you to do anything that's going to put you in danger. You're much too valuable to me. After this, there will be no more cases. This is it."

"Soon as the cow jumps over the moon, I'll believe you."

DARKNESS ENVELOPED BRONSON as he shoved a small, overnight suitcase into the back of his olive-green Honda CRV. He'd been extra careful not to wake Carol, but he need not have bothered. By now she was used to him coming and going at all sorts of hours. Almost nothing disturbed her precious sleep.

Little Carol, on the other hand, had awakened when Bronson opened the camper door. "Daddy, are you going to be in any danger?"

Bronson smiled and walked back to his daughter. "I'll be fine."

"Mom worries about you. She won't let on, but she does. She's worried now. Should she be?"

"I'm going to check on some guy's paperwork. How could that be dangerous?"

Little Carol relaxed. "You sure that's all? Mom didn't ask."

"She never does. I think maybe that's her way of protecting herself. What she doesn't know won't hurt her, but I think what she imagines sometimes is worse."

"I'll tell Mom what you're doing so she won't worry."

"You do that." He leaned over and gave his daughter a kiss.

"When you get back—by the way, where are you going?"

"Two Forks, Wyoming."

"I hear tell that's a quaint little town."

"We'll see." He headed back toward the car, his daughter close to him.

"Before you go, I wanted to ask you something."

Bronson paused and looked at her. "What's that?"

"When you get back from Two Forks, can we go out to eat, just you and me?"

Bronson beamed.

NINE

BRONSON BROUGHT THE CAR to a halt and stared at the mansion that loomed before him. He'd known Linda was rich but hadn't imagined her to be a millionaire. Maybe money was the issue after all.

From the safety of his car, he scanned the neighborhood. Across the street, a car pulled in. A youthful man wearing a chauffeur's uniform stepped out and opened the door for an elderly lady. As she got out, she handed him several packages. Neither paid attention to Bronson.

Two doors down, a gardener pruned a bush. A jogger ran past; a car pulled in next door; a lady walked two dogs, a poodle and a boxer; and two teens on bikes zoomed by him. Active neighborhood. Maybe someone had noticed a stranger lurking around the house. He'd have to do a door-to-door inquiry.

Bronson stepped out onto the street and focused his attention on the next-door neighbor. Instead of going in, the man loitered by his car. When he noticed Bronson staring at him, he drank from the Coke can he carried, set it down on the edge of a nearby planter, folded his arms, leaned against the car, and stared back.

Definitely someone Bronson wanted to talk to. He headed over, noticing details. The neighbor was tall, tanned, and had a stocky build. His athletic body showed he must invest a lot of time in a gym. He was probably in his mid-thirties and kept his coarse black hair trimmed short. "Evenin'," Bronson said.

The man nodded once.

"Bronson's the name. Harry Bronson."

Something flashed through the neighbor's eyes, so quickly he wondered if he had imagined it.

"That's Linda's house," the neighbor said.

"I know. She's my cousin. With all she's been through lately, she decided to get away. She forgot some stuff, though. I'm here to bring it to her."

"How are you going to get in?"

"I've got the keys."

"I didn't see you at the funerals."

"Lots of people there." Bronson hoped that was true. "I just hung back. I'm not the in-your-face type."

"And she gave you her keys."

Bronson fished them out of his pocket and held them up. "Sure did."

The neighbor nodded.

"Nice of you to watch over Linda."

"Her and everyone else." The neighbor made a sweeping motion with his hand. "You'd be surprised how often we get targeted just because we have money."

No surprise there. "You sayin' that makes me wonder about Mitch's death."

"What do you mean?"

"Prior to his accident, did you happen to see anybody— on foot, or in a car—hangin' around here?"

The neighbor frowned. "That's an unusual question."

Bronson shrugged, as if dismissing the question's importance. "I'm lookin' out for my cousin, just like you. With her parents and husband gone, I don't want anyone takin' advantage of her."

"Nice of you. Glad she still has someone to protect her." He glanced away and his eyes narrowed. "Come to think of it, I did see someone. There was this car hanging around here prior to Mitch's death. Haven't seen it since. Wish I had made the connection before now."

"Did you see the driver? What can you tell me about the car?"

The neighbor tightened his features in an obvious attempt to remember. "If I recall correctly, we're looking at a small car. I was never one of those car geeks so I couldn't give you the make or year."

"Color?"

"Gray. Maybe light blue."

"And the driver?"

"Average-looking. Didn't get a very good look."

"Age? Color of hair?"

"I'd say late forties, early fifties. Brown hair, I believe."

Bronson noted the way the neighbor answered the questions. Very precise. "Anythin' else you remember?"

"Yeah, she kept staring at the Randigs' house."

"She?"

"Didn't I mention that?"

"You didn't by any chance get a license number?"

"Nope. Wish I had. One thing I can tell you, though. The car had an out-of-state license."

"Which state?"

The neighbor shrugged. "Can't say. I remember noticing it wasn't a local plate."

"What color was it? What kind of design did it have?"

The neighbor shrugged again and shook his head. "Sorry."

"Did you tell the police this?"

"I believe I mentioned it, yes, but I never connected it to Mitch's death. You don't think it was an accident?"

"I'm not sayin' anything like that. Like you, I'm just watchin' for my cousin."

The neighbor's eyes drilled into Bronson's soul. "Are you a policeman? A detective, maybe? Private eye?"

"I wish." He looked at the Randig mansion. "Best I get those things Linda needs."

The neighbor nodded and turned toward his front door. Bronson watched him walk away before he too pivoted and headed for Linda's house.

BRONSON STEPPED INTO THE black-and-white-tiled foyer, disarmed the alarm long enough to walk farther inside, reset it, flipped on the light switch, and was immediately bathed with light from thousands of crystal drops that sprouted out of the biggest chandelier he'd ever seen. He turned and lowered his head, making his face unidentifiable, just in case someone still manned the security camera.

He headed directly down the hall just as Linda had instructed him. He opened the first door to his right. The immaculate blend of oak furniture and fine paintings spoke of elegance. Bronson headed for the desk and thumbed through the calendar on it. During the two weeks prior to his death, Mitch had met with someone named Ella twelve separate times. No phone number, no address. Just the name followed by the time.

Bronson opened his notebook and jotted down, *Ella: mysterious woman in the car?* He returned the notebook and pen to his shirt pocket and searched the drawers. He found a plain file folder with the words *Henry Clark* written across it. Under the name, an address and a phone number had been scribbled. Bronson retrieved his notepad and recorded the contact information.

He sat on Mitch's chair and thumbed through the papers in the folder. The notes had been written in cursive. The first paper read, *from Henry Clark: add 1.06 more ethoxydiglycol.* A date followed the notation. Bronson checked the calendar. That had been almost a month ago. He looked at the next page. *From Henry C: less carbomer—maybe .007?* The date was three days after the first.

He looked at the next page. *From Clark: check extracts from pansy, cornflower, mallow, sage. Also from Henry...*

Bronson set the papers down and rubbed the bridge of his nose. It didn't make any sense to him, but it would to the right person. Nothing else in Mitch's office attracted his attention. He flipped open his cell and called Linda.

The cell rang several times before Linda picked up. "Bronson, hi. I'm outside. I can talk. Did you find anything? Is everything okay?"

"What can you tell me about Henry Clark?"

"He and Mitch headed the fountain of youth project. He'd come over to the house and they'd talk hours and hours about the ingredients and amounts that should be used. Real boring stuff."

That would explain the notes Mitch left behind. "What about Ella? What can you tell me about her?"

"Ella?"

"Yes."

A small pause followed. "Is that a person's name?"

Hadn't she heard of Ella Fitzgerald?

Linda cleared her throat. "I suppose it is," she said, answering her own question. "But I have no idea who that could be."

"Prior to Mitch's death, did you happen to notice a small sedan, either gray or light blue, hanging around the neighborhood, maybe even followin' you or Mitch?"

"Good God, no. Was someone following us?"

"What can you tell me about your next-door neighbor?"

"My next-door neighbor?"

Bronson shook his head. Yes, the next-door neighbor—only one she had. The other side was the street. Why had she chosen to turn into the million-question lady?

"You must be talkin' about the Oaxacas, Belen and Ross. They're both nice enough."

"Tell me about them."

"What in the world for? What's going on? You don't think they're somehow involved in Mitch's and my parents' deaths, do you?" She sounded as though she were gasping for air.

Bronson removed his glasses and rubbed the bridge of his nose. Again with the questions. "How well do you know them?"

"Better than most neighbors know each other. We used to get together once a week and play bridge."

"Used to?"

"Yeah, they went on a three-month world cruise, and then they're planning to spend some time with their son and the grandkids. Why is this important? What're you trying to tell me?"

Bronson folded his glasses and returned them to his pocket.

"When do you expect them back?"

"Just about anytime now."

"Can you describe Russ and Belen Oaxaca?"

"Belen, she's rather attractive. Knows what to wear and wears it well. Loves to cook. She'd always bring some kind of goodie she'd baked to our bridge sessions. Got a good sense of humor, little wrinkle lines on the sides of her eyes. She—"

"What about Russ? What does he look like?

"Russ? He's short, a bit overweight. Tends to be temperamental, especially when he's losing. He looks much older than Belen. Why is any of this important?"

"It's all part of checking things out—just doin' my job." He opened his notebook, wrote down, *Check on Russ and Belen Oaxaca,* and returned it to his pocket. His glance traveled toward the next-door neighbor's house and he realized his Chief Special was buried in the back of the Honda underneath some tools and a blanket.

His retired I.D. gave him permission to carry concealed. First thing he had done as soon as he retired was to make sure he had a legal permit, but what good would it do him now? He should have known better. Age or retirement was making him sloppy. He'd have to address that.

He walked over to the front window and looked out. The man he'd talked to had disappeared, but his car remained in the neighbors' driveway. That meant he could be anywhere nearby. Bronson's car, along with his gun, was only a few feet away, but for all they were worth, it could have been miles.

He scanned the neighborhood as carefully as possible. He spotted no one. He took a deep breath and reached for the doorknob.

TEN

THAT POMPOUS ASS.

As soon as Carrier had seen Bronson, he'd recognized him as a cop. He could smell them a mile away, and like all cops, Bronson's intelligence shone like charcoal. He'd actually believed that story Carrier had given him about the gray/blue sedan and its female driver. Carrier considered allowing Bronson to live long enough to make a fool of himself. Let his last earthly hours be wasted pursing a fake lead. That would serve him—and the entire police department he represented—right.

Unfortunately, Carrier didn't have that luxury. Bronson had to die and die now. An accident wouldn't be enough. Carrier considered his options. Shooting Bronson in broad daylight in this busy neighborhood would never do. Besides, he refused to use a gun. Carrier hated guns. They belonged to unimaginative, detached, unprofessional people who took no pride in their work.

Carrier stepped back and studied the Randig household. Tall bushes partially obscured the entrance. He could hide behind one of those and when Bronson stepped out, he'd come from behind, throw a garrote around his neck, and pull. He'd drag the struggling Bronson back inside and no one would be the wiser. Once inside, who knows? He might be tempted to release the pressure just a bit, long enough to prolong Bronson's death.

Pull. Release.

Pull. Release.

He could almost hear Bronson's gurgling blood.

The image pleased him.

BRONSON OPENED THE FRONT DOOR, but did not step out. He closed the door and glanced at his watch. He walked back to the study and absorbed every detail. Maybe he had over-looked something. Nothing caught his attention. In the near distance, he heard the wailing of sirens.

Only three minutes had elapsed since he opened the front door. Very impressive. By the time he reached the door again, a security guard had arrived. Bronson swung the front door open. "I'm sorry, I believe I owe you an apology."

The youthful-looking guard unholstered his weapon and pointed it at Bronson. "Don't move. Get on your knees. Turn around. Put your hands up. On the floor. Now."

Bronson stared at him. What TV show had he been watching? Since this was a multiple-choice command, Bronson slowly raised his arms. He saw another security car approach. Two more guards got out. They saw Bronson with his hands up and the novice pointing a gun at him. They ran toward the front door, their hands by their weapons, ready to be released at a moment's notice.

Bronson waited until they were within listening range. "I'm Harry Bronson. Linda Randig sent me to pick up some stuff for her. I accidentally set the alarm off. I have a cell. I'm going to reach for it. It's hanging from my belt." He waited for this information to register in their minds, especially that of the youth. "Any of you know Linda Randig personally?"

"We both do," said one of the new arrivals, a stocky man with beady eyes and bushy eyebrows. He pulled on his goatee, in what Bronson assumed was a nervous reaction.

"Good, then you can talk to her. She'll prove I'm tellin' the truth." Bronson focused his gaze on the inexperienced guard as he retrieved his cell and punched in the numbers. When the phone began to ring, he handed it to the goateed guard who'd spoken up.

The guard talked to Linda, snapped the cell shut, and handed it back to Bronson. "Larry, put the gun away. He's cool. He's telling the truth." He turned his attention to Bronson. "Just to be on the safe side, do you have an I.D.?"

Bronson showed him his retired police identification.

"Sorry to have bothered you." He reached in, reset the alarm, and looked at the other two guards. "Let's go."

Bronson stepped out. "Actually, I was gettin' ready to leave, myself." His eyes scanned the street. "That's my car right there, in the driveway." He didn't notice anything out of the ordinary. Maybe the precaution had been for nothing. He kept pace with the security guards.

"Make sure you disarm the alarm next time," said the second guard.

By now they had reached his car. "By all means." Bronson turned to open the door and spotted the neighbor as he stepped away from the bushes. The first thing Bronson noticed was that Neighbor had slipped on some driving gloves. He wondered why.

With sure steps, Neighbor headed their way. The intensity in his eyes told Bronson he had read him right. He wouldn't be foolish enough to shoot anyone and leave witnesses behind. The security guards and the active neighborhood served as temporary shields.

Neighbor shoved a folded piece of paper toward Bronson. "This is the paper I told you about, the one your cousin is looking for." Without waiting for an answer, he got in his car and drove away.

Bronson stuffed the note in his pocket. Now he knew why Neighbor had worn gloves. No use trying to get prints from this one. This jerk fancied himself some kind of a pro, and he wouldn't allow a small detail like fingerprints to escape his notice.

Bronson glanced at the planter. Maybe Neighbor wasn't that much of a professional. The Coke can was still there. Mistake Number One. He hadn't been wearing the gloves while he drank from it. Bronson looked at the guards. "Do any of you know that guy?"

"Never seen him." The guard pulled on his goatee again as he watched Neighbor drive away. "Should we know him?"

"Thought maybe he's Russ and Belen's friend. Someone takin' care of the house while they're away."

"The Oaxacas would have told us if they had a housesitter. Why do you ask?"

Bronson shrugged. "He looked familiar, that's all. Maybe not." He glanced at the Coke can. "You guys cruise this neighborhood all the time, right?"

"That's our job," the youthful one said. "Around each block, several times. We keep our eyes peeled."

"Did you happen to see a light blue or gray sedan hangin' around here about two weeks ago?"

"Can't say we have." The goateed guard stiffened. "What's with all the questions?"

"Got this broad followin' me everywhere. You know what I mean?" Bronson flashed them a conspirator's smile. "If you happen to remember seein' a blue or gray compact, I'd appreciate a call." Bronson handed them his business card, which consisted of nothing more than his name, cell number, and the words *retired, Dallas police detective*. He doubted he'd ever hear from them. The blue/gray car story sounded as if it was just that, a story.

The guard pocketed the card without looking at it.

Bronson grabbed the Coke can. "I'll throw this away."

The security guards waited until Bronson drove off before they too pulled out.

A block away, Bronson checked his rearview mirror. No one followed him. He made a right turn, then a left, and finally another right. He had gone around a couple of blocks, but remained in the same neighborhood. He knew that with the security guards still around somewhere and the neighbors outdoors, this would serve as a temporary sanctuary.

He pulled off, kept the engine going, and read the note Neighbor had handed him:

> *Go to the police and your "cousin" is dead. I know about The Roost Resort by Custer State Park. I will be contacting you soon.*

And I'll be waiting, Bronson thought. He dreaded the day they would confront each other.

From the glove compartment, Bronson retrieved his fingerprint kit and dusted the Coke can. Several prints appeared. He took the tape out and placed it on top of the prints. Hopefully, he'd soon get a match.

CARRIER LOWERED HIS binoculars and smiled. Bronson had fallen for the Coke can. Soon he would know Carrier's identity—and that would give Carrier the edge.

ELEVEN

BRONSON SWALLOWED HIS pride and made the call. It seemed the last few times he had talked to his old partner, he needed to cash in a marker, but he didn't know what else to do. He felt he had no choice. He punched in the numbers.

"Homicide. Hoover speaking."

"Hey."

"Bronson? Something go wrong with your South Dakota contacts?"

"Far as I know, all's well in that department."

"Oh, oh."

"Oh, oh?"

"That means you're calling to cash in another marker. You're raking them off—all the ones I owe you—real fast. What's going on?"

"I need a creep identified. I have his fingerprints."

"Oh, man, Bronson. Do you know all the work that entails?"

"A bit of computer work, a couple favors."

"Okay, so you know what's involved. I'm not impressed. When can you fax me the print?"

"Prints. Got more than one."

"Great. So when can you fax them?"

"I'm standin' in front of the fax machine."

"Of course. I should've known that."

"Then why ask?"

"Really, don't know what I was thinking of."

"So did you get them?"

"Hold your horses, Bronson. I'm still walking that way." A small pause followed. "Got 'em. I'm on my way to see Paul. Since you've left, he's become a real computer geek."

"So I've heard." Bronson hesitated before adding, "Listen, buddy, I really appreciate what you're doing."

"Don't get sloppy on me, Bronson. Besides, do you know how many times I relied on you? You've save my hide more than once."

"That's part of the job."

"And the friendship."

"Now who's getting sloppy?"

"You started it."

PAUL MCKENZIE SAT IN FRONT of his computer. He loved the challenges that Mike Hoover brought him now and then, thanks to Bronson. These puzzles, as he considered them, challenged and stimulated him. They certainly were much more fascinating than the usual stuff he had to do. Today's assignment didn't provide much intrigue, but at least it offered a break from routine police work.

He entered the information into the computer and clicked the search button. While he waited, he went to refill his coffee cup and thought of Bronson. Ever since he'd left the force, the coffee urn stayed full and often the coffee got old and rancid. No one else craved coffee the way Bronson did.

He returned to his desk and saw that the computer had found a match. He sat down and stared at the image the computer offered him. His muscles tightened and he began to sweat, his mind a jumble of incomplete thoughts and emotions.

A SMALL TOWN IN WYOMING, Two Forks's charm came from its historic, Western heritage and splendid scenery. Its abundant homes and buildings rich in the Western architectural style lined its streets.

For a town such as this to be the home of something as futuristic-sounding as McGory and Stein Pharmaceutical Research Center and Lab seemed inconceivable to Bronson. He expected a renovated warehouse sporting a Western motif to serve as headquarters for the place, located off Interstate 18 outside the city limits.

His eyebrows arched as he pulled into McGory Road. The Research Center loomed before him and filled him with awe. The pond alone, with a water fountain at its center, occupied at least an acre. What seemed to be the original five-story, C-shaped building contained wings that went every which way, as though additions had been built without a plan.

Bronson parked the car and headed toward the receptionist's desk. A youthful-looking woman with a round face greeted him. "May I help you, sir?"

"I'm here to see Henry Clark." He smiled, offering all the charm he could muster.

"Certainly, sir." She looked down at her list. "He's in Room…" She frowned. "Who did you say?"

"Clark. Henry Clark."

Her index finger moved down the list of approximately ten names. "Oh, he works in the lab." She stared at Bronson through huge, round brown eyes.

Bronson had seen more intelligence in a box of rocks. He leaned toward the receptionist. "So where's the lab?"

"Down the hall, but you can't go there."

"Why not?"

"It's a restricted area."

"Then can you please call him and tell him I'm here to see him?"

"He's in the lab, sir. He doesn't like to be disturbed when he's working."

Bronson made a mental note to stop at a toy store and buy an official-looking badge. He retrieved his I.D. card and flashed it. Hopefully, she hadn't seen the *retired* part. "This is police business. I can talk to him here or have him dragged down to the police station. I'll make sure the press knows he works here. Why, I'll even haul you in for obstructing justice."

As impossible as it seemed, her eyes widened further. "I'll call him."

Good girl, Bronson thought.

She picked up the phone and gave him her back.

He occupied his time by studying the floor plan of the research center under the glass on the receptionist's desk. The lab where Clark worked had a door that led outside. Bronson filed that information away.

The receptionist hung up. He stepped away from her desk and saw a thin, wiry man approaching. He was almost bald and wore thick glasses. On a scale of one-to-ten for looks, he scored a negative three. Bronson guessed this must be Henry Clark.

"May I help you?" the man asked.

Bronson bridged the gap between them and offered his hand. "I'm Harry Bronson. Doctor Clark, I presume?"

Clark stared at it as though unsure what he was supposed to do. Hesitantly, he shook it. "I'm Henry Clark."

"Is there a place we can talk?"

"There's a cafeteria on the third floor. I haven't eaten. We can talk and eat."

The receptionist frowned, visibly disappointed that she wouldn't be privy to any gossip.

"WHAT'S ALL THIS ABOUT?" Clark asked as he transferred their plates from the tray to the table and sat down.

"I'm Linda Randig's cousin." Bronson stirred two spoon-fuls of sugar into his coffee.

"The receptionist told me you're the police."

"I am—or was. I'm just tryin' to help my cousin."

"Mitch and Linda never mentioned your name."

"We're not that close, but with Linda being left all alone, I figure someone needs to look after her." Bronson used the last cream on the table and spotted some more on the one to his right. He reached for two more containers and poured them in.

Clark crumbled some crackers and stirred them into his chicken soup. "What exactly is it that you want?"

"I want to talk to you about Mitch."

"Me? Why me?"

Bronson took a sip of his coffee. Way too hot. He put the spoon in and stirred the contents. "You were his partner."

"Yeah, so?"

"Sometimes you tell your partner things you wouldn't tell anyone else."

"What kinds of things?"

"Things. Secrets. Feelings. Thoughts—that kind of thing." Bronson drank his coffee. Ah, good coffee. Freshly made.

"Mitch and I were not personal friends."

"Linda tells me you were often at the house."

"For business." Clark bit into his sandwich. "Strictly for business."

"So you never discussed anything personal." Bronson watched a brown-skinned youth—perhaps part Indian—clear the table to their left.

"No, never."

"What about retirement?"

Clark opened his sandwich and took the tomato out. "What about it?"

"Surely he told you he planned to retire."

"He did."

"How did he feel about that?" The busboy moved to a different table and wiped it down even though it looked clean. Bronson continued to watch him.

"He was apprehensive."

Bronson's attention bounced back to Clark. "Apprehensive? Why?"

Clark opened his mouth to speak, hesitated, and ate more of the sandwich. He took his time chewing and swallowing. "Guess it's just natural to be apprehensive. You know, a new way of life, very different than what he was accustomed to."

"But he never told you why he felt that way?"

Clark set the rest of the sandwich on the plate. He ran a trembling finger over his thin mustache. When he noticed Bronson studying him, he quickly moved his hand away. "Tell me, Bronson, what is this really all about? Are you thinking somebody did Mitch in?"

"Should I be thinking that?"

"That's absurd." He pushed his plate away. "Now if you'll excuse me, I have a lot of work to do." He started to get up.

"Just one more thing. Does the name Ella mean anything to you?"

Clark's eyes bounced around as though searching for an answer. "Can't say it does. Is that all?"

"One more thing. What kind of car do you drive?"

Clark frowned. "How is that any of your business?"

"I can check. Thought maybe you'd want to save me some time. More time I save, less angry I get. You don't want to see me angry. You'd be surprised what an angry cop can do." He drank the last of his coffee and smiled.

Clark sighed, looked away, and shook his head. "I drive a red Toyota Tacoma. Do you want the license plate number?"

"I'm looking for someone who drives a blue or gray sedan, possibly female. Does that ring a bell with you?"

"Not even close." Clark stood up. "Look, I'm sorry to be so abrupt with you, but I see this as a complete waste of time. Mitch met with a tragic and untimely accident, nothing more. No need to alarm Linda with any suspicions where there's no cause. She's a good woman. She doesn't need this. Is that clear?"

"Perfectly clear." The busboy was now wiping the table behind them. Bronson wondered if it, too, was already clean.

Using a softer tone, Clark continued, "I'm happy Linda has someone to watch over her. Please give her my regards." He walked away.

Bronson's gaze shifted to the brown-skinned youth. When he looked up and saw Bronson studying him, he quickly gathered his cleaning dishcloth and hurried to the kitchen.

By the time Bronson reached the kitchen, the youth had disappeared.

TWELVE

As Bronson opened his car door, a white truck with a dented front and a broken window pulled up next to him. The driver kept the engine running and rolled down the window, but didn't stick his head out. Even so, Bronson recognized the busboy.

"I know Ella," he said. "Meet me at Wyoming Café."

"When?"

"Now." He drove off.

For Bronson, the Wyoming Café ranked right up there with heaven. The aroma of coffee teased his taste buds and it took every ounce of discipline he could muster not to run to the counter and order a cup. Instead, he glanced around until he spotted the youth, sitting at the back of the café, his gaze glued on Bronson. Up close, the teen looked even younger than Bronson had imagined.

Bronson pulled up a chair and sat down. "Can I buy you a cup?"

The youth shook his head.

Imagine, turning down free coffee. Amazing, some people. "Something else?"

Again he shook his head.

"Mind if I get me a cup?"

This time when the teen shook his head, Bronson wondered how the conversation would go between them. He stood up, went to order, and returned to the table holding a steaming cup of joe. "You said you know Ella."

The kid nodded.

Ah. He'd gone from shaking his head to nodding. Bronson considered it progress. He leaned back in the chair, his gaze focused on the young man sitting across from him.

The youth bit his lip and looked away.

Bronson reached for his wallet, took out a twenty-dollar bill, and set it on the table.

"I...I am Manuel." He stared at the money, but did not reach for it.

"Nice to meet you, Manuel. I'm Bronson."

"You really be cop?"

"I was. I'm retired now."

"Oh. Then...then..." He rubbed his hands.

Bronson inched the twenty-dollar bill closer toward his possible informant. "Nothin's changed. I'm still willin' to pay for information."

"I have...girlfriend."

"Yeah?"

"She got—how you say?—pregnant."

Bronson glanced down at the money. Twenty dollars wouldn't give him the information he sought. He added another twenty, hesitated, and then added a ten. "Tell me about Ella."

"It is game." Manuel grabbed the money with the speed of an animal not sure it could trust the person feeding it.

"What?"

"A game—you know—for machine." He thought for a moment. "Computers. Cannot buy game at store. Internet, also no. I checked."

Bronson poured three packets of sugar into his coffee and stirred. "What makes you think it's a game?"

"I do two jobs so I can pay for, you know, baby. I be good busboy, but I clean, too. I clean Mr. Randig office. One time, I empty his trash. I see drawing he made and threw away."

"What did this sketch look like?"

"Like boxes you see in computer game. You see woman—she wear—" Manuel pressed his thumb and index finger together, giving the universal sign for small "—little clothes. She hold sword up high. Name of game is Ella. Bottom of drawing say *Ella, A Computer Game.* Maybe she be lady on box."

Bronson took a sip of coffee while digesting the information. "You wouldn't by any chance happen to have the drawin', would you?"

Manuel shook his head. "I no need it. I no want it. Stays in trash."

Bronson retrieved his pocket notebook and wrote down what Manuel had told him. "And this was how long ago?"

"A month? Six weeks?"

Interesting. Bronson had never imagined Mitch as an artist. Normally, scientists and artists came from opposite ends. "Was Mitch an artist?"

"Who?"

"Mr. Randig."

"Oh, him, no. I not think so. Drawing bad."

"Then why would you suppose he'd be designing a computer game box drawin'?"

Manuel worried his lip and shrugged. "I not know."

"What else can you tell me?"

He shrugged. "You want know Ella. I tell you. Ella is game. All I know." He bit his lip again.

His nervousness told Bronson he knew more. Bronson retrieved his business card and handed it to Manuel. "If you remember anything else, please give me a call."

Manuel reached for the card and placed it in his pants pocket. He stood up.

"Wait."

Apprehension swam in Manuel's eyes. His body stiffened.

"Your gal—does she have a doctor?"

Manuel shook his head.

"How far along is she?"

"Three months."

"Her parents or yours know about the baby?"

Manuel looked down and shook his head.

"They need to know. Maybe they can help."

"They no help."

"Have you contacted the Welfare Department?"

"Welfare? They help on this?"

"You bet they do."

Manuel's face lit up. "Yeah? Hey, thanks, Mister." He turned to leave. "Maybe I get more information, yes?"

"What kind of information?"

"You see." With a definite spring to his step, he walked away.

THIRTEEN

BRONSON FINISHED HIS COFFEE, got to his feet, and retrieved his cell as he left the café. "Can you talk?" he said once he heard Linda's hello.

"Bronson, hi. Yes, I'm outside. I've been waiting for your call. What have you learned?"

Bronson flipped through his notebook. "Your uncle—he creates computer games."

"Yes. Why? What does that have to do with anything?"

He flipped to the next page. "What can you tell me about Ella?"

"What? You're so frustrating at times. Can't you ever answer a question?" A small pause followed.

Bronson waited.

Linda sounded annoyed. "What did you want to know?"

"About Ella."

"You mentioned her before. Who is she?"

By now Bronson had reached his car. He opened the door and got in. "She's not a who. She's a what."

"Oh, brother. I finally get an answer and I still don't understand. What are you talking about?"

"Ella is the name of a computer game," Bronson said. "Apparently this game hasn't been released yet, which leads me to believe it's one of the games your uncle created. Mitch had what will probably be the cover drawing for the game. Any idea why your husband would have something like that?"

"Mitch and Uncle Phillip often sat and talked games. At first Mitch had no interest in Uncle Phillip's work. He considered it silly, certainly not something that a respect-able, mature adult should be involved with. So Uncle Phillip started talking to Mitch, showing him the vast amount of knowledge needed to create interesting games. Eventually, he won Mitch over. After that, they would sit for hours and talk about them. As to why Mitch would have a drawing for one of my uncle's games, I have no idea. Maybe they talked about cover designs. I don't really know. Do you think this drawing of Ella is important?"

"Probably not, now that I've heard your take on it, but at least it's one less loose end."

Manuel knew he should head home. His parents expected him soon, but this couldn't wait. He rang the doorbell and waited.

Pedro opened the door and stepped out. "Manuel, what are you doing here?" he said in Spanish.

Manuel replied in the same language. "I met a man who paid me for some information." He retrieved the money and showed it to his friend.

Pedro's face lit up. "What did he want to know?" He closed the door behind him.

"I told him about Ella. Now I'm thinking if you tell him what you know, we'll be rolling in money."

Pedro studied Manuel. "Did you make arrangements for me to meet him?"

Manuel shook his head. "Uh-uh. Let me tell you how it's going to be. I set up the meeting, we both go, and we each get half of what he gives you."

Pedro squinted. "Fifty-fifty doesn't seem fair. I'm the one who's sticking my neck way out."

Manuel thrust out his chin. "Fifty-fifty or I don't make the arrangements."

"Let me think about it." Pedro stepped back inside. "I'll call you."

PEDRO WATCHED MANUEL drive away. He could go with him and earn a little money, or he could make the call and get a lot more money. He didn't like the idea of screwing Manuel. They were friends, and he knew Manuel worked hard to provide for the baby and its mother.

But Pedro also needed money. Next week, Mama would celebrate her fiftieth birthday and Anita—hey, what would she do if he sent her flowers?

Pedro reached for the phone and hesitated. Manuel had to take care of his girl and the baby. But screw it, Manuel knocked her up, let him be responsible for his actions.

He punched in the number and when he heard the hello he said, "Doc Ponce? It is Pedro."

FOURTEEN

As BRONSON DROVE BY Linda's house, he focused on the new BMW parked in the Oaxacas' driveway. An attractive woman in her fifties watered her yard. He stopped the car in front of the house.

The woman continued to water but watched as Bronson approached.

"Evenin', ma'am."

She nodded.

"You're Belen Oaxaca?"

Her eyes narrowed. "Who wants to know?"

"Name's Bronson, Harry Bronson. I'm Linda's cousin."

"Oh, the poor dear. I just heard about Mitch. Right after her parents...I can't believe it." Her eyes filled with sadness. "How's Linda? Where is she? Nobody seems to know."

"She's on her way to see Uncle Phillip."

"Oh, really? And she took the motor home? Whenever she and Mitch go visit up there, they stay at her uncle's house. He's such a sweetheart. Why would she take the camper this time?"

Bronson shrugged.

"I'm glad to hear she took the camper. When we got home and didn't see it in their driveway, I was afraid she had to sell it to pay for the funerals."

Bronson's eyebrows went up. "They had financial problems?"

"Oh, dear. I shouldn't have opened my big mouth." She turned off the water and rolled the hose. "Mitch handled all of the money."

Bronson nodded as if he knew.

"He worried about what would happen when he retired. He didn't think he'd be able to keep Linda in the current fashion. In fact, when I first heard about Mitch, I thought...I thought..." She bit her lip and looked away.

"You assumed Mitch killed himself? Some insurance policies pay double for accidents."

Belen glanced back at Bronson. "Please, don't tell Linda. That's just my thoughts. I don't even know what the police said."

"The police ruled it an accident."

"Thank God." Belen placed her open hand on her chest. "I don't think—no, in fact, I know—Linda had no idea Mitch worried about finances, but he confided in me." She half smiled, still looking tearful.

Bronson nodded. He should check on Mitch's insurance policy. "Glad to see you and Russ made it safely back home. House was okay when you arrived?"

Belen's eyebrows pinched together. "Yes. Why would you ask?"

"Just a question, ma'am." Bronson's cell rang. The caller I.D. read *Mike Hoover*. "I have to take this call. Excuse me." As he headed for his car, he flipped the cell open. "Hey."

"Bronson."

Not good. Anytime Hoover began with his name, it meant bad news. "What gives?"

"Those prints you sent us belong to Benjamin Carrier."

Bronson's hand, holding the ignition key, froze on the way to the slot. "They can't be. He's dead."

"Or so we thought."

Bronson's mind pulsated with questions. He knew his ex-partner'd had a run-in with Carrier before Bronson came along.

"You never worked his case," Hoover said.

Bronson sank back into the car seat, focusing on every word Hoover uttered. "Never had the pleasure."

"What do you know about him?"

"I know his record is longer than our arms put together. I know he's the reason you limp, and I have a rough idea what happened that night. Aside from that, I don't know much. When you were working this case, I was in Missing Persons. By the time I transferred to Homicide, Carrier was dead and history."

"That's what I thought, so I put a package together that I'm faxing you. Carrier is a real badass and you've got to watch your own. He likes to play with his victims. He stalks and terrorizes them for days. Then he moves in for a slow kill. Never with a gun—too impersonal. He gets his thrills by getting so close he can smell their fear. He uses knives and wires. He's even known to beat his victims to death. Three of them, he cut their limbs off while they were still alive."

Bronson inserted the key in the ignition. Angie McKenzie, Paul's wife, popped into his mind. She had been a pretty thing. Dainty, kind, always wore a smile. She and Paul had been married for only three months when Carrier murdered her.

Hoover pursued him and eventually corralled him in a deserted warehouse. In an effort to escape, the bastard set it on fire. Hoover barely escaped as the inferno erupted. He got out with bad burns, mostly on his legs. Carrier had burned to death, or so the police had assumed.

The only time Hoover and Bronson had discussed the case, Hoover said, "I'll never forget the acrid odor of burning flesh. As a child, my mom used to take me to my grandparents' farm. I still hate the smell of burning chicken feathers. This was similar, but worse." Hoover had never mentioned the case again, until now.

Bronson asked, "You're sure those are Carrier's prints?"

"Positive."

"So who died in that fire?"

A small pause followed. When the answer came, Hoover's voice quivered with emotion. "I guess we'll never know. The body had been reduced to ashes, destroying all chance of finding usable DNA, but we found other evidence that led us to believe Carrier burned. His ring. The knife he used— they were there with the body. Other stuff, too. Now it looks like it was all a setup." Hoover cleared his throat. "He led me to that warehouse with the full intention of setting it on fire. The poor guy who burned to death was already there with Carrier's ring, knife, and personal stuff. Maybe he was unconscious or already dead. We'll never know, but Carrier had this planned from the beginning."

Bronson shook his head in bewilderment. "That conniving worm. How's Paul takin' it?"

"He fell apart. He asked for a leave of absence. He plans to fly there and personally hunt Carrier down."

"He can't do that. He's a lab tech. He doesn't have any street experience. He's going to get killed."

"Exactly what I told him."

"What'd he say?"

"I'll quote him: 'As long as that S.O.B. is alive, I'll hunt him down. I don't care if he kills me. I'd rather be dead.'"

Bronson looked out the window. Belen had resumed her watering. "Hoover, you need to stop him. He'll only get in the way and make things worse."

"You know that and I know that, but I might not be able to stop him. If Paul goes, I'm going with him. You'll need all the help you can get."

"Tell him the police will take care of Carrier."

"I have, but Paul's not listening, and speaking of police, your Wyoming police contact is Captain Samuel Marshall. He's eager to talk to you about Carrier."

Bronson wrote the name and number down. "Anything else?"

"Yeah, the captain is getting the same fax you are. I'll send yours to the same place I faxed the other papers. Is that okay with you?"

Bronson waved goodbye to Belen and started the engine. She waved back and Bronson drove off. "Yeah. Give me fifteen minutes or so."

"Can do."

"And speaking of can do, you keep Paul in Texas."

"I'll try, but I'm sure that won't happen."

FIFTEEN

BRONSON SAT IN THE CAR, reading the fax. He read it a second time, making notations. When he finished, he set it aside and reached for his cell. He needed to contact Captain Marshall. Instead, the cell rang in his hand. Bronson didn't recognize the number on the caller I.D. "Bronson here."

"Mr. Bronson? Manuel. We talk. You remember?"

"I remember." The image of Manuel's youthful face popped up before him.

"Huh, good. I talk to Pedro. He—"

"Pedro? Tell me about Pedro." Bronson took out his notebook and wrote the name down.

"Pedro, my friend. He cleans like me. He hears something he not suppose hear."

"Like what?"

"I not say. Pedro tell you."

"Is Pedro willing to talk to me?"

"He say we meet in alley behind Great American Steak House. You see big—what you call it? Trash can?"

"A Dumpster?"

"Yeah, Dumpster. We be there."

"In an alley? Why does Pedro want to meet in an alley?"

"He says you be trouble. In alley no one see we talk. Dumpster hide us. Door goes from steak house to alley. Pedro use door to leave. Pedro cousin, he owns place, so it be okay."

"How long will it take you to get there?"

Bronson heard Manuel discuss it with someone else, presumably Pedro. "Maybe forty-five minutes. Maybe hour."

Bronson glanced at his watch and estimated how long it would take him to talk to the police. "I'll meet you in a bit over an hour."

"Mr. Bronson?"

"Yes?"

"This be big. You want hear what Pedro knows. Fifty dollars not good. Too little."

"I understand." Bronson opened his wallet. It contained four twenties and one ten.

He sighed.

MARSHALL, A BEAR OF A MAN, stood when he saw Bronson approach. "Bronson." He offered his hand. "Sit." He pointed to the chair by his desk.

Bronson shook hands with him and sat down.

Marshall also sat down. "I understand you've got yourself involved with a nasty criminal."

"Not by choice."

Marshall smiled. "I'm sure that's never by choice." He leaned back in his seat. "Tell me what you know."

Bronson told him about David and Irene Hummings's deaths and how that led to Mitch Randig's. He then related details about his first encounter with Carrier at Russ and Belen Oaxaca's house. He concluded with the call he had just received.

Marshall sat straighter. "When did you say this meeting takes place?"

Bronson glanced at his watch. "In less than half an hour."

"But this is just between you and two teens, right?"

"Far as I know."

"We'll have a car in the area just in case something goes wrong."

Bronson stood and eyed the coffee urn. Too bad Marshall hadn't offered him some. "Thanks, I appreciate that, but I don't foresee any problems. Soon as the meeting is over, I'll fill you in."

"I'll send one of my detectives with you," Marshall said.

"As you wish, but it might spook the kids."

Marshall nodded. "You're a veteran cop and Hoover highly recommends you. Besides, like every other place, we're short-handed. I'll wait for your report, then we'll take over from there."

"Sounds like a plan." Bronson walked out.

"HEY, WHERE ARE WE GOING?" Manuel asked as Pedro drove past the street that led to the Great American Steak House.

"I—I've got to do something first. Won't take long." Pedro shrugged and flashed him a smile with trembling lips.

Manuel wished he could reach out and comfort his friend, but Pedro was macho and macho men wouldn't appreciate that. "We'll be okay. Bronson is a good guy. All that's going to happen is, we get lots of money. You'll see."

Pedro looked away and drove faster. They didn't speak until Pedro parked the car at McGory and Stein Pharmaceutical Research Center and Lab. As Pedro got out of the car, he looked at Manuel and said, "Get down."

Manuel looked around. "What are we doing here? Today's Saturday. The place is closed."

"The back door to the lab is open."

"How do you know?"

Pedro reached for the door handle and let himself out. "Come."

Manuel hesitated, listening to the butterflies in his stomach. Pedro knocked on the window and signaled to join him. Manuel swung the door open. "What…?"

"I'll show you." He turned and walked at such a fast pace that Manuel had to almost run to keep up. Before Manuel could ask him anything, Pedro opened the door to the lab and waited for Manuel to step in.

"How did you know the door was open?" Manuel asked. "We're gonna get in big trouble." Then he saw the man sitting at a desk. "Doc Ponce."

Manuel's heart skipped a beat when he noticed the gun Doc Ponce pointed at him.

PEDRO AND HIS COUSIN often frequented the alley behind the Great American Steak House. Most of the time, pot provided the reason for their rendezvous, bringing a sense of familiarity and the rush of a thrill. But today, this same alley filled Pedro with dread. Then, to top it all, he hated the gringo who stood in front of him. His monstrous build intimidated Pedro.

Carrier took a step forward, forcing Pedro to take two back. "I assume Manuel is with Doc Ponce."

Pedro nodded. He couldn't understand why Doc Ponce dealt with this man.

"Good," Carrier said. "You'll be paid well."

"Manuel, he be okay, yes?" How could he have been so stupid? If anything happened to Manuel, it'd be his fault.

"What happens to him depends on the next few minutes. Now, you be a good little boy and stand over there where Bronson can see you as he drives by. I'll be behind the Dumpster."

Pedro inched forward to get a clear view of the street. He wished Bronson would hurry up. He wanted this thing to be over. A few minutes later he got his wish. He spotted the SUV. Its driver—presumably Bronson—matched the description Manuel had given him. Pedro watched as Bronson slowly drove past them, his attention clearly focused on the alley. "Bronson here," Pedro said.

"Good," Carrier answered. "Come here."

Pedro hesitated.

"Get your ass over here or I call Doc Ponce and tell him to kill Manuel. Is that what you want?"

Fear gripped Pedro and he found it impossible to speak. He shook his head and shuffled toward Carrier.

"Let me tell you how it's going to be. Bronson sees me, he won't hesitate to shoot. You stand between us, he won't shoot. Understand?"

Pedro felt his legs turn to Jell-O. Sheer panic forced him to remain standing.

Seconds later, Carrier grabbed him hard from behind.

BRONSON SPOTTED A KID—not Manuel—standing in the alley, looking frightened and confused. Then the kid walked away from his view. Unless the Dumpster hid Manuel, he hadn't come.

Interesting.

Bronson focused on the area before he drove away, parked, and stepped out.

SIXTEEN

PAUL CRADLED THE PICTURE ALBUM to his chest. That's all he had left, the pictures and the memories. Sometimes when he closed his eyes, he heard Angie's gentle laughter—her angelic voice, so unique. A melody that had been silenced forever.

The bastard still roamed the streets. Life wasn't always fair, but he was about to even the score.

Carrier wouldn't be looking for him. Paul had the element of surprise. Carrier would be busy stalking Bronson, and Paul would attack from behind—the same way Carrier had attacked Angie. The same way he attacked his victims. Too yellow to confront them face-to-face.

The only foreseeable glitch in his plan involved Mike Hoover, who would try to stop him. "He'll kill you," Hoover would argue.

So what if he did? As long as Paul killed Carrier first. Paul shook his head. Hoover would never understand simple logic like that.

He shut his suitcase. Fear and anxiety nibbled at him, but he had no choice. He'd told Hoover they would leave tomorrow at noon, but Paul had no plans to wait for him. He was ready to go, eager to confront Carrier before Hoover had the chance to stop him.

OUT OF ALL THE POSSIBILITIES that the establishment next to the Great American Steak House could have been, it turned out to be Just for the Sexy You. Great. Just absolutely great.

Bronson cleared his throat, raised his head, stepped into

the store, and tried not to look—but what the heck was that and how did it fit?

"May I help you?"

Bronson pivoted to face a curvy store clerk, possibly in her late teens. "I need to talk to the owner or manager."

"I'm the manager. How can I help you?"

Lordy, what was the world coming to? "I'm Detective Bronson and we have a deal going on in your alley. You need to keep your employees out of there. I saw three doors leading out into the alley: yours, the steak house, and one more. Please contact them and tell them to stay inside." He started to head toward the back, but stopped. "One more thing. If I'm not back in five minutes or so, call the police and ask for Captain Marshall."

The manager's eyes widened in alarm. "Do you have that number?"

"Yes. Nine-one-one." He stepped into the area labeled *Employees Only*. "There's no way to see into the alley from here?" He'd guessed not, but had to verify it.

She shook her head and pointed to the door leading to the alley. "That's a one-way door."

"Meanin'?"

"Once you step out, it locks behind you. If you plan to come back in, you'll have to jam something in it."

Great, just absolutely great. "Thanks for tellin' me." He took out his Chief Special.

The manager gasped.

Bronson motioned with his head that she should move away from the door. "Go call the surrounding businesses."

She nodded and dashed out.

Bronson waited for a few minutes, giving her time to finish making the calls. He took a deep breath and braced himself. *Lord, here goes nothin'. Please be with me.*

He held the gun at the ready position, point up, ready to swing in any direction. He pushed the door open.

HOOVER'S FINGERS DRUMMED on the desk. He wouldn't put it past Paul to try to sneak out without him. He could call him at home. If Paul answered, he could relax.

On the other hand, if he didn't answer, that wouldn't necessarily mean he'd left town. Oh, what the hell. He picked up the phone.

Paul answered on the second ring. "Checking on me, or is there something you want?"

His abruptness took Hoover by surprise. "I'm not really checking on you, I'm just wondering if you're okay."

A small pause followed. "Yeah, I'm fine." Another pause, then, "Sorry about that. This thing with Carrier has really got me crazy. I do appreciate what you're doing."

"That's what friends are for."

Silence. Hoover rubbed his forehead. He must have pissed Paul off. "Listen, I'll see you tomorrow."

"Yeah, tomorrow."

AFTER PAUL SNAPPED THE cell shut, he felt a twinge of guilt. He shook himself, trying to disperse the feeling. What he was doing certainly wasn't nice, but he felt he had no choice. Hoover insisted that Paul had no idea of police procedure and would get himself killed. Maybe so, but Paul had known enough to transfer all his incoming house calls to his cell. *How's that for knowing proper procedure?*

A hollow, vast feeling consumed him as he boarded the plane.

SEVENTEEN

BRONSON OPENED THE DOOR to the alley. Like all alleys, it reeked of dried urine and rotting garbage. Bronson twitched his nose.

He stepped farther into the alley and saw Pedro on the ground, a pool of blood forming beside him. A note had been pinned to his shirt. Bronson swore. He flipped his cell open as he rushed toward Pedro.

"He…h-help…me." Pedro's eyes, huge as saucers, housed fear and pain.

Bronson spoke to the dispatcher. "Stabs to the kidney. Victim bleeding profusely. Marshall should be in the vicinity. Please notify him." He snapped the phone shut and applied pressure to the wound. "Help is on the way. Carrier do this?"

Pedro stared at him.

"Tall, tanned, stocky built, coarse black hair, athletic body." Pedro nodded. "I…h-h-hurt."

"I know. The paramedics are on their way. I promise. You had something to tell me?"

Pedro grimaced and bit his tongue.

"I promise you, I'll make Carrier pay for this, but you've got to tell me what you know."

Pedro opened his mouth, but nothing came out.

Where were those paramedics? The kid needed treatment now. "I know it hurts, but you don't want Carrier gettin' away with this. Tell me."

"F-f-for-mu-l-laaa…s-s-sell." Pedro's voice trailed off.

Shit! He wasn't going to make it.

"D-d-duck…" Pedro closed his eyes and took his last breath.

Bronson sat down hard on the ground. "Dammit!" In the distance he heard the wailing of sirens.

Without touching it, Bronson read the note attached to Pedro's shirt:

Harry,
You don't mind if I call you Harry, do you? I know everyone refers to you as Bronson, but I like Harry much better. It's so much more intimate.

So tell me, Harry, are you enjoying the game as much as I am? Here's the way it goes. Everywhere you go, I'll be one step ahead. I'll always be there, waiting, watching, and when I'm tired of you, I'll squish you like a roach.

Round One, I won.

It may interest you to know I have Manuel. The police grab me, I don't make the call, Manuel dies. Worst-case scenario, I'm sent to prison. From behind bars, I'll make sure his bitch and baby die. Their deaths will haunt you for the rest of your life.

Who do you think will win Round Two?
Benjamin Carrier

Bronson cringed. This wasn't a game even if Carrier thought so. A breeze blew, causing the note to flip and rip. Automatically, Bronson pushed it back down and secured it with the safety pin that was already there. He looked up and saw Marshall and the paramedics.

Marshall had a frown on his face.

BRONSON LOOKED AT HIS WATCH for the seventh time. He understood the importance of verifying all the details, but dang it, didn't the Two Forks police understand the urgency of the situation? He had to get back to The Roost Resort. With each passing moment, the danger Linda faced wrapped its tentacles tighter and tighter. "Screw it," he muttered under his breath. He flipped open his cell and punched some numbers.

The officer sitting across from him flashed him a disapproving frown.

"Excuse me." Bronson stood up and walked around until he found the best reception.

Four rings later, Linda picked up. "It's Bronson," he said. "I have reason to believe that a very dangerous man is headin' your way, so I want you out of there. Go to the nearest police station and meet me there."

"The police? No!" Linda's voice filled with anxiety. "Bronson, you didn't contact the police, did you? You promised."

"There was a murder. I had no choice."

Linda gasped. "A murder? Who?"

"A young kid, a janitor at the research lab where your husband worked."

"A janitor? I don't understand. Why him?"

"I'll fill you in at the police station."

A slight pause followed. "The Two Forks police can work on that murder. I don't care, but the police here must not get involved."

Bronson rubbed the bridge of his nose. "Linda, that's a dangerous killer we're dealin' with. You've got to—"

"You heard me. No police. I'll sit and wait for him to grab me before I go to the police."

"All right. Go to a public place somewhere filled with people."

"I'll meet you at the Purple Pie Place. You know where that is?"

Bronson knew it. He and Carol had recently enjoyed ice cream sodas there. "In town on the main highway?"

"That one. How soon can you get there?"

"I'm still several hours away. That's why I'd feel better if you went to the police."

"It's the Pie Place or nothing. I'll bring my needlepoint to keep me busy."

Damn her stubbornness. Unfortunately, he was in no position to argue. "You're sure you'll be safe?"

"Very sure. The place is always crowded."

"Okay, just get out now and don't forget to take the trackin' device off the car." Bronson disconnected as a feeling of dread overcame him.

A BIT OVER AN HOUR LATER, Bronson walked out of the police building. The image of Pedro's eyes begging him for help haunted him. He pushed his glasses up and rubbed his eyes. Pedro's last words had been "Formula…sell…duck."

Formula…sell…duck.

The words raced through his mind again and again. The first two were easy to decipher. If Mitch planned to sell his formula to a rival pharmaceutical lab, or if he knew someone who planned to do so, that could easily lead to his so-called accident. If the company knew of his plans, they would want to stop him—enough to kill him? If the formula were sold, how much would McGory and Stein stand to lose? Bronson needed answers to those questions. Maybe that last word—duck—would serve as the key to complete the puzzle.

Bronson reached his car and got in. He recalled the pond in front of the research center. Did it have any statues of ducks? He didn't recall seeing any, but he hadn't been looking. Maybe Mitch's partner would know.

He opened his notebook and found Henry Clark's address. He had no idea where that was, but since this was a small town, he'd have no trouble finding someone who could give him directions. Right after talking to Clark, he'd head back to The Roost Resort. He knew Carrier never bothered his victims' families, perhaps the only honorable trait he possessed. Still, Bronson wanted to reassure himself of his family's safety. Afterward, he'd focus on Linda. By now she should have left the campground and be safely waiting for him.

As Bronson drove down the narrow streets of Two Forks, his thoughts returned to Pedro's words. "Formula…sell… duck." What was the connection?

EIGHTEEN

HENRY CLARK LIVED ON THE historic side of town. Once the elegant home of cattle baron Randolph Schilsom, the house had been modernized without forsaking its Western look. Its surrounding gardens had been restored to their full splendor, providing stunning visual effects. Bronson stepped back and took it all in. The house was elaborate and flamboyant, something Carol would love, something Bronson didn't care for.

Working for the pharmaceutical lab paid well. Both Clark and Randig had homes that stood as testimonies to that fact. Why, then, would Mitch be tempted to sell the formula? Unless, of course, retirement pay wasn't up to par. Bronson made a mental note to check on the retirement pay system.

He rang the doorbell. A maid opened the door. She wore a frilly white apron over a black dress. "May I help you?"

"I'm here to see Henry Clark."

"Do you have an appointment?"

"I wasn't aware I needed one. This is urgent. Please tell him I'm here. I'm sure he'll see me. My name is Harry Bronson."

The maid led him into the foyer. "Wait here. I'll talk to Mr. Clark."

From where Bronson stood, he could see into the living room. The interior wore the same grand manner as the exterior. The marble fireplace and the heavy gold mirror hanging above it blended perfectly with the elaborate ceiling cornices. Chandeliers graced the frescoed ceilings while graceful door frames lured the visitor in.

"Bronson."

He turned to face Henry Clark. "It's nice outside. Let's go talk on the patio."

Clark opened the French doors and stepped out. Bronson followed him. They sat in the ornate wrought-iron table-and-chair set. The maid brought a pitcher of lemonade and two glasses with ice. Bronson would have preferred coffee.

Clark poured himself a glass. "I told you everything I know. Why are you here?"

Bronson swallowed the urge to return the rudeness. "Today, someone died in my arms."

Clark paused with the drink halfway to his mouth. "Died? Who?"

"You probably know him. He worked for the same research center you do. His name was Pedro Lopez. He was only seventeen years old."

Clark set the glass down and stood up. "Pedro? Yes, I know him—knew him." He locked his hands behind his back and paced. "I can't believe he's dead." He stopped in front of the table but didn't sit down. Instead, he reached for his glass and took a large swig. The dull look in his eyes and the tautness around his mouth revealed his turmoil. He didn't ask how Pedro died, Bronson noted.

"Is that why you're here, to tell me Pedro died? I'm sorry he's dead, but I hardly knew him well. What does his death have to do with me?"

Bronson leaned back in the seat and scanned the surrounding gardens. His imagination took him back in time. The sheer glamour of the foliage reminded Bronson of the gardens depicted in the grand scenes of a movie about the Renaissance. "You and Mitch—you were workin' on a special project."

"Yeah, so?"

"So tell me about it."

Clark frowned at Bronson and sat back down. "How's that any of your business?"

Bronson smiled, leaned back, and admired the row of multicolored lantanas that graced the walkway. His gaze traveled back to Clark. "Humor me."

Clark glared at Bronson and drank his lemonade.

Bronson glared back.

Again, Clark frowned and shook his head. "We came this close to finalizing the formula that would wipe the years off people's faces." He squeezed his thumb and index together.

"What happened?"

Clark shrugged. "Mitch died. That's what happened."

"So it's unfinished."

"As of now, yes. But I plan to pick up where we left off. It's just a matter of time."

Bronson reached over and poured himself some lemonade. "What if I told you Mitch found the answer?"

Clark's eyes widened—in fear or bewilderment, Bronson couldn't tell. Seconds later, his bland look returned. "He couldn't have. I would have known about it."

"You sure now?" A movement to Bronson's right caught his eye. He turned very slightly so as not to be noticed. He scanned the area, but didn't see anyone.

"Of course I'm sure. Why wouldn't I be?"

"What if I told you that not only did Mitch successfully complete the formula, he planned to sell it to a rival company?"

Clark's eyes mirrored confusion, then slowly transformed into genuine astonishment, or maybe panic. "Then I would say you're either misinformed or you're allowing your imagination to run away with you." His voice came as a hoarse murmur.

"Why would you say that?"

As Clark reached for his lemonade, his hand trembled. He

cleared his throat. "Because even though Mitch and I were not the best of friends, I knew him well enough to know he wouldn't do something like that."

"The way I see it, sellin' the formula would bring him millions of dollars. A nice cushiony sum that would ease his worries. You said he felt apprehensive about retirin'."

"Everybody is apprehensive about retiring. That doesn't mean they'll sell out."

A maid Bronson hadn't seen stepped outside. She carried a bucket of water and a sponge. She hosed a window, dipped the sponge in the bucket, and wiped the glass. Bronson gestured her way. "If you had to live on your retirement pay only, I bet you couldn't afford her."

"Not her, or the gardener, or the other two servants. What's your point?"

The maid finished wiping the window and moved onto the next. "That's why you haven't retired? Pay is lousy?"

"It's adequate, but certainly way below what I'm accustomed to. How's this relevant or any of your business?"

Bronson picked up his glass of lemonade and raised it as if in a toast.

"I continue to work because I enjoy my job," Clark said. "The formula isn't complete and that provides me with a challenge."

Again a movement by the bushes caught Bronson's eye, but when he glanced that way, he saw no one. "Let's assume for a minute that Mitch was willin' to sell. If you were him, who would you sell it to?"

Clark tightened his features like a fist. Through clenched teeth, he hissed, "I would have no idea." He set his empty glass down and stood up. "It's late. I still have things to do. This isn't getting us anywhere. I don't understand why you insist on frightening Linda."

"Maybe you're right. Let's hope so." Bronson remained

seated. "Just one more thing. Before Pedro died, he said the word *duck*. Does that mean anything to you?"

Clark's eyes narrowed slightly. "You talked to him before he died? What else did he say?"

"Nothing much. Do you have any idea what he was talking about?"

Clark shook his head and looked down. "No, sorry."

The maid finished her task and moved to the side of the house, away from Bronson's view. "That pond in front of the research lab, does it have any statues of ducks?"

"No, but we do have ducks that come and go, depending on the time of year."

Bronson watched the bushes sway. "About Mitch selling that formula."

"I told you before, that's ridiculous." Clark frowned and sat back down.

"And why's that?"

"We've been through this."

"Humor me."

"For one, the formula isn't his to sell. The patent to the formula is under his and my name jointly. He can't sell it without my consent, but even putting that aside, the lab owns the rights."

"So if Mitch sold the formula..."

Clark closed his eyes and shook his head. He rubbed his eyebrows as if attempting to chase a headache away. "He wouldn't."

"If he planned to sell the formula, the one who would lose the most is the company itself."

Clark stared at Bronson.

"I suppose Mr. McGory and Mr. Stein are real people," Bronson said.

Clark flashed him a look that clearly meant *obviously*.

"What can you tell me about them?" By now the bushes stood still, but that told Bronson more than their movement.

Clark poured himself the last of the lemonade. "I don't know what to say about them. They're rich and powerful. Mr. Stein is the head behind the organization, the true chief. Mitch and I are—were—directly accountable to him." Clark shrugged. "I guess I'll still be reporting to him, which is the part I don't care for. He runs the lab like a tight ship. We have to justify every single penny we spend. I personally feel that Mr. Stein is the one who makes all the decisions. Mr. McGory just goes along for the ride. Mr. Stein is a worrywart. Mr. McGory is more relaxed."

"Worrywart?"

"Yeah. Sometimes during our meetings, he goes over and over the same items. The way he talks sometimes makes it seem the company is ready to collapse."

Bronson retrieved his notebook and jotted down the new information. "And is it?"

"I have no idea. I'm part of the lab, not an accountant. All I know is that in the past few months, the company let several employees go."

"You said you and Mitch were very close to finalizing the formula."

"Yes."

"How long until you finish?"

"A month? Maybe less. Maybe more. Close enough."

"Then what happens?"

"I'll turn the results in to Mr. Stein and that will generate big bucks for the company and for both Mr. Stein and Mr. McGory."

"Exactly how much?"

"Initially, at least three hundred million, but billions of dollars in sales after that."

Once again the bushes moved. Bronson scooted his chair, making it easier for him to get up. "You've got a beautiful garden."

"I think so, too."

"I'm a bit of a plant bluff, but I don't recognize those ones there." He pointed to his right. "Mind if I take a closer look?" Within seconds, he reached the bright red flowers but went past them.

From behind him, he heard Clark ask, "What are you doing?"

Bronson stepped behind the bushes. He saw a man sitting on the ground, his hands covered with dirt.

The gardener looked at Bronson through startled eyes.

"Just wanted to let you know what a nice job you're doing maintainin' these gardens," Bronson said.

The gardener nodded. "Thank you." He returned to work.

THAT ARROGANT SON-OF-A-BITCH knew.

Doc Ponce swept the papers off his desk and watched them float down to the floor. He picked up one, looked at it, and realized he didn't need it. He crumpled it and threw it toward the trash. He missed. He kicked the trash can. It tumbled over.

Doc Ponce let out an angry growl that sounded like a duck quacking. He hated Bronson. The sooner he died, the better off Doc Ponce would be.

He had heard every single word Bronson said out there in the gardens, and also every word he hadn't said. Bronson knew about selling the formula. He knew Mitch's death hadn't been an accident. His knowledge spelled danger for the entire operation.

He needed to be eliminated. Why hadn't Carrier done him in? What was he waiting for?

Doc Ponce picked up his cell and called Carrier.

He answered on the first ring. "This better be important."

"You killed Pedro."

"Oh? He died? Too bad. Or maybe not. He was a punk. I did the world a favor."

"He talked to Bronson before he died."

"Yeah?"

"He said something about a duck. Do you know anything about that?"

Carrier burst out laughing. "Think about it."

His superior attitude bothered Doc Ponce and he wished he could strangle the man. "How much does Bronson know?"

"It doesn't matter."

"Of course it matters. Why is he still alive? The Chief is paying you thousands of dollars to—"

"He's paying me to do the job. I decide when and how to do it. Neither you nor the Chief have any business telling me that. It'll be done at my leisure within my own time frame. Which reminds me, how's Manuel?"

"Scared shitless. What do you expect?"

"He's still with you?"

Doc Ponce knew what Carrier did to anyone who crossed him. "No, I took him to your cabin and locked him in the room. I followed your instructions to the T."

"Nobody saw you?"

Did Carrier think he was a moron? "Of course not. The place is so damn isolated."

"Did anybody follow you?"

"No, I made sure, just like you said. Manuel is tucked away safely and ready to be enjoyed at your will."

Carrier disconnected and Doc Ponce heard the silence at the other end. His jaw ached as he clenched his teeth. He took several deep breaths. "Calm down," he said aloud even though no one would hear him. "Calm down."

He regained control and reached for the phone. This time, he dialed the Chief's number.

NINETEEN

FOR THE SECOND TIME TODAY, Bronson sat facing Marshall's desk. "I'm here to tell you that I sort of bumped into Henry Clark."

Marshall looked up toward the ceiling's corner as though attempting to recall the name.

"Mitch's lab partner," Bronson said.

"Gotcha." Marshall retrieved his notepad, clicked the pen, and looked at Bronson. "And how did you sort of happen to bump into Clark?"

"He was home."

"Hmm." He glared at Bronson and shook his head. "So tell me what Clark said."

Bronson proceeded to tell him about the conversation he and Clark had.

Marshall waited until Bronson finished talking. He made the final notations, set the pen down, and looked at Bronson. "So you think McGory and/or Stein are at the bottom of this?"

"I think they're worth paying a visit, and I think we need to find out if the company is financially stable."

"We, Bronson? This may come as a shock to you, but I do know how to do my job."

Bronson slowly nodded. "Of course you do. Sorry. It's in my system, and I can't seem to shake it." He stood up. "I'm out of here."

"Can't say I'm sorry to hear you're leaving."

BRONSON HEADED OUT OF TOWN via the less traveled road that would eventually hook up to Highway 18. By doing so, he'd drive past the area where Linda's parents had met with their so-called accident. Linda told him that she and Mitch had erected two crosses on the side of the road. Bronson slowed down, hoping to find them.

If he did, he'd search the area—for what, he wasn't sure, but maybe something would jump out. He drove down the narrow, winding road, focusing his attention mostly on the ditch. He glanced at the rearview mirror. Not a car in sight. He understood now how an overturned car could have remained unnoticed for a week on this desolate road.

He surveyed the area. Tall grass and occasional white firs and quaking aspens covered the rolling hills. Several dirt paths branching from the road weaved their way to barns, ranch houses, and other farm structures. If he didn't find the crosses, he'd take one of the roads and ask the first farmer he encountered.

The sudden screeching of tires somewhere behind him grabbed Bronson's attention. A beige sedan had pulled out from one of the branching roads. It skidded onto the highway, screaming toward Bronson.

Bronson took the gun from his belt and placed it on the seat next to him where it would be readily available. Being a Chief Special, he knew it would be more dangerous in a crowded elevator than on an open road. His best bet was to outrun the sedan.

He jammed the gas pedal to the floor.

The car behind him closed in.

Bronson flipped the cell phone open. The display read *No Service*. Shiiit. He dropped the phone and kept the pedal floored, but still the sedan narrowed the distance between them.

His only option left meant driving like hell. Nothing new to him.

The sedan bumped him from behind, pulled back a bit, then rammed him harder.

Bronson braced himself. Just as the car was about to hit him again, he steered sharply to the right. His Honda left the pavement for the uneven, almost nonexistent shoulder. He fought for control over the car and brought it to a stop.

As the beige sedan zoomed past him, Bronson's and Carrier's eyes connected in the snap of a second. Carrier flashed an eerie smile that filled Bronson with dread. He shook himself and watched Carrier slam on the brakes, bringing the car to a screeching halt. Then he reversed, heading at a high speed toward Bronson's car.

Bronson grabbed the Chief Special, jumped out of the Honda, and dove for safety behind a tree. He aimed the gun and fired.

Carrier's back passenger window burst, but that didn't prevent Carrier from ramming into Bronson's car. The impact caused the car to skid several feet downhill.

Carrier slid down in the seat, threw Bronson a finger, and sped away.

Bronson watched the sedan disappear. He knew he'd made a statement. He stepped away from the tree and assessed the damage. The front bumper looked like a raisin. He'd have a lot of explaining to do. He got in the car and started the engine. It coughed once but caught. Bronson threw the engine a kiss.

He popped out the empty shell, reloaded the gun, and replaced it in its holder. He took a deep breath, the cool air invigorating him. He felt thankful to be alive. He turned on the radio, found a classical station, and drove off. Within ten minutes he reached Highway 18, which headed toward Custer.

Now that Carrier had disappeared, anxiety gnawed at him. He reached down to the floor, retrieved the cell, and checked it. Finally, he had service. He called Marshall, told him what happened, and gave him Carrier's approximate location.

"Give me the description of the car again," Marshall said.

"Medium-sized. Beige. Buick Le Sabre. First two numbers on the license plate are six and one. Couldn't get the rest."

"And you're sure that was Benjamin Carrier."

"Positive."

"I'll notify the Highway Patrol. They'll set up roadblocks. We've got the bastard."

"Let's hope so," Bronson said, but his gut told him it wouldn't be that easy.

TWENTY

BRONSON'S CELL RANG and he frowned. He knew he shouldn't be driving and talking, but often life offered no choices. He glanced at the caller I.D. Mike Hoover. "Hey."

"Bronson."

Oh, oh. His ol' partner was in business mode. "What's going on?"

"About two hours ago, I called Paul and talked to him. He seemed fine, getting ready for our trip tomorrow, then I got orders from up above. They're sending me with the file on Carrier to assist the Wyoming and South Dakota authorities."

"How did Paul take the news?"

"That's just it. I called to tell him and he's out of pocket. Thinking the worst, I drove to his house. He's not there."

"He could have gone out to eat."

"Yeah, I keep telling myself that, but I've got a bad feeling. He might have left without me. If so, I don't know how to find him, much less help him."

"I'll keep an eye out. Thanks for lettin' me know." Bronson disconnected and silently cursed. On top of everything, now he might have to babysit. Great, just great.

Just what he needed.

As he pushed on, he found himself fighting to keep his eyes open and on the road. He couldn't drive much longer. He passed a sign that read *Rest Area One Mile*.

Great. Just what he needed.

More out of habit than necessity, Bronson scanned the area as he pulled into the parking lot. He spotted a motor home with its jacks down. Its owners probably planned to spend the night. Next to the camper, he saw an eighteen-wheeler, pulling a white trailer with the words *ARK Exports*. Across from them, a motorcycle, a Harley with sidesaddles, awaited its owner. Next to the bike, two cars and a truck were parked: a red Dodge, older model, and a black sedan, Chevy, fairly new and well kept. An empty space occupied the spot between the cars and a blue Dakota.

He parked next to the Chevy and headed for the men's room where he splashed water on his face. A big, burly guy with a bandana on his head and a leather jacket washed his hands and walked out. Probably the motorcycle dude.

From a vending machine, Bronson bought a cup of coffee, small, the only size they offered. Maybe he'd buy another. He watched a frenzied mother juggle two small kids and one large dog. An elderly man passed him and nodded.

Bronson nodded back and watched as the man joined his wife.

He kissed her cheek. "Ready?"

"You bet." She smiled at him and her eyes lit up with love. "I'm so excited that we're going to see our little girl."

The man whispered something. She giggled, and they walked away, holding hands.

Bronson turned away from them. The elderly couple was on their way to see their daughter. A note of regret struck Bronson's heart. He should be home, helping Little Carol sort out her problems. But instead, he was in the middle of nowhere chasing—no, being chased by—a killer.

He could walk away now. The police had control. They—

A woman's shrill scream pierced the air. He ran in the direction of the sound.

The elderly man he had been studying had his arm wrapped around his wife, attempting to comfort her. Big sobs shook her body.

"Can I help?" Bronson asked.

"Our…c-car," she sobbed.

Bronson glanced at his car and noticed a note had been stuck under the windshield. He saw the gap next to his car where the older couple's car had been parked.

"Someone stole our car." The elderly man pointed to the empty space.

Bronson flashed them his retired I.D. card. "I'll call it in for you. What did it look like?"

"It's a Chevy."

Bronson recalled the car. "Black sedan, newer model, very well kept."

The elderly man's eyebrows shot up. "Yes. How did you know?"

"What year?"

"Two-thousand eight."

"Do you know your license number?"

"M-K-seven something or the other. That's all I remember."

"State?"

"Minnesota."

"Wait here." Bronson flipped his cell open and called it in. As he did, he worked his way through the small group of people who had gathered to watch the commotion. Touching only the corners of the note, he retrieved it from the windshield and read it.

Harry,
Oh, Harry, Harry, haven't you learned? I'll always be one step ahead of you. Round Two is over and I've won that one, too. So far, the Mighty Harry has batted zero. Good going. Now I see why you had to retire.
  See you in South Dakota for Round Three.
Benjamin Carrier

Bronson returned the note to the windshield. The state troopers would want to see that. As he walked back toward the elderly couple, he repeated the words on the note. Carrier had won Round Two. How the hell had he won Round Two, and what exactly did Round Two consist of?

Round Two. Round Two...the roadblock. He looked around. Several cars had pulled in since he had taken inventory, but the beige Buick with a dented back bumper and a shattered back window drew his attention.

Carrier had changed cars. The police wouldn't be looking for him in a black Chevy. Bronson flipped his cell open and called Captain Marshall. "Carrier is no longer drivin' a beige Buick Le Sabre," he said once he'd been connected.

"Explain."

Bronson could hear the frustration in Marshall's voice. "He hijacked a car at the rest area." Bronson described the Chevy.

"That son-of-a-bitch," Marshall hissed. "I'll notify the state patrol. Hopefully, we're not too late."

Bronson saw the troopers arrive and head toward the elderly couple. They talked for a few moments before the man pointed at Bronson. "State troopers are here," Bronson told Marshall over the phone. "And I forgot to mention, Carrier left a note on my windshield."

"Don't let the troopers get it. I'm on the way. Tell me about the note."

Bronson did and disconnected. He watched a trooper approach.

"Good evening. Are you the one who called this in?"

Bronson nodded as he retrieved his I.D. He wondered how long this would delay him.

Forty-five minutes later, Marshall arrived, and Bronson watched in amusement as the state troopers and the captain exchanged words over custody of the note. As far as Bronson was concerned, it belonged to him. But he didn't want it.

He was about to walk away when he spotted another trooper working his way toward them. His flushed face told Bronson he had something to say. Bronson decided to stick around to hear the news.

"We found it!" The trooper yelled loud enough for everyone to hear him. "We found the Chevy, off road, partially hidden behind some trees. It's been abandoned up ahead from here, walking distance. Nothing seems disturbed. It's in good condition."

"How about Carrier?" Marshall asked. "Did you get him, too?"

The trooper looked at him. "No, I'm afraid not. I found the car, but no sign of Carrier. Who are you?"

Marshall introduced himself and Bronson walked away. Apparently, Carrier was on foot, but that didn't make sense. Maybe he had hitchhiked, but that wasn't Carrier's style. Some piece to the puzzle needed to be solved.

Bronson stepped back and studied the rest area. He recalled seeing the cars, the truck, the motor home, the eighteen-wheeler, and the motorcycle. He remembered the old couple, the bike rider, the young couple with kids and a dog. As he brought each of these details to mind, he walked the rest area, concentrating on its perimeter. The eighteen-wheeler had driven away and so had the biker. Bikes make noise, and Bronson hadn't remembered the revving of the engine. Maybe he hadn't been paying attention.

He doubled his efforts and expanded his search. It didn't take him long to find the biker's body. His throat had been slit and he'd been stripped of his leather jacket, chaps, and head scarf.

"Shiiit," Bronson said.

TWENTY-ONE

At 8:55, BRONSON REACHED the Custer exit sign. He knew the Purple Pie Place closed at eleven o'clock, which meant he didn't have to worry about Linda waiting outside. Still, he wanted to reach her as soon as possible. He checked his cell for phone availability. As soon as his cell showed he had service, he called Linda.

The phone rang once…

…*pick up, Linda.*

Twice…

Pick up.

Three times…

Be there.

Four times…five. Finally, "The party you're trying to reach is unavailable."

Bronson snapped the phone shut. *Damn.* Why hadn't she answered? *Relax,* he told himself. Maybe she didn't have service. He punched in Carol's number.

"Dad, hi."

"Sweetie, are you and Mom okay?"

"Of course, why wouldn't we be? But I'm glad you called I have something to tell you. A man stopped by to see you He—"

"A man?" Carrier? No, he wouldn't do that. Who, then? Paul? He would have identified himself. "What man? Wha did he look like? What did he want?"

No answer.

"Carol, sweetheart?" A lump the size of a lemon formed

in his chest, blocking his airway. "Carol?" He looked at the cell. The call had ended.

A bad connection. Had to have been. Bronson tried calling again, but the phone read *No Service*.

He floored the accelerator and prayed he'd reach them in time.

FOR THE PAST TEN MINUTES, Eric had stared at his parents' picture. It had been snapped long ago when they were a family. Dad, now dead. *Murdered*. And Mom...Mom, that bitch.

Eric's mouth filled with an acid taste. He set the picture down. He could no longer stand and do nothing. The truth had to come out, and he was the only one who could set the events rolling. The immediate problem involved the two silly bodyguards Bronson had hired to protect him and Brad. Somehow, he'd have to shake them.

Best way was to split them. Eric picked up the phone and dialed the babysitter's number.

Five minutes later, he came down the stairs carrying Brad and his backpack.

Jay and Pete looked up from the TV program they were watching.

"I'm taking Brad to the sitter's. I'm feeling restless. I'm heading to the movies."

Jay and Pete exchanged looks. "It's your turn to watch the kid. I'll go with Eric," Jay said.

"How come you get to see a movie and I get stuck with the kid?"

Jay shrugged. "Call it fate. It's my turn to do the fun stuff."

Pete sighed. "Might as well. I didn't want to go see a movie anyway."

"Glad you got that settled," Eric said as he retrieved the car keys, "because I'm leaving now."

Jay and Pete grabbed their jackets and followed Eric out.

Eric drove to the sitter's a block away and dropped Brad. Pete stayed behind.

One down, one to go, Eric thought. "I have no idea what's playing. I'm going to the first movie available."

"No problem," Jay answered. "A movie is a movie."

The animated movie had just begun when Eric and Jay arrived. Eric purchased the tickets and headed inside. Once they were seated, Eric leaned over and whispered, "A movie isn't a movie without popcorn and a drink. What do you want? My treat."

"Thanks. A soft drink would do. Any kind."

"You got it. I'm going to make a pit stop first."

Jay nodded and turned his attention to the movie.

Using long strides, Eric headed out the door, reached the car, got in, and drove off.

So far, so good.

Being late at night, he imagined that the pharmaceutical tycoons McGory and Stein would be at home. He'd visit one, then the other, if necessary. He hoped the confrontation would go well.

He doubted that.

TWENTY-TWO

BRONSON GLARED AT THE CELL, willing it to have service. Frustration gnawed at him like a giant insect. He stepped on the accelerator and watched the needle climb past eighty.

He picked up the cell. Finally, full service. He called Carol. She answered on the first ring. Relief flowed through his veins. "You and Little Carol, you're okay?"

"We're both fine. Why? What's wrong?"

Bronson sat up straighter in the car. "Wrong? Sweetheart—"

"Harry Bronson, don't you *sweetheart* me."

Dang that woman. Even over the phone she knew. "I'm headin' home now. But I've got one stop to make."

"You're avoiding the question."

"I was about to tell you where the stop would be."

"Harry Bronson, you know exactly what I mean." A small pause followed. When she spoke again, her tone had softened. "Should I be concerned?"

The world slipped away from Bronson. She had spent countless sleepless nights worrying, wondering. She didn't deserve this. "No, never."

"Oh, Harry."

She knew. Bronson rubbed his forehead.

"When you get home, Harry Bronson, we'll talk."

Oh, oh.

TWO BLOCKS AWAY FROM THE Purple Pie Place, Carrier brought the motorcycle to a stop and dismounted. He was glad to be rid of that thing, couldn't wait until he hijacked a car instead—maybe Bronson's. That would teach him.

Carrier sighed. He wished he could do that. It would serve Bronson right, but that would be a stupid move, and he would never do anything to jeopardize his assignment.

He walked away from the bike, stopped, and turned. Earlier he had checked out the saddlebag's contents and found the gun. He immediately knew the biker had been a weak jerk. Anyone who relied on guns qualified as a poor excuse for a human being.

Not that guns didn't have advantages. Often, situations called for the exclusive use of them. Such as today. Yes, he could see how the gun would be beneficial. He returned to the bike, opened the saddlebag, got the gun and a handful of extra ammunition, and stuffed the ammo in his pants pocket. He tucked the gun in his waistband.

He glanced at his watch. Bronson would have sent Linda to some safe place. He'd probably suggested going to the cops, but she'd never do that. She'd go to some public place where tourists gathered. Good thing Custer was a small town. He'd track her down in no time, grab her, and find an ideal hiding place. He'd be waiting by the time Bronson got there.

Carrier's footsteps echoed his urgency as he rushed toward destiny. He reached toward his waistband and felt the cool metal.

He smiled and wet his lips in anticipation.

BRONSON SNAPPED THE CELL SHUT. Linda still wasn't answering. The knot in his stomach tightened. He spotted the sign for the Purple Pie Place. He slowed down and pulled into the semidark parking lot. Only two cars—a black jeep and a beige Toyota—remained parked in the Employees Only area. In the visitors' parking lot, he spotted Linda's Mercedes and a dark blue Chevy Cobalt.

He looked toward the building's windows. He detected movement. Linda would be there, working on her needle-point and perhaps a bit anxious for Bronson to show up.

He drove toward the back of the building, backed up, and parked next to Linda's car. He turned on the headlights. The parking lot lit up like Las Vegas at night. He watched for any movement, concentrating on the area beyond the light. Soft gray shadows followed by deeper, darker areas greeted him. He killed the lights and waited.

The only sound he detected was his breathing.

He reached for the door handle and stopped. Assuming Linda was inside, why wasn't she answering her cell?

He focused his vision on the area immediately outside the car. Darkness surrounded him.

Could it be a bad cell connection? How many times had he been inside a building and never received the call until he stepped out?

Bronson focused on the darker shadows. No movement, not even the swaying of leaves in the cool breeze. The tall pines that Carol so loved blocked the view of the area outside the parking lot. He swung the door open but remained inside.

No shadows sprang toward the car.

He pulled his gun and held it at the ready position. He stepped out, crouched, and aimed—at nothing. He could hear his heart beat in his ears.

He waited—still aiming—for four, five seconds.

Nothing.

Six, seven seconds.

No movement.

Bronson closed the car door. The slam became a resounding bang in the night.

Still, he waited. Watched.

With almost robotic movements, he put the gun down,

stood up, and glanced inside Linda's car. He saw an empty soda can and nothing else. She had to be inside.

A shot rang out.

Immediately followed by another.

TWENTY-THREE

JAY DREADED CALLING PETE to tell him Eric had gotten away. He should have been more attentive, but hindsight thrived where foresight didn't. Jay had no options left. He opened his cell and punched in Pete's number. When Pete answered, Jay told him what happened.

"What do you mean, you lost him?" Pete's tone clearly stated that he thought Jay was a moron.

Jay frowned. What kind of an idiot question was that? "Exactly what I said. Eric told me he was hitting the can and then stopping at the concession stand. When he didn't come back, I went looking for him but he was nowhere around."

"What's your theory?"

"Someone saw us going to the movie. Soon as Eric was alone, he grabbed him."

"So what do you think we should do?"

"Go back to his house and see if someone contacts us. We should also call Bronson."

"What about the police?"

Jay's first instinct had been to contact the police but he had decided against it at the last minute. "At this point, we don't know if he's been abducted or he gave me the slip."

"Why would he give you the slip?"

"I'm not saying he did—"

"—but the police would want to know that."

Jay nodded, then felt foolish when he realized Pete couldn't see him. "Yeah. Tell you what, I'm going back to Eric's. Maybe he'll show up, maybe not."

"Call me."

"I will."

Jay never got the chance to call him back.

"SHIIIT." BRONSON KICKED ONE of the two flat tires. That S.O.B. had shot them, and now he was stuck. He wouldn't be getting back to his Carols any time soon. Might as well do something useful while he waited for the police. From his car, he retrieved a flashlight and headed toward the area from where the shots had been fired.

He pointed the light at the ground where he thought the shooter might have crouched and moved the beam around the area. Some insect scurried out of sight. The wind scattered the leaves. No papers, no cigarettes littered the place. Interesting.

Bronson concentrated on the pine tree, the one that had hidden the shooter from his view. He shook his head in disgust. The *shooter* didn't exist. Carrier did.

Knowing this bothered the hell out of Bronson and filled him with dread. Carrier hated guns. They conflicted with his principles. Why then had he chosen to use one?

Bronson flashed the light on the lower part of the trunk and slowly moved the beam up. At eye-level, he spotted a note thumtacked to the tree. The folded paper read *Harry*.

"That's you, buddy boy."

Bronson jumped around, heart pounding, to stare at his expartner's smiling face. The area behind Hoover swarmed with red flashing lights and police cars. A plainclothes policeman bent down by Bronson's tires as he dictated something to other policemen.

Bronson smiled back. Up to now, he hadn't realized how much he missed seeing Hoover's goofy face. "Hoover."

"Bronson."

A wave of relief and nostalgia hit Bronson. "Good to see you."

"Even under these circumstances?"

"Especially under these circumstances."

"You seem surprised. Didn't you hear us?" Hoover spotted the note. "Never mind. When you're in a detecting mode, nothing disrupts you."

Bronson reached for the note. "Let's see what Carrier has to say."

"You're sure this is Carrier's work?"

"I'm willin' to bet a week's pay."

"You're retired. You don't have a week's pay."

"Nice of you to remind me."

"Hey, that's what friends are for."

"Does that mean you're willin' to give me some money?"

Hoover smiled, retrieved a pair of plastic gloves, and handed them to Bronson. "Read your note."

"As you wish." Bronson put the gloves on, opened the note, and read:

Harry,
Just so there's no doubt in your mind, that was me who shot your tires.

I could just as easily have shot you instead, but we've only played two rounds.

It's not your turn to die in Round Three. Whose turn, then? Figure it out and maybe you can finally win a round.
Benjamin Carrier

Bronson felt the sting of defeat erupt like a volcano.

"What's wrong?"

"Each round ends with a death. If he kills someone, he wins. If I prevent him from killing, then I win. We're in our third round and so far, I've let two people die."

"Bronson, you're not responsible."

"If I'd figured it out sooner, they would be alive."

"That's exactly what he wants you to think. It's all part of his twisted game. This is just one way to demoralize you. That's why he's calling you Harry instead of Bronson. He's trying to get to you. Don't let him."

Easy to say. Hard to do, and Bronson realized Hoover knew it. Bronson nodded and watched the policemen gather around his car. "The bullets will lead them to Carrier's gun."

"Let's hope so."

A flatbed tow truck pulled in. "You called them?"

"Helps if you have connections, but let me set the record straight. I called, you pay."

"I'd say that's a bargain."

"Getting shot at is never a bargain."

"Carrier didn't shoot me. He shot my tires."

"Yeah, and that worries me."

Bronson nodded. "We're on the same wavelength. Why do you suppose he changed his M.O.?"

Hoover shook his head. "Don't know, buddy."

A wave of anxiety smothered Bronson. What other rules had changed? The whisper of a cold wind brought back his daughter's message. A man had stopped by, asking for him.

A man—Carrier.

Carrier had been in his camper, had talked to his daughter. Bronson was convinced of it. A freezing chill engulfed him, increasing his heartbeat. He turned toward his disabled Honda. "My car."

Hoover watched Bronson's car being loaded. "We'll use mine. Let's go."

Bronson bolted toward the vehicle. Hoover followed close behind.

"What's going on?" Hoover fished the car keys out of his pocket.

"Carrier's been at my camper, talkin' to Little Carol."

For a second, Hoover froze. "She's okay?"

"Yeah. I guess. I'm just…"

"—worried."

"Yeah." Bronson continued to head toward the rental while Hoover approached a plainclothes policeman. He pointed at Bronson.

As Bronson climbed into Hoover's passenger seat, he looked at his watch, thought of calling Carol again, but decided against it. That would give her one more reason to worry. He watched Hoover talking to the detective and wished Hoover would hurry. The detective nodded and Hoover ran back to the car. "He wants to know if you want a police escort."

Bronson shook his head.

"Figured as much." Hoover started the engine. "He made me promise to bring you back as soon as possible."

Bronson nodded. "I just need to see them—be sure they're both okay."

"I understand." He pulled out.

TWENTY-FOUR

"RELAX, WILL YA? I CAN SEE your camper from here and it's intact. Take a deep breath," Hoover said as he pulled into The Roost Resort.

Bronson sat up, leaned forward, and scanned the area. Nothing unusual stood out. Bronson relaxed, but a small twinge of worry hung on. "Seein' is believin'."

"You bet." Hoover slowed down as he entered the campground.

He pulled in behind Bronson's camper. "Get out of here. Go check on your wife and kid."

As Bronson stepped out, he glanced at the empty lot next to his. Linda's unit should have been there. Had she taken the time to hitch her Mercedes to the back of the camper and then drove the camper to the Purple Pie Place? He remembered seeing her car, but not the motor home. That meant she had to unhook the car and park the camper elsewhere. Why? It didn't make any sense. He made a mental note to check on the camper.

But first, his family. Seconds later, he stood in the motor home's living room, glancing, searching.

"Dad, you're home." Little Carol sat, curled up on the couch, a magazine by her.

Bronson stared at his daughter. Her thick black curls framed her round face. Her warm smile filled him with relief mixed with pride. She looked so beautiful.

"Dad, you look dorky. What's wrong?"

So much for pride. "Your mom, she's home?"

"No. Tonight they're meeting at Leslie's."

"But she's okay?"

"Of course. Why?"

A knock on the door interrupted them. Bronson looked out the window and Hoover waved at him. Bronson swung the door open.

Little Carol sprung to her feet. "Uncle Mike." She hugged him.

Great. Hoover gets the hug. I get the I-look-dorky statement.

Little Carol stared at Hoover, then at Bronson. "Dad, something's going on. What's wrong?"

"You're gettin' to be more and more like your mom every day."

"I'll take that as a compliment. Now tell me what's going on."

Bronson led the way to the brown plaid couch, and both he and Hoover sat down. Little Carol curled up in the reclining rocker with her feet wrapped under her.

"You told me a man stopped by to see me. I need you to tell me exactly what he said and what he looked like."

"He was nice enough looking and had a real good body."

Bronson cocked his head and stared at his daughter.

Hoover smiled and Bronson glared at him.

"Oh, sorry, Dad. You didn't let me finish. He may have been a looker, but something about him seemed to be off."

"What does that mean?"

Little Carol shrugged. "He was, well, creepy." She got to her feet. "Mom told me you'd want me to describe him, so I did one better. I drew a picture of him."

Drew a picture? When had she learned to draw? What else didn't he know about his daughter?

Little Carol retrieved a piece of paper from the magazine rack and handed it to him.

Carrier's face stared back at Bronson, the image chilling him. His daughter had captured Carrier's harsh, cold gaze. The image hypnotized him and drew him in. Maybe Carrier's victims felt the same way.

"You did this from memory?" Hoover asked.

"Yeah. I memorize people's features. Took me a while to master the skill, but I'm getting better."

"We need you in the police department. Anybody who can be so observant and remember details like this..." Hoover pointed to the picture. Then he saw Bronson's glaring eyes. Hoover hushed.

Little Carol looked at her father, then at Hoover. "Oh, Dad. It's sweet of you to be concerned, but I don't need to be protected anymore. I'm old enough to make my own decisions." She smiled at him, perhaps in an attempt to soften her words.

Amazing how much she reminded him of her mother. "What exactly did he say?" Bronson asked.

"Exactly?"

"As close as possible."

"He said, and I quote, 'Tell him Round Three is almost over.' I asked him what he meant by that, and he smiled and said you'd know. Then he said, 'Remind him I'm still one step ahead and always right behind him.' What did he mean by that? Is he dangerous?"

The message cut through Bronson's heart with the precision of a sharp blade. He forced his fears down. "He's very dangerous and if you see him again you're to steer away from him. Is that clear?"

"Dad, I'm twenty-five years old."

Hoover smiled.

"Sorry, sweetheart. It's just that— Sometimes I—"

"I understand, Dad."

"Thank you." Bronson looked at his daughter. She had blossomed into a beautiful, strong woman. Suddenly, her nickname, Little Carol, seemed inappropriate. "You're sure your mom is okay?"

"I just left her less than five minutes ago. What about you, Dad? Are you in danger?" She bit her lip and looked at him with concerned eyes.

Bronson opened his arms and drew her in. "Nothin' to be worried about." His gaze traveled over his daughter's shoulders and landed on Hoover.

Hoover flashed him a hard look.

Bronson released his daughter from his embrace. "Linda Randig, the lady next door, where did she go?"

Little Carol shrugged. "I don't know. She was here this morning when Mom and I went to Leslie's to rehearse. When I got back, I noticed the camper gone."

"I'm going to the office to see if they know anythin'. You wait here for your mom."

She cocked her head and pinched her eyebrows together.

"Sorry." Bronson reminded himself that his daughter was now a grown woman. "I'll be back in a minute." He stepped out and Hoover followed him.

"That son-of-a-bitch was in my motor home," Bronson said once they were out of his daughter's hearing range. He spoke between clenched teeth.

"I know how you're feeling. He wants you angry and afraid so you won't be able to think straight. Clear your emotions and keep a level head. You need to come up with a plan. Let's hear it."

"I'm gettin' the hell out of Dodge."

"Which direction are you heading?"

"I'm going back to the Purple Pie Place, talk to the police, and hopefully hook up with Linda. Her destination is Minnesota, so I think I'll head that way."

"Sounds doable, but I have one worry."

A squirrel scurried across their path, leaped onto a pine,

and wiggled its way up. Bronson switched his attention from the squirrel back to his ex-partner. "Carrier's message."

"Exactly. 'Round Three is almost over.' Who's going to die?"

"Only one I can think of is Linda, but if she's with me, I'll be able to protect her."

"Then there's you."

Bronson shook his head. "By his own admission, too early in the game." He paused and looked back at his camper. "That's why I'm leavin'. He'll follow me and hopefully leave my family alone."

"I'll stay with them. I'll tell them I can't afford a motel. I'll be here twenty-four–seven. When I have to leave, I'll make sure there'll be someone to watch them. They'll be safe. Don't worry."

Bronson recalled doing that for Hoover's family. Families should be left alone, but criminals seldom, if ever, followed a set of ethics. "I appreciate that." They reached the front office and waited while the owners checked an elderly couple in. The minutes dragged and Bronson wished he could jump to the back counter, check them in, and dismiss them.

When they finally headed out, the clerk looked up at Bronson and Hoover and said, "I'll be with you in a minute." She pounded on the computer keys. When she finished, she looked up at them. "Need a spot?"

"Got one already. I'm just wonderin' about my neighbor, spot seventy-one. Do you happen to know when she left and where she went?"

The clerk shook her head. "No idea. We don't check 'em out. They just leave."

"Would there by any chance be a message for me?"

"What spot are you holding?"

"Seventy."

She checked and shook her head. "Sorry."

"Thank you anyway." Bronson and Hoover headed back to Bronson's motor home.

"Now what?" Hoover asked.

"Now I leave." Bronson's cell rang. The caller I.D. read *Jay*. A sinking sensation hit Bronson. "Jay, is everythin' okay?"

"Not really. You need to get over here as soon as possible."

"What's wrong?"

"Can't say over the phone. I'll explain when you get here. Eric's disappeared. I've contacted the police."

Shiiit. Bronson rubbed his forehead. "The baby?"

"He's fine. He's with the babysitter, one block away from Eric's. Pete's with them."

"What's the babysitter's name?"

"Brookes Berry."

Bronson wrote the name down. "I've got some unfinished business to take care of. I'll meet you as soon as I get free from here. Where will you be?"

"At my house." Jay gave him the address along with directions.

Bronson recorded it and snapped the cell shut. "We may have the victim of Round Three."

"Who?"

"Eric."

TWENTY-FIVE

WHEN BRONSON PULLED INTO the Purple Pie Place's parking lot, Detective Chuck Gorman approached him. "You're Bronson."

"I am." Bronson stood by the cruiser, digesting his surroundings.

"Took you long enough to get back. When I said you could go, I thought maybe it'd take you fifteen minutes, not half an hour." He peered inside the cruiser. "Where's Hoover?"

"He stayed behind. He's watchin' over my family." *As though you cared.*

"I need him here. I'll send a cruiser to babysit your family." He looked around and signaled one of the young officers to approach.

The rookie's body stiffened and for a second, Bronson assumed he would salute Detective Gorman. Instead, he headed their way.

Gorman turned to Bronson. "Tell him how to get to your place, then join me." He looked at the officer. "You, get over to Bronson's camper and watch his wife and daughter. You suspect anything, call for backup." He turned and walked away.

Bronson nodded a greeting at the officer and gave him directions. "Please take good care of my wife and daughter. Your presence might scare them."

"I'll watch them from the distance. They won't even know I'm there."

The rookie seemed familiar with procedure, but maybe all he knew about protecting a family, he'd learned in a classroom. "I appreciate that."

"You're right, you know," the rookie said.

Bronson looked at him.

"I've never done this before, but I graduated top in my class. I know what I'm doing." He threw his shoulders back, making him look taller. "What are their names?"

"Both are Carols."

"Let me assure you, Mr. Bronson, that I'll keep a real good eye on them."

Bronson believed him. He nodded. "I know you will. Thank you."

The rookie got in the car and Bronson watched him disappear over the horizon. As the police car vanished from his view, he wished he could be the one to protect his family. He shook himself and focused on the current dilemma. He approached Gorman. "Where's Linda?"

"Who?"

"Linda Randig. She was supposed to meet me here. I don't see her."

"Sorry, I don't know who you're talking about. Those are the employees lucky enough to be working this shift. Maybe one of them is this Linda Whatever. If not, then I don't know. No one else is inside the building." He pointed to a group of bored-looking teens.

"Thanks." Bronson headed their way. "I was supposed to meet a lady here. Her name's Linda Randig. She's in her late fifties or early sixties, about yay tall." He raised his hand to the appropriate height, approximately to his cheek. "Chocolate-brown eyes, reddish hair, angular, diamond-shaped face. Did you happen to see her?"

"Bronson." Detective Gorman signaled for him to come.

Bronson continued talking to the teens. "Any of you see her?"

They looked from one to another and shook their heads.

Somebody had to have seen her. "Are there any employees who already went home who had an earlier shift?"

"Bronson." Gorman's bright red face told him the detective wasn't pleased with him.

A tall, skinny waiter stepped forward. "My shift began at four. Me and my buddies came over here for lunch. It's free, you know. So I've been here since around two. Nobody like that has been here since then."

"Bronson!" The short, sharp command pierced the approaching night.

Bronson thanked the teens and worked his way toward the detective.

Even before Bronson reached him, he began snapping at Bronson. "I expected this to be a routine killer-stalks-ex-cop. Get the facts, file a report, be on my way. I have—"

"Linda Randig is missin'."

"What?"

"That's why I came. I was supposed to meet her here. No one's seen her and I know Carrier was here. That's her car over there." Bronson pointed to the Mercedes. "I checked the front and back passenger seats, but not the trunk." His nerves tightened in a knot. He had promised Linda to keep her safe. He had failed.

Gorman snapped his fingers and two officers rushed toward him. They all approached the car. The trunk looked pristine. No one had made any attempts to break in, but that didn't mean much.

The officers opened the trunk. Bronson held his breath and released it only when he saw the empty space.

Where was she? Why wasn't she answering her cell? And what of Eric? What did Jay have to tell him that he couldn't say over the phone?

Bronson felt the world crumbling around him.
Round Three is almost over.
Who's going to die?

TWENTY-SIX

As far as nights went, this one had all the makings of a perfect one. Millions of tiny lights sparkled in the velvety moonless sky. A touch of a breeze blew away the day's oppressive heat and called for people to gather outdoors to unwind. Under normal circumstances, Bronson would have been captivated by the night's enchanting beauty.

Instead, he cursed the night. He didn't want to have to wait until morning to try to find Linda and Eric. Time had become his enemy. He pressed the gas pedal and watched the needle climb to eighty.

Jay had told him that he had contacted the police. That meant Captain Samuel Marshall was aware of the problem. That should have set his mind at ease, but it didn't.

Bronson sped even more.

Almost two hours later, Bronson located the address Jay had given him. Nothing distinguished the modest-sized home. The front lawn had been trimmed and watered. A row of yellow and red marigolds led up the pathway. The house, however, could benefit from a new coat of paint. Light shone through the two front windows like eyes luring him in.

Bronson walked up the pathway, staring at the door. His heart pounded in his chest at a steady beat. The front door stood ajar. Was this the norm? Did Jay always leave his front door slightly opened? Bronson didn't know. A lump the size of a lemon formed in his throat, and he found it hard to swallow.

He took out his gun and held it at the ready. He pressed his back against the wall and rang the doorbell.

No answer.

"Jay?"

He waited and pushed the door all the way open.

He waited some more.

No sounds. No movement. Nothing.

Bronson stuck his head in. The first thing he noticed was the overturned lamp, then the pool of blood that had already started to congeal on the floor. "Shiiit," Bronson murmured under his breath.

Jay's body lay on the floor, a spilled can of Sprite by him. His throat had been so severely cut that he'd almost been decapitated. The note rested on top of his stomach.

Bronson bent down and read it:

Harry, Harry, Harry,
Round Three is over and I won again. I can't believe you let another innocent person die.
*   What's wrong, hot shot? You're beginning to bore me.*
Benjamin Carrier

Bronson called the police and then snapped the phone shut. He'd had enough. The best defense was always a good offense. He stepped outside. While he waited for the police, he retrieved his pocket notebook and read through his notes, focusing on the details, looking for something he might have missed.

His cell rang and he looked at the caller I.D. Pete Acevedo. Bronson wanted to talk to him. He snapped the cell open. "Bronson here."

"It's Pete."

"Do you know about Jay?"

A long pause followed. "We need to talk. Meet me."

"Where?"

"There's an abandoned warehouse outside of town. It's called Mensa Enterprises. I'll wait there. I'm already on my way." His voice sounded almost robotic. Either that or very tired. It reminded Bronson of the voice that informs the listener that his call is very important and to please hold for the next available representative.

As soon as the connection ended, the cell rang again. The I.D. read *Restricted Call*. "Yes?"

"Harry, it's me." Laughter followed. "I won." The line went dead.

The sound of Carrier's gloating laughter chilled Bronson like a serpentine hiss.

From behind him, someone said, "Why is it, Bronson, that wherever you turn up, there's a body? It's really making me think and I don't like where my thoughts are leading."

Bronson pivoted and faced Detective Samuel Marshall.

TWENTY-SEVEN

"HE WAS DEAD WHEN I walked in," Bronson said.

"So you say, Mr. Bronson." Marshall held his hands behind him as he watched the photographer snap shots of the corpse from different angles. "Thing is, can you prove it?"

Bronson bit his tongue to keep from snapping at Marshall. "I don't have to prove it. What possible motive would I have?"

Technicians swarmed around, dusting the place for prints, recording information, discussing the murder among themselves. "Let's step outside where we can talk a little more freely." Marshall led Bronson past the living room and out onto the porch.

A cool gust of wind blew, chilling Bronson and rattling the windows. Bronson preferred the cool outdoors to the stuffiness of the house.

Marshall rubbed his upper arms. "We can go inside my car, if you want."

Not on your life, Bronson thought. From there to jail would be just a hop and a skip away. "Actually, I like the breeze."

"Suit yourself." He walked over to the edge of the porch and sat down. Bronson joined him. "Let me tell it like it is. You've worked long enough in a law-enforcing capacity to know rumors get started and often are damaging."

Rumors had destroyed many solid cases and tainted otherwise perfect careers. Bronson, as well as his fellow officers, tried to ignore them but as human beings, they couldn't help wondering if they were true. The seeds of doubt had been planted. "Haven't heard any gossip about me," Bronson said.

"I have. It's loaded and I'm not sure it's gossip."

Bronson felt the vice of his stomach turn a notch tighter. "Explain."

"First time I see you in action, you're bending over Pedro's body, pinning a note on him, which you claim Carrier wrote and attached to him." From his tone and manner, Marshall could have been talking about something as trivial as the weather.

Bronson knew he shouldn't justify that comment with an explanation, but he decided to anyway. "A breeze almost ripped the note off. I was just fixin' it."

"So you say." Marshall raised his hand, the index and middle fingers extended. "Two, all these notes Carrier has left you are fingerprint-free. No one's seen Carrier leave the notes behind. Hell, no one's even seen Carrier. Only you. And Carrier, I understand, is a dead criminal who's resurfaced. Miracles never cease to amaze me."

Bronson's mind, wrestling with incomplete thoughts and emotions, struggled to anchor his thoughts. "The Dallas Police Department confirmed his fingerprints."

Marshall snapped his fingers. "That's right. They did, but wait, let's see. Weren't those fingerprints the ones you sent them?" His eyes were as hard as crystal and he sniffed the air. "What's that smell? Wait, don't tell me. I know. It smells like a dirty cop, and one thing I hate more than anything is a dirty cop."

Bronson stood rigidly, sweat running down his back and chest. "I could never be dirty, goes against my grain, and I have lots of people who would testify to that."

"For your sake, I hope so. Thing is, it can happen so easily. Take me, for instance. My wife got cancer. Even with insurance, I couldn't afford the payments. Accepting bribes would have solved my problems. But I stood firm against temptation."

"I'm sorry about your wife, but I have no temptations."

"That's not what I hear."

Time froze. "Meanin'?"

"I have a witness who's willing to testify that you and Linda Randig are having an affair."

"That's ridiculous. I just met the lady." Bronson felt his blood boil. What if Carol heard these rumors? "Who's this witness?"

Marshall screwed up his face. "Oh, come on, Bronson. You know better than that. You know I'm not going to tell you. If I did, I'd have another body in my morgue."

An icy tentacle of uneasiness pierced Bronson's heart. "I can't believe I'm hearin' this. Even if Linda and I were havin' an affair, why kill Pedro?"

"I'm going to bend the rules a bit here and tell you what I know. We've established that you and Linda are lovers. The rest is speculation, but give us time. We're working on it. What we think happened is, Mitch found out about the affair and threatened to tell your wife, so you killed him. Only you didn't see the gardener next door, a kid trying to earn extra money for his mother's upcoming fiftieth birthday. His mistake was contacting you to blackmail you. Naturally, you agree to meet him in the alley. But instead of handing him money, you stabbed him and then devised this fantastic story about a dead man killing him."

The information hit Bronson like a straight shot just below his heart. A little grunt escaped him as his mind roared with white noise. "Tell me, do you actually believe this?"

Marshall half smirked. "Doesn't matter what I believe. It's what they believe." He pointed to the people inside the house.

"What about you? What do you plan to do?"

Marshall took a deep breath. "I'm going to gather evidence and when I have enough, I'll start proper procedure and get the judge to issue a warrant." He looked at Bronson straight in the eye.

"What about Carrier?"

A small, twisted smile escaped Marshall's lips, a smile lacking any humor. "I'm going with the assumption that Carrier exists. For now. I know you being from the big city, you'll think our efforts are insignificant, but you'd be surprised what my men can do. We don't hold much hope of finding Carrier because I think you resurrected him to cover your dirty deeds. You could have gotten away with it until Jay's death."

"How did that change things?" Bronson knew he wasn't going to like what he was about to hear.

"Jay needed extra money, so when I could, I'd hire him to do odd jobs. I recently hired him to look into your background. He called me today and told me he'd found some very interesting things about your maverick reputation. We were to meet tomorrow. Now he's dead." He stepped forward so Bronson could clearly see him. "You've got to realize, we protect our own, retired or not. Jay has—had—an untarnished police record. In this community, he's very much respected and loved. His death will not go unpunished, and the cards are stacked against you."

Bronson walked away but heard Marshall's parting words. "Wherever you go, we will find you. You haven't seen the Two Forks police at work."

Feeling as though he'd been thrown into a bottomless pit with no hope of escape, Bronson walked faster, rushing to his car, praying he'd get away.

TWENTY-EIGHT

THE SILENCE OF THE ROAD accompanied by dense air hovered over Bronson as the highway stretched out before him. Anxiety gnawed at him and he wished he could freeze time. But being unfamiliar with the area kept him driving at a slow, steady speed, making sure he could spot the vague landmarks the gas station attendant had given him.

"On your right, you'll see a bare area where trees have been cut and a new crop of seedlings has been planted," the attendant said. "That'll be followed by a cluster of white fir. Shortly after that, you'll see a dirt road—it's not labeled. You follow that road for maybe five miles or so. Then you'll come to a Y. Keep left for another two miles and you'll see Mensa Enterprises. Can't miss it."

Bronson thanked him as he paid for the coffee and candy bar. He turned to leave.

"Hey, Mister."

Bronson stopped and pivoted.

"You don't mind me asking. Why are you going there? Used to be a big thing couple of years back. I worked there, myself, but the place is empty now."

"I'm thinking of buying the building. Wanted to see it before money changed hands. What can you tell me about it?"

The attendant shrugged. "Used to be part of that big pharmaceutical lab we have here in town. You know which one I'm talking about?"

Bronson nodded.

"Been deserted now maybe three, four years. I heard Mr. Stein planned to burn it, but I guess he's selling instead. Makes more sense to me. If you buy and reopen the facility, keep me in mind. Wouldn't mind having my job back. Being a gas station attendant for the rest of my life isn't exactly my life's ambition."

Bronson opened his candy bar and sipped his coffee. "What did you do for Mensa?"

"I was a gofer."

"A what?"

"A gofer. You know. Go for this—go for that."

Bronson smiled. "And what exactly did you gofer for?"

"Mostly deliveries. I dropped off creams and all that fancy goo to rich people's houses."

"You ever actually see the product?"

"Nah, didn't have to. Products were always boxed up. Didn't have to open them to know there's cream inside."

"What can you tell me about Stein or McGory?"

The attendant leaned forward, clearly savoring the conversation. "McGory never showed up. He stayed mainly at the research lab. Stein was the one I dealt with, and if you excuse my French, he's an arrogant son-of-a-bitch."

"Why's that?" Bronson looked at his watch. He didn't want to keep Pete waiting longer than necessary.

"He had to stick his nose in everything. He'd personally inventoried each box that left the place, even when I loaded the van myself. Seems he didn't trust me to do the job right. He's such a jerk. But I was always real careful to deliver the right package to the right person, specially the ones out of town."

Bronson thought about the creams. If all he did was deliver them, why not mail them? Why the personal touch? "Were there many of those deliveries?"

"You sure ask a lot of questions."

Bronson shrugged. "What can I tell you? If I'm buying, I want to know what I'm getting into."

"Place is deserted now."

"Right. Anything else you can tell me?"

The attendant squinted as though attempting to remember. He shook his head. "Haven't been there in about two years, but back then, the place was in a real bad condition. It was a rat's nest. A fire hazard. Sure you want to go there now?"

Bronson knew he didn't have a choice.

Soon as Bronson reached his car, he took out the cell and speed dialed Hoover.

Hoover answered on the second ring. "Yo, buddy, what mess have you gotten yourself into now?"

"Do you ever answer the phone in a normal way?"

"Do you ever answer any questions people ask you?"

"Should I?" On the side of the road Bronson spotted a deer and its fawn. He slowed down. "I got somethin'. It may be nothin', but it's a loose end we'll need to close."

"I'm all ears."

"Seems that some of the pharmaceutical creams were delivered by truck and not by mail. That piqued my interest. Why the personal touch?"

"That should be easy to check," Hoover answered. "I'll get back to you."

They disconnected and Bronson concentrated on his driving. Just as the attendant had said, seven miles down the road, he came across an area where saplings of all sizes covered the ground. He wondered how many of those would actually survive.

He slowed down, searching for the dirt road.

A fire hazard, the attendant had said. Now deserted.

Pete had chosen a strange place to meet. Had Carrier been holding a gun to Pete's head as he made that call? That would explain why his voice has sounded like a robot's. He'd been scared.

Bronson spotted the road and turned. Images flashed in his mind. Hoover running toward the deserted warehouse, crouching. Minutes later, the place a living inferno. Hoover trapped. A body burning to ashes, beyond recognition. Hoover desperately attempting to find his way out.

A fire hazard, the attendant had said. Bronson neared the area where Mensa Enterprises should be. He killed the headlights.

TWENTY-NINE

Paul stood at the airport in Rapid City, South Dakota, looking, wondering. He had no idea how to find Carrier, but his determination would lead him to that sorry excuse for a human being.

One good thing about being a computer whiz, Paul knew how to get into ATF's database on illegal gun dealers in South Dakota. When Freddie's name popped up, Paul contacted a police informant who had a reputation for working on either side. Paul made sure he paid this two-bit Dallas hood above the amount he would have expected to make all the proper arrangements. The informant had done so, and now Paul stood in the airport, ready to meet Freddie. He opened his cell and made the call.

"Yeah? What do you want?" came the answer at the other end.

Paul remembered the code and hoped he wouldn't make a mistake. "Certainly not information about the weather."

"Why? Too cold for you?"

"No, actually the weather is perfect." Paul waited. Had he forgotten a phrase? Said one wrong?

He'd almost given up when the voice came back. "About a ten-minute drive from the airport, there's a park, Buffalo Gap City Park. There's a bench, facing the pond. Meet me there."

"How will I know you?"

"I'll know you."

The line went dead. Paul put the cell away, hailed a taxi,

and instructed the cab driver to take him to Buffalo Gap City Park. He found the bench, plopped down his luggage in the space beside him, and sat down. While waiting, he thought of Bronson and Hoover. If they were sitting on this bench, they would have memorized by now where each person stood and what each wore.

He watched two kids feed corn to some ducks. An elderly woman stood by them. Their grandmother? A handful of teens, each on Rollerblades, zoomed up and down the street. A man in his mid-forties read a newspaper. A couple with their arms wrapped around each other stared at the pond. No one paid attention to him. He'd been stood up. Good thing money hadn't been exchanged.

Paul looked around once more. No one of interest. He looked at his watch. He'd wait five minutes. To help pass the time, he studied the people again. The couple by the pond was now kissing. Grandma gathered the kids and dragged them screaming to the car. The guy reading the paper had vanished. A man walked his dog. A car pulled into the parking lot, but no one got out.

Paul looked at his watch again. Seven minutes had lapsed. Time to head—where? He didn't have a motel room, and he didn't have a frigging car to get there. He picked up his carry-on luggage and headed out of the park.

A maroon sedan pulled up in front of him. The driver reached over and opened the passenger door. "Get in."

Paul stared at the man. He was the one who had been in the park reading the newspaper.

"Do you want the merchandise or not?" he asked.

"I'm interested," Paul said, but now wondered if that had been a good move. His experience with gun dealers had been restricted to seeing their names in the computer, reading about them, filing information away, and checking on evidence that would hopefully lead to their conviction. He'd never confronted one, until now. The idea filled him with fear, but as soon as he closed his eyes, he saw his wife's smiling face followed by the image of her lying in her coffin. He'd do this, no matter where it led him.

"Get in," the man said again.

For a second, Paul hesitated. Then he took a deep breath, opened the door, and climbed in. "I'm Paul McKenzie."

"Who cares? I'm here to do business with you, not be your friend."

Paul opened his case, retrieved an envelope, and handed it to him. "It's all there. Where's my piece?"

The driver reached under the seat and handed him a box. Paul opened it and stared.

The criminal made a noise that sounded more like an animal's cry. "Do you even know what that is?"

Paul looked at him. Did he look that stupid? "A gun."

The man closed his eyes and shook his head. "I meant what kind of gun."

"Oh." Paul shrugged.

"It's a .25-caliber automatic. You can put five rounds in some dude's head while a guy with a .38 is getting one out."

"Sounds good to me."

"Do you know how to fire it? Load it? There's some extra ammo in the box."

Paul had never fired a gun before and knew little about them. Other guys in the lab dealt with guns and other weapons. They were the experts. Not him. Not that it mattered, or at least not until today. "I'll only need one bullet."

"I don't want or need to know that."

"Sorry." Paul closed the box and put it in his carrying case. He had the weapon now. All he needed was Carrier. "You wouldn't by any chance be for hire, would you?"

"I may be a lot of things, but a killer, I'm not."

"That's not what I want to hire you for. That pleasure will be all mine."

"Too much information."

"Sorry." Paul cleared his throat. "I'm looking for a man, and I've no idea how to find him. He's extremely dangerous, so all you'll have to do is find him and report back to me."

"Tell me about this person you want me to find."

Paul did, then thought maybe he had said too much. Had he spooked Freddie?

Freddie sat back in the car seat and studied Paul. "All you want me to do is find Carrier. That's all? Nothing else?"

"Nothing else."

"I'll see what I can do. I'll get back to you within twenty-four hours. It's going to cost you, though."

"I figured it would. Do a good job and you'll be paid well."

The man's gaze focused on Paul. "Fine." He inserted the key in the ignition. Paul remained sitting in the car and made no attempt to leave. "Anything else I can do for you?"

"Yes, you can take me to a clean, but inexpensive motel."

The driver glared at Paul.

SOON AS FREDDIE DROPPED Paul off at the Happy Trails Motel, he retrieved his cell and pressed speed dial number four.

Stuart Ruggiero answered on the first ring. "Hope this is about a job. I could use one just about now."

"Then you're in luck."

"Speak."

"I'm looking for a man named Carrier."

A small pause followed. "Benjamin Carrier?"

Freddie brightened. That had been easy. "That's the one."

"Take my advice, from one cell mate to the other. Steer away from him."

"Bad news, eh?"

"Real bad."

Freddie considered this, but the good part was that he didn't need to get involved with Carrier. "All I need is a phone number and an address. Then I hand the information to a customer. No sweat off my brow. I get paid. You get paid."

"Sounds easy."

"Does that mean you can get me Carrier's contact info?"

"Oh, yeah." Stuart paused. "You really don't remember, do you?"

"Remember what?"

"Back a couple of years when we did time at the Federal Correctional Institute."

Freddie recalled that he and Stuart had been cell mates for a bit over a year. That hadn't been the best part of his life. "Yeah, what about it?"

"Remember that guy two doors down from us?"

Freddie squinted, trying to recall the name. Then it dawned on him. "Weird Jimmy."

"That's the one. He's Carrier's cousin. Used to talk about him all the time."

Freddie recalled all the tales Weird Jimmy had spun. At the time, Freddie had doubted that Carrier existed or at least did half the stuff Weird Jimmy gave him credit for. "Can you get hold of Weird Jimmy?"

"You bet. I hire him now and then to do odd jobs for me. I'll give him a buzz. I should have Carrier's contact information in an hour or two."

THIRTY

Approaching an unfamiliar place in the dark ranked high among Bronson's list of Things I Hate Most to Do. He slipped the gun into his hip holster for easy access, grabbed the flashlight, and stepped out of the car.

He stood at the top of the cliff, staring at the valley that housed Mensa Enterprises. The well-lit single building beckoned him, but instead of making him feel welcome, it filled him with dread. This certainly was no abandoned site as he had been led to believe. Someone had been taking care of it, or at least was paying its electric bill.

He started his descent, thankful for the full moon. As he worked his way down the hill, he watched his surroundings as carefully as a bird preparing to take flight. Still, he advanced at a steady rate. During the few times he knew the beam of his flashlight couldn't be seen by anyone who might be watching from one of the windows, he'd turn the light on, always directing its beam downward.

The cool night breeze blew, chilling Bronson's bones. The anxiety gnawing at his gut drenched him with a cold sweat. He ignored the discomfort. Off in the distance, he heard the shriek of birds. Other guttural creature sounds surrounded him, making his descent seem unreal, menacing. Still, he pushed on.

When he reached the bottom of the hill, he made a wide circle, enabling him to get a good view and approach the building from the back. He crouched and waited from behind some shrubs, watching the warehouse that loomed before him. He didn't detect any movement.

Keeping low, he advanced at a snail's pace. He crouched under a window, the only sound stemming from his pounding heart. He raised his head high enough to peek. Row after row of stacked cardboard boxes filled the area from floor to ceiling. Carrier could easily hide behind any of those.

Bronson moved on to the next window and encountered the same setup. He sat hard on the ground, trying to think of an alternate solution. Nothing came to mind. If Carrier held Pete prisoner, his chances of survival diminished with each passing second, but Bronson knew better than to try to use shortcuts. He would check the rest of the windows. Hopefully, he'd be able to spot something different, something that would give him the upper hand, no matter how slim.

Luck evaded him.

Resigned, he worked his way to the back of the building. He took out his gun and held it at the ready position. He plastered his back against the wall and swung the door open. He waited and listened for the slightest noise. In the far distance, an owl hooted and the wind whistled around him.

Bronson stuck his head in just long enough to enable him to see. The place seemed deserted.

He stepped in, knowing a trap awaited him.

AT 9:03 THE CALL CAME IN. Hoover checked the caller I.D. and sprang to his feet. "Got to take it." He looked at Little Carol and pointed to the TV show they were watching. "Fill me in?"

"Of course." Little Carol returned her attention to the TV.

Hoover stepped out of Bronson's camper, the cool night air hitting his face. "Hoover."

"You'll want to see this."

Hoover recognized Detective Gorman's harsh voice. "What is it?"

"Just get your ass over here."

Hoover glanced at Bronson's camper where Little Carol sat tucked in the recliner, her legs folded under her. Two doors down, over at the Watsons', Carol rehearsed her part for the play. Hoover had promised Bronson he'd watch his family. He wouldn't go back on his word. "You'll need to send someone over here before I can leave."

"You're talking about that protection thing, right?"

"Yeah."

"Don't see what good that's going to do. That's just a waste of taxpayers' money."

Exasperation consumed Hoover. "What are you driving at?"

"Get here, now."

Hoover knew Gorman had no authority over him, but Gorman could call the Dallas department and demand Hoover be sent home. Dallas would frown at Hoover's failure. He didn't want any harsh reprimands from his superiors. After all, he had his career to consider. He knew Bronson wouldn't have cared about commands. He would've stayed, and that's why Bronson was now unemployed, while Hoover hung on to his job. He wasn't Bronson. He opened his mouth to say he'd be right there, but nothing came out. He took in a deep breath and held it. "I'm not leaving until I know someone is here to protect them."

"Fine, fine. I'll send someone."

Relief flowed through Hoover's veins. He returned to the camper and watched through the window for a sign of a cruiser. Ten minutes later, he spotted the police car pulling into The Roost Resort. His gaze went to Little Carol, who continued to enjoy the TV movie—some romantic comedy Hoover had no interest in. She opened a can of Diet Pepsi and a bag of chips and offered Hoover some.

"No, thanks. I've got to go out for a little while. I'll be back as soon as possible."

Little Carol bolted to her feet, spilling most of the chips. "Everything is okay, Uncle Mike? Dad's okay?"

Hoover bent down and helped her pick up the chips. "Everything is fine. Captain Grouch wants to talk to me."

Little Carol giggled. "Captain Grouch?"

"Actually, it's Gorman, but he's a grouch with a capital G. I've got to be careful not to call him that to his face." He pocketed the car rental keys. "Lock the door behind me."

"You're beginning to sound like Dad."

Hoover smiled and stepped out. He wondered what was so important that Gorman couldn't tell him over the phone.

GORMAN THREW A FILE FOLDER Hoover's way. "How well do you know Bronson?"

Hoover reached for the folder. "Very well," he said. "Why?"

"You'd stand by him?"

"You bet. What's all this about?"

Gorman pointed at the file. "That just came in."

Hoover read in amazement the report listing Bronson as the man responsible for Mitch Randig's, Pedro Gonzalez's, and Jay Pilot's deaths. Bronson was considered armed and dangerous. Hoover slammed the report on Gorman's desk. "That's bullshit."

"Yeah. So now you see why I can't provide police protection to Bronson's family. Seems Carrier doesn't exist."

The image of the inferno surrounding him momentarily paralyzed Hoover. "Oh, he exists all right."

"Granted, he does—or at least did. Thing is, as the report shows, the only one who's seen him is Bronson. No prints, nothing to trace back to Carrier."

"We have the prints—the ones that made us aware Carrier is behind all of these murders."

Gorman leaned back on his desk and interlocked his fingers behind his head. "Tell me, Hoover. Where did you get these prints?"

"Bronson sent them to us. We matched them against the computer listing and got a hit."

"Uh-huh. Ever consider the possibility that Bronson might have been planning this for years? He could have gotten the prints from an old file or something and sent them as brand new."

"That doesn't make sense, and Bronson wouldn't do that anyway."

Gorman's nostrils flared. "How's this for making sense? I'm removing police protection."

THIRTY-ONE

BRONSON STARED AT THE AISLE created by the large shipping boxes piled just high enough to prevent him from looking over them. The passageway dead-ended ten feet down, but at that point, he could turn right or left. He scooted down to the next aisle. The layout remained consistent, as it did in the next aisle and the one after that. *It's a freaking maze,* Bronson thought, and the realization unsettled him.

Bronson tried moving a box. To his surprise, it didn't weigh much, but it'd take him forever to knock them all down. Besides, he didn't know which rows he should destroy. He doubted that he'd maintained the element of surprise in spite of his earlier efforts. He felt sure Carrier was watching him. He looked for cameras, but saw none.

If he took a right every single time he might not get lost. He headed up the first aisle and turned right. One row down, he executed another right and heard a low moan.

Bronson paused, his gun at the ready. He listened to the night's noises, then mostly to the lack of noises. He pushed on until he heard the moan again, followed by gasping, whimpering sounds.

Bronson braced himself, sucked in huge swallows of air, and executed a turn. The maze opened to reveal a large, open space. At its center, a kid sat in a plain wooden chair, his legs tied to the chair, his arms bound behind him. Duct tape held his mouth shut.

Bronson recognized Manuel. He had expected Pete. "Are you alone?"

Manuel's wide-open eyes pointed to somewhere behind him.

At that moment, the room went dark. The great engulfing blackness swallowed Bronson, temporarily disorienting him. He dropped to the ground, holding on to his gun with his right hand, his left hand reaching for the flashlight.

He listened to the screaming silence around him. The seconds stretched into hours, the hours became days. Manuel's muffled cries led him to turn the flashlight on, focusing the beam on the area behind the kid.

From behind Bronson, an explosion erupted, followed by three more, to his right, to his left, and in front of him. The distinct smell of burning boxes filled his lungs. A pulsing whoosh of air grew in his ears and swept past him, the sound reminding him of a panting animal. The air fueled the flames.

He pocketed the gun and flashlight and rushed toward Manuel. Fear swam in the kid's eyes. "I'll get you out." Bronson forced his own choking fear aside, hoping against hope he could pull it off.

The flames surrounded them like giant tidal waves, the smoke scorching Bronson's lungs. He untied Manuel. "Stay low. Follow me."

Manuel's limbs trembled uncontrollably, his hands a shaking blur. He remained frozen, staring at the inferno that surrounded them.

Cardboard burns fast and hot, and only in a few scattered areas had the structure caught fire. This little bit of hope provided Bronson with the edge he sought. He reached for Manuel's arm, jerked him to the floor, and dragged him along, always heading toward his left, toward the exit.

Manuel let out a pained yelp, but followed Bronson.

They dodged several leaping flames as the fire continued to dance around them. Bronson had almost given up hope when he spotted a window. He kicked the glass out, wrapped his jacket around his arm, and swept the shards away. He helped Manuel climb out, and then did the same.

They staggered a little ways from the burning warehouse before collapsing on to the ground. Bronson and Manuel swallowed large gulps of fresh air. "Are you all right?" Bronson asked.

Manuel nodded and made a gallant effort to control his whimpering.

"My car's on top of that hill. I'll take you home."

"Can't walk." He pointed to his leg.

For the first time, Bronson noticed the deep cuts on the kid's left leg. Bronson looked at the wounds. "Some of those may need stitches, but mostly you'll be okay. I'll help you get to the car."

"We wait. Maybe pain go away. We wait one minute, yes?"

Bronson nodded. The building behind them crumbled as the fire consumed it. Bronson thought of Pete. "Who was in that building with us? Who tied you up?"

A chill covered Manuel and he trembled uncontrollably. "He said he name Carrier."

"Anyone else there?"

"No." Manuel placed his quivering hands over his lips. "Last time I come here is for party."

"Yeah?"

"Me and Pedro, we stack boxes. We build—what you call it?"

"A maze?"

"Yeah, maze for little kids. They come, children and mothers and fathers from lab. They come have fun. Now it is trap. I made trap." He lowered his head as heartfelt sobs escaped him. "I hate Pedro."

"Why?" Bronson had thought they were best friends.

"He traitor. He take me to bad man."

"Carrier."

"No, Doc Ponce. He take me to Doc. Doc take me to Carrier."

Bronson listened to the accent. He had pronounced *doc* like *duck*. "Who's Doc Ponce? Where can I find him?"

Manuel shook himself and wrapped his hands around his arms. "He hurt my girl, my baby. I not say."

The vacant look in his eyes warned Bronson that this wasn't the best place or time to interrogate him. Let him calm down first. Take one step at a time.

Bronson scanned the area. "Are you ready to make the walk up the hill to my car?"

"You bring car here. Better, no? I wait."

Bronson glanced at the steep cliff. No way he'd be able to drive the car down it. He also had to consider Carrier. By now he was probably miles away, but Bronson wasn't willing to gamble. "I'd rather you come with me."

"Can't walk."

Bronson considered carrying him, but the kid was big and Bronson's age didn't help any. He cursed time. His aging body showed him his limitations.

"You go get car. Please. I wait."

Not much of a choice there. He'd have to find the road that led to the burning warehouse. From there to where Manuel waited was flat ground. Bronson nodded. He picked up a branch that could double for a baseball bat and handed it to Manuel. "I'll be back for you as soon as possible."

"I know." He flashed Bronson a timid smile.

Bronson scanned the area once more, this time using the flashlight. Satisfied no one lurked nearby, he turned and stopped. He couldn't leave the kid behind. "I'm sorry, but you have to come with me."

Manuel frowned. "You go ahead. I follow."

Bronson waited until Manuel joined him. They moved slowly and Manuel often fell behind.

Bronson detected movement ahead of him. He stopped, pointed the gun, and aimed the flashlight beam in that direction. He watched and waited. Nothing. From behind he heard his name called. A chill covered his body as he paused and turned.

Carrier held Manuel in front of him with an iron grip, the useless branch by Manuel's feet. Carrier's lips twisted into a sadistic, mocking smile that Bronson had seen before.

Bronson pointed the gun at Carrier's head. "Release him and step back."

Carrier crouched down behind Manuel, blocking Bronson's clear shot. With a swift, practiced move, he broke his prisoner's neck. "Message received," he said as Manuel slumped to the ground.

He turned and ran into the dark.

Bronson fired three shots into the vast darkness, knowing full well the bullets would miss their target. Keeping the gun aimed at the darkness Carrier had disappeared into, Bronson squatted down by Manuel and checked for a pulse he didn't expect to find. "Shiiit," he cursed under his breath. He broke into a run, pursuing Carrier, his flashlight beam scanning a wide scope of terrain. He looked for footprints but found none. Behind him, the faint glow of the dying fire did little to light the area. The night's darkness protected Carrier.

A roil of despair hit Bronson, leaving him utterly defeated. If Carrier's intent had been to make him feel like a failure, he had certainly done an excellent job. Bronson had been robbed of his sense of worth, marking him as Carrier's next victim.

THIRTY-TWO

"Ms. Biebesheimer. Sit down." Detective Gorman pointed to the vacant chair by his desk.

Ellen Biebesheimer gladly reached for the chair. She'd been flying all day, and a police escort had met her at the Rapid City Airport. Then it had taken two hours more to arrive in Custer. She had yet to check in at the motel.

She read the nameplate on top of the detective's cluttered desk. It would have been nice if he had introduced himself. "What can I do for you?"

"Your job."

Ellen sat up straighter, tilting her head slightly down. "I beg your pardon?"

Gorman's fingers drummed his desk. His eyes narrowed and Ellen could feel him scrutinizing her soul. "Correct me if I'm wrong. At one time you were with the FBI's Behavioral Science Unit, right?"

"That is correct, but I quit when I found out I can make more money if I freelance." Gorman must have known that because he'd hired her, but for what? And why her? She looked away from Gorman's desk and out toward the main room. She saw Mike Hoover standing by the entry door. That explained it. When their eyes met, he waved at her.

She waved back and focused on Gorman. "What's he doing here? He's the reason I'm here, I bet."

Gorman looked past Ellen's shoulder at Hoover. "You know him? He's a big-city cop and full of himself."

Ellen smiled. Not quite how she'd describe him, but it'd do. Not that she'd know what to say about him if someone asked. In spite of all of her efforts to forget him, even after all these years, she still kept up with his whereabouts. She knew exactly which case he currently pursued and where each case led him. She shouldn't have been surprised to see him standing just a few feet away from her. Still, seeing him had unnerved her.

If she were truthful with herself, she felt relieved to see him alive and well. She had heard Carrier had resurfaced. That thought made fear rise like a scream at the back of her throat. She remembered how Carrier had stalked him. She had lived with Mike through that ordeal. They'd been married then, but not any longer. "This is about Carrier, right? You want me to analyze him? If so, I'm afraid you wasted your money and my time. Carrier was one of Dallas's most wanted criminals, and tons of reports exist about him. All you have to do is access them." She scooted her chair back, getting ready to leave.

"Don't get your feathers in a ruffle. It's not Carrier I'm telling you to analyze."

Ellen's eyebrows knit slightly in puzzlement. "Then who?" She settled back in the chair.

"A new killer has surfaced in Two Forks. I'm doing this as a special favor to Captain Samuel Marshall from the Two Forks Police Department in Wyoming. This murderer has already killed a handful of people in Two Forks, and I know he's been here, too, so I'm doing it for myself as well. Marshall's resources are a lot more limited than mine, so I offered to help." Gorman leaned back in his seat, a smile that said see-what-a-good-guy-I-am plastered on his face.

Ellen leaned forward. "You said he's been here—I assume you mean he's killed—both here and in Wyoming. If so, why hasn't the F.B.I. been notified?"

Gorman's features hardened. "We handle our own here. We don't need any help from any of those fancy guys in suits."

Attitudes like that always irritated Ellen. First thing she'd do is call the F.B.I. "Tell me what you know."

"That's why you're here. I don't know much, and I'm sure Marshall knows even less. The little I know is this guy is smart and devious. He knows all the tricks of the trade and won't hesitate to use them. Marshall thought an analysis would be appropriate. I agree. It might help us catch this lowlife. Maybe your report will show us what kind of pattern he follows and that's what we'll use to catch him."

"We're talking about a serial killer, right?"

Gorman leaned back again. "Not quite, but he is a multiple killer. We feel that only you can provide us insight into his behavior."

"Why me?"

"Because you know him."

Something gnawed at her, perhaps nothing more than her inner voice warning her to leave. She shifted positions. "So who is he?"

"Harry Bronson."

THIRTY-THREE

SHATTERED GLASS SYMBOLIZED Bronson's life. No matter which way he turned, he would cut himself on a sliver. Each cut deeper, more threatening. He couldn't turn to the police, but he also didn't want to leave Manuel's body out here in the woods.

He called Hoover. The message went to voice mail. Bronson told him about tonight's events. "Call me as soon as you get this."

He disconnected and checked messages received. The last call had come from Pete. Bronson wondered if he knew about his partner's death, and if he had gotten a whiff of the rumors. Maybe Pete thought Bronson had killed Jay. Was that why he called? Had he sent Bronson to Mensa Enterprises knowing Carrier and Manuel would be waiting for him?

Only one way to find out. He punched in the number and pushed the send button.

Pete picked up on the second ring. "Bronson, I've been meaning to call you. There's a whole bunch of nasty rumors circulating about you. We need to talk." His voice came in clear and distinct, not robotic like before.

"Yes, we do, but let me first assure you I had nothin' to do with Jay's or Pedro's or Mitch's deaths." He might as well add Manuel's name to that list.

"I figured as much. I'm a good judge of character, but you have a lot of explaining to do. Why don't we meet and talk?"

A cool breeze swept by, rattling the branches and swaying the boughs of the small nearby evergreens. Bronson zipped his jacket and remembered what had happened the last time he had made arrangements to meet Pete. "The expression goes, if you fool me once, shame on you. If you fool me twice, shame on me."

"What are you babbling about? I haven't talked to you since you left Jay and me to protect Eric and the baby, so how could I have fooled you?"

Something didn't register. "Are you sayin' you didn't call me to tell me to meet you at Mensa Enterprises?" If Pete hadn't made the call, who then? Carrier? The call had come from Pete's cell.

"Why would I do that? I've never even heard of that place."

Bronson decided to play his game. "Someone, using your cell and claiming to be you, called me to set up the meeting."

"That's not possible. I never called you."

"If you didn't, who did?"

"I have no idea. You sure it came from my cell?"

"Positive."

"Somebody must have borrowed it without my permission. Let me think about that one. Maybe by the time we meet, I'll figure out who and how that person used my phone."

If he'd made the call, he would've had a solid excuse for doing so. Maybe he really didn't know someone had used his cell. "When, where can we meet?"

"Hold on." Pete returned to the phone a few seconds later. "Just as I thought. I'm here at home and I looked out the window. I saw a van parked two doors down. I'm sure it's the police. They figure you're going to contact me, and they'll grab you when you come."

Bronson rubbed the bridge of his nose. The world closed in on him. "Can you sneak out the back door?"

"Maybe. Maybe not. They're probably watching the back door, too. Wouldn't you?"

"Yeah, of course." His options narrowed.

"Tell you what I'm going to do. I'm going to walk out the front door and make sure they follow me all the way to the movie house. They'll see me buy the ticket, popcorn, and drink. They'll watch me go into the theater. They'll figure they'll have maybe two hours. I'll sneak out the back door. If I'm successful, we'll meet."

Pete's plan might buy them the time they needed. Bronson liked the idea and his respect for Pete increased a notch. "Where?"

"I'll think of a place. In the meantime, is there anything I can do for you?"

Yes, get me out of here. Lead me to Doc Ponce. Better yet, lead me to Carrier. Bronson closed his eyes for a second. He hadn't realized until now how tired and hungry he felt. He couldn't remember what or when his last meal had been. He could sure use a steaming cup of coffee. "Do you know Doc Ponce?"

A slight pause followed. "Yes. Why?"

Bronson noticed the hesitation. "He's involved in this. I'm not quite sure how."

"I would have thought this to be Carrier's work, not Doc Ponce's."

"Carrier's the killer, Doc Ponce the mastermind. What can you tell me about Doc Ponce?" Bronson realized he was pushing Pete, but he had limited resources and Pete, at least for the moment, seemed to be his best source of information.

"He's one of the technicians at McGory and Stein. There was an article in the paper a while back about his work on that miracle anti-aging formula."

Seemed like the anti-aging formula wasn't much of a miracle. It brought death to everyone it touched. "I want to talk to Doc Ponce."

"I can arrange that, but first we meet."

If I can trust you. "Have you been with Doc Ponce?"

"Yes."

"Any chance he made the call? Did you set the cell down somewhere, and he picked it up and used it?"

"Maybe." A small pause followed. "Yeah. In fact, I did. This really bothers me. Let's talk more about this when we meet."

"I'll wait for your call."

Bronson closed his cell and looked down at Manuel's body. Just a kid. God, he was just a kid. "I promise you I'll get to the bottom of this. I'll get that bastard and help your gal and baby." He placed his opened hand on Manuel's chest and lowered his head.

Bronson's cell jangled a tune, and he snapped it open. "Hey, Hoover."

"You're in a hell of a mess."

"You're tellin' me."

"Where are you?"

Bronson looked at his surroundings. The giant pines and quaking aspen stretched out their arms, casting even darker shadows in the night. Beyond him, the ashes of the fallen structure glowed bright red like lava threatening to erupt. Every now and then he'd hear the angry pop of a fire refusing to die. "I'm still in the forest outside Mensa Enterprises. I can't bring myself to leave the kid's body alone."

"I'll call the police as soon as I hang up. I guess they'll take maybe fifteen minutes or so to reach you. Get out of there before they arrive. Do you have somewhere you can go?"

Bronson looked at his watch. It read 10:24. He hadn't even thought of where he'd be spending the night. Maybe Pete would help him. "Possibly."

"Figure it out. I'll call you back for details. I'm here in Custer but as soon as I talk to Ellen, I'll leave for Two Forks. Hang on. I'll be there."

"Ellen? As in Ellen Hoover?"

"No, as in Ellen Biebesheimer. She went back to using her maiden name."

"I'm sorry."

"Yeah, well, me too, but there's nothing I can do about it."

"Why's Ellen there?" Bronson thought about it. "I'll save you the trouble. She's here to analyze my behavioral patterns, mental disturbances, and so on."

A long pause followed. "Yeah, buddy, she is. I'm sorry."

Bronson's frustration became a lump in his stomach. "Don't worry about it. It's not your fault."

"Yeah, I know, but still. Listen, Ellen's getting ready to leave the grouch's office, and I still have to make that call to the Two Forks police. Will you be all right?"

"Always."

"Stay safe."

"Yeah." Like that was really one of his options. Bronson returned the cell to his pants pocket and pulled the lapels of his dark jacket up tight around his neck. Hopefully, that would keep the relentless chill from seeping into his bones.

Fifteen minutes, and then he'd leave. Fifteen minutes. He sat next to Manuel's body and waited. The time had almost elapsed when his cell went off. The caller I.D. told him that Pete was on the other end. "Pete, that's you?"

"Yeah. I did it. I snuck out and I even found us a place. A friend of mine is in Florida and I'm watering his plants. No one would think of looking for you there. I've got an address and instructions. I can meet you there in about ten minutes." He gave Bronson the address and instructions.

Bronson took one last look at Manuel's body and walked away.

THIRTY-FOUR

WHEN HOOVER SAW ELLEN head out of Gorman the Grouch'
office, he moved, blocking her exit. "You're not really goin
to do it, are you?" he asked her once they faced each other

Ellen looked to her right and left, perhaps searching fo
a way to bypass her ex. "Hi to you, too. It's good to see yo
and all that jazz."

Hoover smiled, taking comfort in the thought that som
things don't change. The love of his life had as much spur
today as she did thirty-three years ago when he married he
"Ellen, you know how I feel. It's always a pleasure to se
you."

She looked around the office as though wondering
anyone was listening to them. "A simple hi would do."

"Hi."

"Goodbye. I'm tired. I'm going to find a motel room ar
sleep the rest of the night away."

"You'll need a ride."

"Are you offering?"

"It's a small town. I haven't seen any taxis around, esp
cially this time of the night. Besides, your suitcases are
my car."

Ellen looked at the corner where she had left her bag
"Imagine that, my suitcases were stolen right out of the poli
department. I guess that leaves me no choice but to go wi
you."

"That's not so bad, is it?"

"It could be worse."

As soon as they stepped out, Hoover said, "Bronson's in a lot of trouble."

"Tell me."

Hoover filled her in. "He needs us. I'm on my way over to Custer. I'd like you to join me."

"Why? What can I do besides get in the way?"

"I'm sure your special trivia knowledge will come in handy." He snuck a look at her and when he noticed that she was staring back, he quickly looked away. "Okay, it's more complicated than that. I want you around."

She shook her head. "Don't go there, Mike." She turned her head so he wouldn't see her eyes. Silence hung around them like dark, dense clouds. "Actually, I like Bronson. I still consider him and Carol my best friends. That hasn't changed."

Hoover felt as if a thousand needles embedded themselves in his heart. They reached the car and Hoover opened the door for Ellen. He wished he could come up with a snappy, amusing answer, but nothing came to mind. "Does that mean you won't create that analysis report?"

"Mike, that's not fair. I told Gorman I couldn't do it because of the relationship between Bronson and me. He said that was the reason he hired me over anyone else. I know him so well, they could rely on the information I provided. He said I was a professional and as such, it was my responsibility to write that analysis. I'd like to agree with him. I am a professional." She got in the car.

Hoover closed the door, walked around, and slid into the driver's seat. "You're right. I'm sorry, but in order to do your job correctly, you need to be in the same place the criminal is. I'm taking you to Two Forks." He started the engine and looked at her.

She nodded.

ANGER AND DEPRESSION, like sisters of sorrow, reached down Bronson's gut and shook him. He felt the acid in his stomach. Unfortunately, he didn't have any antacid pills. Main Avenue, the street he drove on, had a lot of commercial stores but at this time of the night, all were closed.

He continued driving and stewing. He had thought himself incapable of hating someone. Every criminal he'd ever known had at least one redeeming factor, even if minute. Maybe the murderer had been a victim of society or cruel parents, and Bronson always felt at least an ounce of compassion for him.

But not Carrier. He was a genuine asshole with a capital A. The fury Bronson felt consumed him, making it hard to focus on the road.

He reached into his shirt pocket for the directions Pete had given him, but instead pulled out Carrier's last note. He'd found it stuck to his windshield. He didn't need to read it again. He'd already memorized it.

Harry, oh Harry,
Tsk. Tsk. Tsk.
   Manuel was just a kid, wasn't he? And you had res-
cued him, but in the end, you let him die. What's wrong
with you?
   If it's any consolation to you, Round Four is a tie.
You were supposed to die in the fire.
   Now we'll have to go to Round Five. Who are you
going to let die this time?
   Tsk. Tsk. Tsk.
Benjamin Carrier

Bronson crumpled the note and threw it on the passenger side floor. He retrieved the piece of paper where he had scribbled the directions.

Off Main Avenue, turn right on Monroe. He glanced at the

street name. Jackson. Shit. Jackson was two presidents ahead of Monroe. He had missed his turn. Bronson glanced at the rearview mirror and side mirrors, checking for any patrol cars. Last thing he needed was a ticket. He made an illegal U-turn and continued to head to his destination.

As he pulled up to the address Pete had given him, he searched the street for an unmarked car. Satisfied no one watched him, he pulled into the driveway.

Pete greeted him. "Perfect timing. I just got here, myself." A set of house keys dangled from his hands. "I'm thinking. You'll need a place to stay. This is ideal for you. I'll stay away so the police won't follow me here. Do you have your luggage with you?"

"Thanks, that's mighty nice of you. I might just take you up on that offer. Let's talk first."

"As you wish." Pete unlocked the front door but didn't open it. "My friend, the owner of this house, is deeply religious. He doesn't want any guns inside. He calls them the Devil's Weapons. He's strange that way, you know?"

"I've met a couple of people like that," Bronson answered. "I've learned that you just accept them for what they are."

"I like your attitude and I agree. Every time I'd come for a visit when I was still a police officer, I'd leave my gun out here on the porch. Are you carrying?"

"It's out in the car."

"Good." Pete opened the door and they stepped in.

Bronson briefly scanned the room. "You know, I'm really thirsty. Does your friend have any coffee? If not, cold water will do."

"I'll check." Pete headed toward the kitchen.

Bronson removed his jacket, revealing the gun tucked under his belt. He took the gun, placed it between the couch's cushions, and dropped his jacket on top, concealing the hiding place. He joined Paul in the kitchen, who had busied himself preparing coffee. "Mind if I use the head?"

Pete pointed to the hallway. "It's to your left."

Bronson thanked him and headed down the hallway. As he went past each of the bedrooms, he peeked in. In the bathroom he used the facilities, washed his hands, and rejoined Pete. By that time, Pete had two steaming cups of coffee waiting on the kitchen counter.

Pete retrieved the milk and sugar bowl and offered them to Bronson. "You must have a lot of unanswered questions."

"I do." Bronson poured in three heaping spoonfuls of sugar—after tonight's events, he felt he deserved them.

"I'll answer each question as clearly as possible." Pete watched Bronson dump sugar into his coffee.

Bronson poured the milk, stirred, and led Pete back to the living room. "You know Jay's dead."

Pete dropped his shoulders and nodded. A sick, vacant look glazed his eyes. "I know." The words came barely above a whisper.

"I'm sorry."

"You didn't do it."

Bronson sipped his coffee. He'd had better, he'd had worse. He set the cup down. "You know this for a fact."

Pete nodded.

"Who killed him?"

"Carrier. He called you pretending to be Jay and told you he needed to talk to you. He then went to Jay's and killed him so that when you arrived you'd find his body. He knew you'd call the police."

"So Carrier set me up to be a killer." Bronson recalled how when "Jay" called, his voice had been indistinct, almost mechanical. The digital display had identified Jay as the caller, and Bronson had believed it. "How do you know that's what happened? Have you been talking to Carrier?"

Pete nodded.

"When? How?"

"Ask me something else."

Bronson reached for his coffee, using the time to assess the situation. "Tell me about Doc Ponce."

"What about him?"

"Who is he?"

"I told you. He's a lab researcher. He's also Mitch's partner—or at least was."

Bronson retrieved the spiral notebook from his shirt pocket and thumbed through it. "It says here Henry Clark is his partner. Did they have a third one?"

Pete clasped his hands tightly in front of him. Everything about his posture suggested tension. "Do you remember Ponce de Leon?"

"The conquistador?" Bronson searched his mind. He recalled hearing that name in one of his high school history classes. If he remembered right, Ponce de Leon had led his men through the Southwest in a quest—no, a search—for gold. Bronson shook his head. That didn't sound right. When the correct answer dawned on him, he smiled at the simplicity of the significance behind the name. "Ponce de Leon's fame lies in his search for the Fountain of Youth. Clark's task involved developing an anti-aging cream. In essence, he's seeking the same fountain. Doc Ponce and Henry Clark, a Ph.D., are one and the same."

Pete almost smiled. "Very good."

"I'll be damned," Bronson said and leaned back.

"You have been—by Carrier. He's having too much fun with you to kill you. But you're next on his list."

"How are you involved in all of this?"

Pete took a deep breath. "That's the ironic part. I wasn't until you hired me. Carrier approached both me and Jay. He offered us money if we helped him. You've got to realize we're both retired police officers. That puts us barely above the poverty line. I always wanted to have money and enjoy the finer things of life. I deserve them. I always worked hard and what did I get? A damn gold watch when I retired. But Carrier offered us money, lots of money. Jay refused. Now he's dead. I accepted and I'm alive."

Bronson nodded. Pete had answered every single one of his questions truthfully, incriminating himself to a T. Only one reason he had done that. "I'm not going to make it out of this alive, am I?" He reached for his coffee, took a sip, and held on to his coffee mug.

"No, sorry."

Bronson stared at the barrel of Pete's gun.

THIRTY-FIVE

FREDDIE YOUNG DRUMMED his fingers on the telephone. He liked the small sum of money he'd made by equipping Paul McKenzie with the .25 caliber. He would make another small bundle once he called Paul with Carrier's whereabouts. But what if, instead of calling Paul, he called Carrier? Stuart had told him Carrier had money. Why shouldn't he get some of it? Freddie picked up the handset.

The phone rang three times before Carrier picked up. "Yes?"

Sweat prickled Freddie's forehead when he heard Carrier's voice. Had he made a mistake? Too late to change his mind. Carrier probably had caller I.D. and could identify him.

"Speak now or I'm hanging up," Carrier said.

Freddie swallowed the lump in his throat. "Mr. Carrier, sir, you don't know me."

"Get to the point."

"I have valuable information."

"I'm listening."

Freddie felt his heart slowing a bit from its rapid pace when he first dialed Carrier's number. Probably the rumors he'd heard had been nothing more than exaggerations. Even if they weren't, he'd get his money and be done with Carrier. He mentally patted himself on the back. He'd made the right decision. "Does the name Paul McKenzie mean anything to you?"

"I'm not in the mood for games. If you have something to say, spit it out."

"Paul McKenzie bought a clean gun from me and plans to use it on you." Freddie paused, waiting for a reaction, or at least a comment. When none came, he continued, "He also hired me to locate you."

"Is he a professional?"

"He works for the Dallas Police Department, but he's no policeman. He's some kind of technician, and he's as green as they come."

"Paul McKenzie." Carrier stretched out the words as though rolling them in his mouth. "I remember him now. I should have done him at the same time I did his wife. Rather a shame. She was such a pretty thing."

Carrier's cold tone frightened Freddie. He should have left well enough alone.

"Did you tell Paul where to find me?"

"No, I haven't. I thought I'd talk to you first."

"You're calling from Custer."

Freddie closed his eyes. Carrier did have caller I.D. The area code revealed his location. "Yes. McKenzie's here, too."

"I want you to pick him up and bring him to me. Call me when you're close to Two Forks and I'll tell you where to meet me."

"What if he doesn't want to come with me?"

"Then force him."

BRONSON RELEASED HIS GRIP on the coffee mug. It landed with a loud *thud* and shattered, spilling its contents everywhere.

Pete's gaze went to the falling cup. That one second of distraction provided Bronson with an edge. He twisted and dropped to the couch, making himself a smaller target. His right hand reached under the jacket and found the gun. He pointed without precise aim and pulled the trigger. The bullet found its target. Pete *whooshed* aloud as the bullet penetrated his chest. He staggered forward and fired, but Bronson had found refuge behind the couch.

Pete's body crumpled to the floor. Bronson waited. When Pete didn't move, he approached him, eyes peeled for the slightest movement. He kicked the gun aside and bent down. He felt for a pulse.

Pete moaned. A bright red spot formed on his chest as the blood seeped through his shirt. His half-open eyes stared at Bronson. "All I wanted was money." He spoke slowly and breathed through his mouth. "Was that so wrong?"

"You tell me. You're responsible for your partner's and Manuel's deaths. Is that so wrong?" Bronson stood, pointing the gun at him, wishing he could shoot the worthless excuse for a human being.

"I'm sorry…about Jay." His eyes filled with tears. "I loved him. You had a partner. You know how it is."

Bronson lowered the gun and stepped back. Pete wouldn't be trying to make a getaway. "Yeah, I do know. That bond keeps me from betrayin' him."

Tears streamed down Pete's cheeks. He made no attempt to wipe them away. "I know…I've got…what I deserve. You've got…to believe me." He gasped for breath. "I never made that call." Gurgling and whimpering sounds escaped from his mouth. "I didn't set Manuel up."

Bronson reached for his cell, dialed nine-one-one, gave them the necessary information, and disconnected. "Where are Eric and his mother?"

"Ask Doc Ponce." He paused. "He knows."

"The ambulance is on the way."

"I know. What gave it…away?"

"The plants."

"What?"

"You said you had to water your friend's plants." Bronson looked at his watch. He didn't want to be here when the sirens arrived. "There are no plants to water. I checked the bathroom, the bedrooms, and kitchen. Nothing. Not even plastic ones."

"The gun."

Bronson smirked. "Did you think I'm a fool? Did you really think I'd come in unarmed? When I stepped in and noticed not one statue of Jesus or any other religious artifacts lying around—not even a Bible anywhere—I knew."

Pete's face was smeared with sweat, and he gasped involuntarily. "It's not safe...for you here. Go."

"If you see Carrier, give him a message for me?"

Pete nodded and took in a deep breath.

"Tell him I won Round Five, and Round Six is also mine."

"Sure. I don't understand...but I guess he will." He slurred his words and was often hard to understand. "Get out of here. It's time for me to pay my dues."

Bronson hesitated.

"Go."

"God bless you."

"It's too late for that."

Bronson dashed out.

THIRTY-SIX

Fatigue encompassed Bronson as he massaged his heavy eye-lids with his fingertips. His mind, however, refused to turn off or even slow down. Somehow he had to rescue Linda and Eric. That burden sat heavy in his heart.

His watch read 12:25. He bet he'd find Henry Clark at home at this time of the night. Time to pay him a surprise visit. As he pulled out of the driveway, his phone went off. The name Paul McKenzie appeared on the caller I.D. display.

He'd forgotten about Paul. Not surprising, considering what he'd been through in the past several hours. At least Paul had thought to connect with him. "Hey, Paul," Bronson said, expecting to hear Paul's chirpy voice.

The silence that followed attacked Bronson's nerves. "Paul?"

"Help me."

The call ended. "Talk to me, Paul. Talk to me," Bronson whispered as he hit the redial button. With a growing sense of dread, he listened to the unanswered ring. "Pick up, Paul. Pick up."

The call went to voice mail. "Hi. This is Paul. I'm currently unavailable. At the tone, please——"

Bronson snapped the cell shut and let it fall out of his fingers. Adrenaline flowed through his veins as he pumped the gas pedal. He reached down for the cell. The car swerved. He cursed, grateful that the road was deserted. He slowed down and located the cell.

He punched in Hoover's number.

"Yo, Bronson. You okay?"

"I am, but Paul's not." Fatigue settled in his nerves and he rolled down the window.

"Tell me."

"I just got a call from him." The light turned red. Bronson looked both ways. Not a car in sight. He ran the red light. "All he said was *help me*. I called him back, but the voice message came on."

"You didn't hear anything in the background? Anything that would tell us where he is?"

"No. Nothin'." He came to a stop sign and made a California stop. "I'm on my way to Clark's. I have a lot of questions for him, and one way or the other, he'll answer them all. We'll soon know where Paul, Linda, and Eric are."

"Be careful, buddy."

Good thing Hoover wasn't there to witness his reckless driving. "I am."

"We're an hour away from you. I've got Ellen with me. We'll meet you at Clark's house unless I hear otherwise from you. I'll hand Ellen the cell and you give her directions, but before I do, remember you asked me to check on the creams being delivered instead of mailed?"

"Yeah."

"Sorry, buddy, it's a dead end. Those who are rich, influential, or repeat customers get the special treatment. Creams delivered the same day they're ordered."

"I thought it'd be something like that, but I had to make sure."

"I hear ya. Here's Ellen."

Bronson rattled off the instructions and disconnected. He floored the gas pedal and reached Clark's mansion in record time. As he ran up the walkway, he considered breaking and entering, but decided to do it the old-fashioned way. He rang the doorbell and waited. Seconds dragged by. He leaned on the doorbell.

The house came alive with lights and Bronson heard the faint murmur of voices. A maid opened the door barely wide enough to speak to him. "Yes? What is it?"

"I need to talk to Clark."

"It's the middle of the night. Come back tomorrow." The door started to close.

"No, now." Bronson pushed the door open, making the woman stumble backward. He stepped into the foyer, a large entryway that opened to the kitchen area and living room. Off to his left was a large staircase. Bronson turned to the maid. "Are you okay?"

She shrunk back, eyes wide with fear. Three other servants, all in matching white robes, huddled together a few feet away. Another, a man in his late thirties, opened a kitchen drawer.

Bronson pulled out his gun and pointed it at him. "I wouldn't do that if I were you. Put your hands up."

The man gasped and shot his arms up in the air. A carving knife clattered to the floor.

"Join your buddies," Bronson ordered.

The man wet his lips and obeyed.

"Put your arms down, for Pete's sake. I'm not going to hurt you." He must look like a bully. He sure felt like one.

The woman behind him whimpered. He looked at her and he cringed. "I'm sorry about this," he said. Sometimes innocent bystanders ended up getting hurt. Bronson hated that. He always tried to avoid it, but sometimes, like today, it couldn't be done. He looked up toward the staircase. Clark stood halfway down it.

Clark's eyes bored into him. "Bronson, what the hell are you doing here at this time of night frightening my help?"

Bronson pointed his gun at Clark. "You know damn well what I'm doing here."

The air seemed to seep out of Clark, like a deflated balloon. "You don't understand. My niece has cancer. She's all I have. The medical bills are eating me up. I had to do something."

Bronson looked at the chandelier dangling in the entryway. He eyed the designer curtains, the original paintings, the expensive furniture, and finally he looked at the servants who stood clustered together, mesmerized by the events unfolding before them. "Yeah, I can tell. I feel sorry for you." He signaled for Clark to join his hired help.

Clark descended a couple of steps and stopped.

"Come on. All the way down." As Clark joined them, Bronson turned to the woman he had pushed. "Anyone else here?"

She shook her head.

"Good. Let's all mosey into the kitchen." He pointed to the dinette table. "Sit." All but Clark sat down. He stood by a chair, arms folded in front of him, glaring at Bronson.

"Tell me about Eric and Linda." Bronson directed his comment at Clark, but kept a watchful eye on the servants. They might be fiercely loyal to their employer.

"Who?"

"Don't play cute games with me. I know you've got them."

A small whoosh of air escaped Clark. "I never meant for anyone to get hurt."

"Tell me where they are."

"You've got to understand. My niece. She's all I've got." He reached for the chair and flopped down in it.

"For her sake, tell me where they are. Is Paul with them?"

Clark's eyebrows knit slightly in puzzlement. He lowered his head and looked down.

"That's three innocent people," Bronson said. "You can save them. Don't let their blood be on your hands, too."

The maid Bronson had pushed gasped. The others held as still as if suspended in time.

"Do any of you know where these people are?" Bronson asked them.

They shook their heads.

Bronson looked back at Clark. "I've had a rotten day and an even worse night. The kind that makes you boilin' mad. You don't want to see me mad."

Clark sighed and seemed to shrink, a defeated man. "Before I say anything, can you guarantee that you'll tell the police I fully cooperated? That'll get me reduced charges, won't it?"

"I can't predict what the police will do, but I promise to speak on your behalf."

Clark stared straight ahead, his face a mask of despair. "I told you I need money for my niece, and about Mitch worrying over having enough money once he retired."

Bronson nodded.

"Although we're being paid very well at McGory and Stein, it's the company that'll make billions of dollars, not us. After all our hard work, all we'll see is maybe a couple million each. So Mitch and I planned to sell the formula to the highest bidder. Our setback, of course, was that the formula wasn't complete. We were this close to finding the answer." Clark put his index finger and thumb together. "Every single cream that's out there on the shelves can only reach the epidermis, the outer skin. But it's the layer underneath, the dermis, where the wrinkles form. No matter how hard we tried, we couldn't get past the epidermis. Then Mitch locked himself in the lab, day and night. A week later on a Sunday, he called me, his voice filled with excitement. He'd done it, he said. Ours would be the first cream to reach the dermis where the damage occurs. I told him I'd be right over, and his entire attitude changed."

"How's that?"

"He seemed hesitant, as if he regretted calling."

"Why would he regret that?"

"I guess at first he was so excited, he had to share the news with someone. I was a logical choice. Then, after talking to me, he realized he could make more money if I wasn't in the picture. I feared he was up to something, so I rushed to the lab, but by the time I got there, he and all the research notes were gone. You can imagine, I was very upset."

"Gone? What do you mean *gone?*" Bronson asked.

"That son-of-a-bitch destroyed all our notes and hid the formula in a computer game that only he or Linda could successfully play."

"Ella," Bronson said.

Clark's eyes widened. "You knew this."

Bronson nodded. "But what I don't know is where Linda, Eric, and Paul are."

"In due time." Clark waved him off. "I need to tell the story my way." He took a deep breath. "The next day when I went to work, I contacted the Chief."

"Who?"

"The guy we were going to sell the formula to."

"Does he have a name?"

Clark frowned. "Of course. We'll get to that." He paused and Bronson wished he could put Clark on fast-forward.

He retrieved his notebook and pen and jotted down the important information, then looked at Clark.

"Naturally, the Chief was furious," Clark continued. "He hired a man who's despicable but always gets the job done."

"Carrier."

Clark clapped. "Bravo, Mr. Bronson. Your knowledge impresses me." He paused before continuing. "Carrier trie reasoning with Mitch, but Mitch wouldn't listen. Figuring he would frighten Mitch into cooperating, Carrier killed Linda's parents, whom Mitch was close to. But that didn't change Mitch's determination. He figured he was safe because they needed him to play that game. He didn't count on Carrier knowing Linda could just as easily play it, and Linda, of course, would be easier to handle. So Carrier killed Mitch."

"All very interestin', but it's not leading me to Paul or to Linda and Eric. Tell me where they are before I lose my patience."

"I can do one better. I can show you. There's a map in that drawer." Clark indicated a cabinet with a nod of his head. He stood up.

"Uh-uh." Bronson pointed to the chair. "Sit. I'll get it." He walked to the cabinet. "This drawer?"

Clark nodded.

Bronson opened the drawer and peeked in. It was full of papers. He moved them around but didn't find a map. He grabbed a handful of papers, set them down in front of Clark, and froze.

Clark wore a grin from ear to ear.

Bronson wondered why.

CLARK COULDN'T HELP IT. He continued to grin. While Bronson was busy looking for the map, Clark had reached into his pocket for his cell, found the number four button by touch, and pushed it, sending Carrier a warning signal. Carrier would soon arrive and take care of things.

Bronson was a dead man.

Clark smiled wider.

THIRTY-SEVEN

CARRIER ROLLED DOWN his window. The cool night breeze invigorated him. The car's digital display read 1:06. That meant by now Bronson was dead.

Too bad. Carrier had wanted to be the one to snuff the life out of him, but since Carrier had considered hiring Pete for odd jobs, he needed to see where Pete's capabilities lay.

The light turned red and Carrier stopped. Even if the streets were deserted, he always followed traffic laws. He'd never take a chance on being arrested for violating a simple rule.

When the light changed to green, he accelerated through the intersection. With luck, he'd be home in fifteen to twenty minutes. First thing, he'd reassure himself of Bronson's death. What was that expression? Seeing is believing?

Then he'd teach Pete how to properly dispose of a body, especially one with a high profile like Bronson's. Carrier had high hopes for Pete, but if he messed up, Carrier would kill him. No big thing. Someone else would replace him.

An approaching siren pierced the night. Carrier looked at his rearview mirror and saw a vehicle several blocks away. He couldn't tell if the siren belonged to a cruiser, an ambulance, or what. He slowed down and pulled to his right, clearing the lane for the emergency vehicle. He took the gun and put it next to his seat.

An ambulance zoomed past him. Carrier relaxed, hid the gun, and drove off. Ten minutes later, he neared his street. He turned the steering wheel, guiding the car to make a left

Then he saw, three blocks down, his house lit up with flashing lights. He straightened the car and continued heading up the road.

Sudden naked rage overwhelmed him. Pete had let him down. Carrier should have known better than to trust him. If Pete wasn't dead, he would soon be.

Carrier slammed a fist against the steering wheel. On top of everything, the police would soon put two and two together and realize that address belonged to him. He had lost the use of his rental home.

Down the block, he turned left, and executed another left at the end of that block. He parked the car and walked the rest of the way. He knew the police wouldn't be looking for him, at least not yet. He felt safe, but still he used the night's shadows to conceal himself.

From behind some bushes, he watched as two officers strung yellow crime-scene tape between sawhorses. Light bars pulsed, piercing the night with yellow and red flashing lights. The paramedics loaded a stretcher into the ambulance.

Carrier couldn't tell whether the body on the stretcher was Bronson or Pete. Either one meant bad news. He focused on the people hanging around the crime scene, but spotted neither Bronson nor Pete.

His cell phone went off. He reached into his pocket for it, looked at the digital display, returned it to its place, and headed back to his car.

Bronson was alive.

Damn.

THIRTY-EIGHT

BRONSON WAITED FOR CLARK to sort through the pile of papers. "You don't have to show me where they are, just tell me. I'll find them."

Clark pushed the papers away. "Might as well. I can't find the map anyway."

One of the servants, the young upstairs maid, leaned forward as if eagerly following the conversation. All eyes focused on her. She shrank back.

"You were about tell me where they are," Bronson said.

Clark leaned back, crossed his arms, and stared at Bronson.

Two could play that game. "Tell me about Ella. Where is it?" Bronson thrust the gun closer to Clark's face.

"I don't know."

Bronson flashed him a hard look.

"I really don't know. All I know is that the game consists of a couple who have to make all sorts of decisions. They make the right ones, they survive. They choose the wrong ones, they die. The only way to know which paths to follow is to use all the details that only Mitch and Linda know about their personal lives. If the character dies at any time, the game self-destructs."

"Very ingenious, but why bother? Wouldn't it be a lot easier to recreate the formula?" Bronson took a step backward, away from Clark's reach. One-handed, he retrieved his notebook and pen and made a couple of notations.

"Mitch—and Mitch alone—had found a way to penetrate

the epidermis. The notes I have—had—are no good without his information. And without my notes, I have to start from scratch. That's not an easy thing to do. I know what I used, but I don't remember the exact quantities—or even the order I put them in."

"But you have Stein and McGory to back you."

Clark leaned back and smiled.

Dread clutched at Bronson's heart. Clark was holding back, stalling. He knew something and he wasn't telling. Before heading down the stairs, had he called Carrier? If he had, Bronson had to get the servants out before they too became Carrier's victims. Forcing his voice to remain neutral, he said, "You know, I don't like all these people here. This should be a private conversation between you and me."

He heard a couple of groans and complaints. The help watched him closely with eyes that missed little and revealed less. "Send them upstairs."

"Why? So you can torture me into telling you what you want to know?"

"I'm a police officer. I wouldn't torture you. Look, if it makes you feel any better, have them call Captain Marshall and tell him I'm here. He can come and listen to your confession. You tell us where Paul and Linda and Eric are, and we'll go easy on you. We'll make sure your lawyer knows you fully cooperated. What about it? It's your only way out." Bronson signaled for the servants to leave.

They stood up. Clark didn't complain.

"You want us to call Captain Marshall, sir?" the man who had opened the knife drawer asked.

Clark looked at him for a long time before nodding. "Make sure you talk to the captain directly."

"Yes, sir." He began to herd the others out of the kitchen and up the stairs. "Will you be all right, sir?"

"I will be if you can get the captain here to protect me from Bronson."

"I'll make that call right away, sir." He turned and went to join the others who were already at the top of the stairs. Halfway up, he paused and turned. "You want me, sir, to stay with you until the captain arrives?"

"Thank you, but no. That won't be necessary."

"Very well, sir." He joined the rest and they went down the hall.

Bronson's interest in them ceased. The captain and his crew would arrive soon. He hoped that meant Carrier would be nowhere near Clark's house. He turned his attention back to Clark.

"I'm good to them," Clark said. "I pay them well and I treat them right. In return, they're faithful to me even after finding out that I involuntarily got involved in some wrong-doing."

Bronson didn't quite agree with the involuntarily part. "You were going to tell me where I can find Paul and Eric and Linda."

Clark raised his eyebrows and tilted his head. "No reason for you not to know. There's a good-sized basement—"

The house went dark. Bronson felt a garrote around his neck, choking him, cutting him, sucking his life away.

THIRTY-NINE

FREDDIE IMAGINED THEY WERE maybe half an hour away from Two Forks. Paul sat next to him chatting all the way from Custer. He was either stupid or very trusting. Possibly both. People like him needed to learn a lesson about real life. Freddie was glad he'd notified Carrier, which reminded him. It was time to call him. He pulled off to the side.

Paul sat up straighter and looked around. "Something wrong with the car?"

Freddie's lips formed a small, twisted smile. "Car's fine. I'm getting sleepy. Thought I'd pull over and catch a bit of fresh air."

"I'll drive."

"Not necessary. I'm fine. I just need a five-minute break, that's all." He stepped out of the car and walked away.

Paul got out, too, leaned against the hood of the car, folded his arms, and watched Freddie.

When he figured he was out of listening range, Freddie called Carrier. He heard the phone ring, but no answer. When the voice message came on, Freddie said, "It's Freddie Young. I've got your merchandise, which I'll deliver in half an hour or so. I'll call back in about fifteen minutes if I don't hear from you." He replaced the phone in his pocket and headed back to the car. "You ready?"

Paul stared at him.

BRONSON FELT A TRICKLE of blood ooze out of his neck. For the first time in his life, he felt helpless. At first he had tried reaching for the wire, to force it away from his neck. He wanted to breathe, he wanted it to stop hurting. He quickly realized that the more he struggled, the deeper the wire cut. If his assailant had wanted him dead, he'd be dead by now. Instead, he would live a bit longer, knowing that any minute could be his last. Bronson decided to play the game, hoping against hope that the police arrived in time.

Mustering every ounce of courage and self-discipline he had, Bronson stopped struggling and stood still. His hands hung beside him like broken tree limbs. Blackness wrapped its tentacles around him, smothering him.

From the far distance he heard a familiar sound, the ringing of a cell. Carol? *I love you.* Little Carol? *There's so much I have to tell you.* His other daughter, Donna? The grandkids? He wanted to see them all again.

As the cell continued to ring, he felt a slight release of the garrote's grasp. His eyes snapped open. Adrenaline rushed through his veins. He thrust both elbows back, striking his attacker's body. At the same time, he raised his right leg and thrust it down, hoping to break his attacker's foot.

Carrier yelped and lost his grip on the garrote, which fell limply to the floor. Bronson spun around and threw a fist, aiming for Carrier's chest, but by then Carrier had moved and Bronson only struck the air. He stood, panting, listening to the night noises.

Movement came from his right. Carrier had opened the door and stepped out. Bronson stood in the kitchen, feeling like a quarterback who had been sacked and dazed. He was slightly disoriented but very much ready for the next play. He followed Carrier outside.

He stood halfway in, halfway outdoors, his gaze searching the shadows. He reached for his gun.

Carrier rammed him from the left. Bronson landed with

a loud *thud*. Carrier grabbed a steel bar that lay among a pile of pipes on the patio. He brought the bar down hard.

Bronson rolled and the bar struck the cement, sending a clanging sound rippling through the air. Bronson hurt like hell from Carrier's tackle, but bounced to his feet despite the pain. They circled each other like a pair of wolves. Carrier swung the bar each time, closing the gap between them. Bronson reached for his gun, but time was against him. He saw Carrier's lips spread in sharkish anticipation as he advanced, like a caged animal that had just been released. Carrier brought the bar down toward Bronson, who ducked away.

As Carrier moved to regain his balance, Bronson made a fist and swung it full force into Carrier's stomach. Carrier doubled over and dropped the steel bar. Bronson cupped his hands and brought them down on the back of Carrier's head, while bringing his knee up to connect with Carrier's chin. The impact jarred him. Carrier stood in a dazed crouch, not falling, but also not standing.

Bronson paused to catch his breath. Carrier made a right forearm hammer, thumb down, and smashed Bronson on the inside of his right forearm. Bronson heaved like a weight lifter.

Triumph glowed on Carrier's face as he moved in for the final blows.

Bronson braced himself, waiting for the right moment. When it came, he raised his wide-open hand and aimed for Carrier's face. He caught Carrier with the heel of his hand under his nose.

Carrier shrieked and put both hands to his face. Bronson drove an elbow into Carrier's Adam's apple. Carrier dropped slowly to the floor, gurgling like bathwater leaving the tub.

When he hit the ground, he looked at the steel bar, but then grasped at his pocket. Bronson whipped out his gun and shot Carrier in the chest.

With his revolver cocked and pointed, he approached, reached into Carrier's pocket and grabbed the man's gun. He located a pulse, weak but present. Bronson flopped down, weak and dazed.

Headlights blinded him. He raised the gun.

"Put it down. It's Marshall."

"Captain." The fight had taken its toll on Bronson. Twenty years ago, he could have done this. Not today, not anymore. He uncocked the revolver and stuck it in his belt.

Carrier's phone went off. Bronson took it out of Carrier's shirt pocket and looked at the caller I.D. He didn't recognize the number and the name *Freddie* didn't ring any bells with him. "Yes?" He lowered his tone, hoping to sound like Carrier.

"We're about ten minutes away from Two Forks," the voice at the other end said. "Did you get my call?"

Bronson remembered hearing the cell ring while the garrote sliced into him. "Haven't checked messages."

"No problem. I have Paul with me and we're real close to Two Forks. What do you want me to do?"

Bronson wondered how this Freddie character fit in the picture. He drew a blank. "What model car you drivin'?"

"What?"

"So I can recognize it."

"Oh. It's a Chevy Impala, older model, pale blue. So where do we meet?"

We? Did he also have Eric and Linda? "How many of you came?"

"Just me. I can handle Paul. He doesn't even suspect."

Bronson searched his mind for a location. Somewhere out in the open where he could spot them, but also somewhere he could hide. "There's a huge park here in town."

"I know it."

"Meet me there, first bench as you approach the park. It may take me a while to get there, but wait for me."

"I can do that."

"And I don't want Paul harmed." Bronson thought of other innocent bystanders who might be visiting the park. "Or anybody else. The less people get hurt, the easier we get away. Is that clear?"

"I understand, Mr. Carrier. You can rely on me. How will I recognize you?"

"I'll know you."

Bronson shut the phone and looked at the captain. Marshall had squatted beside Carrier's body, examining his wounds. "He's not going to make it," Marshall said.

"That breaks my heart."

"I bet." He pointed to Carrier's cell. "What was that about?"

"Carrier's holding one of my friends from the police department hostage. I arranged to meet them at the city park." Bronson found it hard to talk even though his breathing had started to come at more regular intervals.

"Fill me in."

Bronson took a deep breath. "I don't know much. All I know is that some guy named Freddie, no last name, has Paul McKenzie, a lab technician for the Dallas Police Department, and he's bringing him to Carrier. Paul is going along with it because he doesn't know what Freddie is really planning to do. Freddie called Carrier for further delivery instructions. I sent them to the park and told them to wait for me—he assumed I was Carrier."

"I'll get my men on it." Marshall headed back toward his car.

"They're about fifteen minutes away, driving an old blue Impala."

Marshall nodded an acknowledgment as he walked away. The silver bolts of pain Bronson had been experiencing began to recede. He stood up and almost fell to the ground, but managed to regain his balance.

Marshall approached him. "Where's Clark?"

"I left him in the dining room. The lights all went out."

Marshall walked to the side of the house and flipped the switches. The area flooded with lights. Bronson stared at Marshall.

"Clark had a New Year's party here. At midnight, he had this huge fireworks display. I was in charge of killing the house lights so everybody could see the works better," Marshall said. "Let's go find Clark."

They found him sitting where Bronson had left him. Clark smiled when he saw Marshall. He nodded a hello.

Bronson squinted, focusing on Clark, but addressing Marshall. "If it's okay, I'd like to be there at the park to rescue Paul."

"I'm afraid that'll be impossible."

Bronson pivoted.

Marshall's gaze met his over the barrel of the captain's gun. "Very carefully set your weapon down on the table and walk away."

Bronson suspended his gun from the handle using his thumb and index finger. He set it down and stepped away. "Clark will vouch for me. Carrier's the one behind all these deaths."

Marshall leaned back against the kitchen counter and kept his gun aimed at Bronson. "Is he, now? Too bad he killed you before you had a chance to proclaim your innocence."

Bronson's eyes widened.

FORTY

PAUL FELT THE GUN IN his pocket. Freddie had to know he was carrying, but he hadn't asked. That alone had suggested, at least at first, that Freddie was on the level. He'd driven Paul to Two Forks because he wanted to help, or because it earned him an easy buck. That didn't bother Paul. In fact, he'd welcomed Freddie's offer to come along.

But now he wasn't so sure. Twice, Freddie had stopped to use the phone. Ever since then, he'd had *betrayal* written all over him. Paul could read it in his shifty eyes. He felt sure Freddie planned to hand him to Carrier, but that wasn't about to happen.

Paul leaned back in the car seat and closed his eyes, his mind busy devising plans. He could overpower Freddie, catch him by surprise. Problem was, Paul had no idea how to pull off something like that. Freddie was a professional. He wasn't.

That didn't matter.

One way or the other, Paul would make sure they never reached the park.

BRONSON CAST MARSHALL a disapproving stare. "I don't know who's the bigger scum of the earth, a serial killer or a dirty cop."

Marshall's lips curved upward, but the smile, heavy and thick like motor oil after being used thousands of miles, lacked humor. "Look, we all do what we have to do. Don't be so quick to judge. Just remember who's holding the gun."

Bronson's gaze held Marshall's stony gray eyes for several seconds. They reminded him of a graveyard. He glanced away from Marshall, past a window, then briefly back again.

Hoover waved at him.

Bronson's thoughts strayed to the door. Had Marshall locked it behind him? "My friend Paul needs help. There's no reason why you can't send some unmarked cars to that park." Bronson noted Marshall's cold, hard look. No way Bronson could hope to check the door. He didn't dare move and give Marshall a reason to shoot.

Marshall smirked. "I wouldn't be so concerned about your friend. I'd be more worried about me."

Bronson assessed his situation. He had to unlock the door if Marshall had locked it. Maybe if he took one step at a time. He inched toward the door.

Marshall raised the gun further, his features firm, his determination clear.

Bronson froze.

"I didn't say you could move. What the hell do you think you're doing?"

Bronson's hope vanished like a puff of smoke swallowed by air. "I'm tired. Sorry I moved. It was unintentional."

He heard a door open somewhere upstairs. Then the servants appeared by the staircase, huddled together. "Go back to your rooms," he ordered.

Marshall threw Clark an accusatory stare. "You didn't tell me they were here."

Clark shrugged.

The back door flew open as Hoover crashed in, throwing his body against the floor, his gun aimed at Marshall.

Bronson rushed Marshall, throwing his full body weight against him. Marshall landed on the floor. His gun skittered across the room. Bronson straddled him and punched him hard just below the breastbone. Next, just to be on the safe side, he landed another one on Marshall's face.

Marshall whooshed as his breath shot out of his lungs. Blood streamed down his nose.

Bronson straightened up, grabbed him by the lapels, and shoved him into a dinette chair. He bent down to reach for Marshall's gun just as Hoover stood up, his own gun still in his hand.

Bronson felt cold metal against the back of his head.

"Back off," Clark said. Bronson froze. "You." Clark indicated Hoover. "Drop your weapon." The coldness and toughness in his voice sent Bronson a warning signal.

Hoover set the gun down on the floor and raised his hands.

"Shiiit!" Bronson said.

FORTY-ONE

Paul pulled out his gun and pointed it at Freddie. "There's been a change of plans."

Freddie's head swiveled as he gaped at Paul. "What are you doing, man? I'm just trying to help you."

"I think not." The gun shook in his hands. Paul had never pointed a gun at anyone. "You made arrangements with Carrier to meet me at the park, didn't you?"

"Well, yeah. I thought you wanted me to hand you Carrier."

"You had it planned the other way around."

Freddie looked at the road in front of him and then checked the mirrors. He steered sharply to the right, then the other way. The car swerved. Paul reached for the door, trying to maintain his balance.

Freddie continued to drive in sharp S-curves. He reached over and gave Paul a karate chop on his wrist. The gun dropped to the floor and slid under the seat. Paul leaned forward to reach for it.

Freddie slammed on the brakes and Paul hit his face on the dash. When he looked up, he saw Freddie's gun pointed at him. "Don't move." Freddie's foot felt for and located the lost gun. He scooted it toward himself, leaned down, and grabbed it. "Get out of the car."

Paul glared at him.

"Now."

Paul got out. A fresh gust of cool air hit his face, stinging his wounds.

Freddie got out and headed toward Paul, gun in hand. The two men stared at each other. "Turn around," Freddie said.

Paul gasped. Suddenly, nothing mattered. He would embrace death. At least then he'd be with his beloved Angie. He turned around, giving Freddie his back.

ENOUGH'S ENOUGH, BRONSON thought as he threw his body weight backward, knocking Clark off balance. He pivoted toward Clark and smashed him in the face. The blow sent Clark stumbling to the floor.

Bronson raised his fists, ready for a fight.

Clark stood up, covered his face, and whimpered.

Bronson lowered his fists.

Hoover removed Marshall's belt, grabbed the cop's arms, and pulled them behind him. He tightened the belt around Marshall's hands. "Good job, buddy."

Bronson pocketed Clark's discarded gun, and smiled the first genuine smile in a heck of a long time, even though his body screamed with pain. "We still make a good team, don't we?"

"The best."

Bronson massaged his shoulders. "Think I can go back to work for the Dallas Police Department?"

"I doubt it."

"I thought so, too."

The maids and butler had worked their way down the stairs.

Bronson's gaze sought them out. "Are we going to have any trouble from any of you?"

They shook their heads.

"Good. I know you all feel loyalty to Clark, but somewhere along the way, you've got to choose between right and wrong. What's it going to be?"

The servant who had originally taken control stepped forward. "What do you want us to do?"

"A friend of ours, an employee from the Dallas Police Department, is in grave danger. We've got to rescue him. Call the police, but be careful. Marshall here is dirty. We don't know how many more cops are. You may want to call the newspapers first. Have them send lots of reporters, lots of photographers. Then have them snap a lot of pictures of you handing Marshall over to the police."

"Easy enough," the man said. "By the way, my name's Joe."

Bronson nodded and pointed at Hoover. "My partner, Mike Hoover." It felt good to say that again.

Hoover and Joe shook hands. Then Joe pointed to Clark. "What about him?"

Bronson and Hoover exchanged looks. "He'll come with us," Bronson said.

Hoover nodded.

"We still need to find Linda and Eric, and Clark will lead the way."

"Fat chance," Clark said.

Hoover relieved Marshall of his handcuffs. "Where are the keys?"

"In my pocket." Marshall's face had swollen and it was hard for him to speak.

Hoover reached in and found the keys. "Have a good life, Marshall. May you rot in jail." He took the manacles, spun Clark around, and cuffed his hands behind him.

"Ready?" Bronson asked.

"Not just yet. Some of those cuts, especially that one around your neck, need to be looked at."

"Paul's waiting."

"Ellen is out in the car. She's probably scared half to death. I'll bring her in. If I remember right, she was a real good nurse." Hoover looked at the help. "One of you please bring some alcohol and bandages."

"Right away, sir." The youngest of the servants ran out of the room.

Hoover stepped out and brought Ellen in. When she saw Bronson, she said, "My God, Harry. Look at you. Carol is going to kill you when she sees what you've done to yourself."

"Yes, it's good to see you, too," Bronson said.

The young lady returned, bringing a large first-aid kit. Ellen got busy cleaning Bronson's wounds.

FORTY-TWO

ELLEN PIVOTED TO LOOK AT Bronson, who sat in the back seat next to Clark. Clark's hands remained cuffed behind his back. "Bronson, are you sure you're up to this? You look like hell."

"Thank you, Ellen. I have always appreciated your truthfulness." Truth was, he felt like hell.

She smiled. "You're welcome."

"While you still have me as a captive audience, anything you'd like to ask me for your report?"

Ellen met his eyes. "There won't be one."

"Oh, I'm sorry."

She stuck her tongue out at him. "I bet you are."

They fell silent for a couple of blocks. Then Hoover broke that silence. "Bronson, buddy, I can do this by myself. You stay in the car. Keep an eye on Ellen and Clark."

"Not on your life. No offense, Ellen." Bronson wanted to be there to rescue Paul so he could punch him in the face for pulling such a dumb stunt.

"No offense taken," Ellen said in a sing-song voice.

Bronson flashed her a forced smile. He retrieved a pocket flashlight, turned it on, and read his notes. He paused on the page labeled *Pete*. "Listen, you two. Somethin' is botherin' me. Supposedly, Pete called me on my cell and told me to meet him at Mensa Enterprises. But instead of Pete, Carrier showed up. I was sure Pete had set me up, but Pete swore it wasn't him even though my cell said the call came from his He never did explain how Carrier made that call using his cell. According to Pete, Carrier never borrowed his phone. Any ideas?"

Hoover shook his head. "Seems to me like Pete told you a lie to cover his ass."

"I thought of that. Had it been just that one call, I'd agree with you. But I also got a false call from Jay, and that very strange *Help me* call that supposedly came from Paul. That's three calls I can't explain."

Ellen eyed Bronson through the rearview mirror. "I know how he did it."

"Tell me."

"Carrier spoofed you."

Bronson frowned. He'd been beaten, threatened, lied to, and now *spoofed*. "What the heck is that?"

"You know, spoofing, as in Internet spoofing."

"Enlighten me."

Ellen turned so she could see Bronson's face. "You get on the Internet. Go to any search engine and type *spoofing, caller I.D.* That'll give you the website for spoofing. Once you're on their website, follow their prompts. It'll tell you to enter the phone number of the person you want to call, then enter the number you want the cell's caller I.D. to register. When the cell rings, it'll show as coming from that person, when in essence It's coming from a computer."

Bronson leaned back. "I'll be. Anybody can call you pretendin' to be someone else."

"As long as they have access to the Internet."

Hoover turned to his ex. "Told you your trivia knowledge would come in handy." He winked at her.

"I'm sure that solved a lot of problems," she said and turned around.

"Park's about four blocks from here," Hoover said. "Front or back?"

The phrase brought a smile to Bronson's face. First time

Hoover had used it, they had cornered a killer in a house. Bronson banged on the door and identified himself. The killer snuck out the back door and straight into Hoover. Ever since then, Hoover covered the back and Bronson the front, but each time, Hoover asked. "I'll take the front." Bronson knew that wouldn't surprise Hoover, but still he felt he had to explain. "Since I was the one who talked to him, he might remember my voice."

"Fine with me," Hoover said. "Why break tradition?"

"Exactly."

Hoover drove to the opposite end of the park where the benches were located. He turned off the engine and pointed directly in front of him. "I'll head that way and surprise him from behind." He reached for the doorknob and felt Ellen's hand on his arm. He paused and turned.

"Be careful out there," she said.

Their eyes locked. "Do you care?"

She let her eyes slip away from his. "Yes."

He raised her chin, kissed her lips, and stepped out.

Bronson got out and motioned for Clark to follow him.

Clark's eyes snapped opened. "Why? What are you planning?"

"Get in the trunk."

Clark's eyes widened with fear. He began to sweat.

"Don't worry, you're not going to suffocate. It'll only be for a few minutes. Did you think we would leave you alone with Ellen? Come on, let's go." Bronson helped him out and half dragged him to the back of the car. "You make any noise—"

"I'll be quiet."

Clark climbed in and Bronson slammed the lid. He climbed in the driver's seat next to Ellen and restarted the car. "I'm going to leave you the keys. If somethin' goes wrong take off. Is that clear?"

Her eyes opened wide and her eyebrows shot up. "And leave you both here? I'm not going to do that."

"Is that clear?" Bronson gave her a hard look and she seemed to shrink.

"Fine, fine. I understand." She folded her arms. "You're worse than my husband—ex-husband."

"You still love him."

She looked away. "Maybe so, but that doesn't mean I want him back. I can't take too many nights like tonight. Not anymore."

Bronson thought of Carol and wondered if she ever felt that way. "If you love someone, you should be with them."

"Not necessarily so," she said.

They reached the parking lot. Bronson spotted the only other car there, an older model, pale blue Chevy Impala. Freddie's car.

"Be careful," Ellen said, "and take good care of Mike."

"Always."

Bronson shut off the engine and stepped out.

FORTY-THREE

As BRONSON WALKED PAST the Impala, he peeked inside. Discarded soda cans and wrinkled hamburger wrappers littered the floor. An opened map rested on the back seat. Nothing unusual. Bronson resumed his pace.

He scanned the park. No one visible, including Hoover. He looked at the empty bench where he'd told Freddie and Paul to wait. He headed that way and scanned the park one more time. This time, he spotted a lone figure coming toward him. He checked his pocket for easy access to his gun.

Once they were within hearing distance of each other, Freddie called out, "Carrier?" The man watched him through keen brown eyes. He had a common face, as nondescript as the guy who hands out tickets at the movie theater.

"I was expectin' two of you," Bronson said.

"I had to make sure—" Freddie paused and bit his lip.

"—that I wouldn't double-cross you?"

Freddie's eyes widened in alarm. "That's not what I meant."

"Where's my merchandise?"

"Where's my money?"

Bronson wished he had brought Ellen's attaché case with him. "You know the rules. You show me the merchandise, I give you the money. You give me what I want. Simple rules. Always work."

Freddie looked down and shifted uncomfortably. "Doesn't work for me that way, Carrier." He cleared his throat. "Give me the money."

An icy tentacle of uneasiness pierced Bronson's heart. He

wrestled with his emotions, trying to anchor his feelings. "Where's Paul?"

"He, huh, he…look, it wasn't my fault."

Bronson saw Hoover approaching and wished he'd go away. If this little piece of insignificant dirt had hurt Paul in any way, Bronson would make sure he'd regret it for the rest of his life. He took a step toward Freddie, putting them almost face-to-face. "Where's Paul?"

Freddie pulled a gun from his pocket and pointed it at Bronson. "Back off."

Bronson rolled his eyes. If one more person shoved a gun in front of him, threatened him, pushed him, he'd…he'd…he couldn't think of the right phrase. He kicked Freddie's wrist. The gun flew through the air. Hoover dove forward the last five steps and grabbed Freddie from behind.

Bronson stood back, his muscles taut. Hoover's tackle had thrown Freddie to the ground. Freddie moaned. Hoover looked at Bronson. "Very good, buddy. I didn't know you knew karate."

"I didn't either." Bronson rubbed his leg. "And now I hurt in a brand-new place." He hobbled toward the discarded gun, grunted as he bent to reach it, and pointed it at Freddie. "You were going to tell us where Paul is."

"I want my money first," Freddie said through clenched teeth.

Bronson stepped forward, cocked the gun, and shoved it against Freddie's cheek. "You have ten seconds to tell me what I want to hear."

Freddie's lower lip trembled visibly even in the shadows of the night. "My money."

"Nine."

Fear shone in Freddie's eyes like twin spotlights. "It's not my fault."

Bronson shoved the gun deeper. "Eight."

"He…he…" Freddie closed his eyes, whimpering.

"Seven."

"He attacked me." His breath caught absurdly in his throat.

"Six."

"It's not my fault. Do you hear me?"

"Five."

Hoover tightened his grip on Freddie, making him yelp. "Just tell us where he is."

"Four."

Silence.

"Three."

"All right. All right."

Bronson sighed as his muscles relaxed. He eased the pressure on Freddie's cheek, but didn't remove the gun. "We're all ears."

"He's…" He stopped.

Bronson shoved the gun harder against his cheek.

"…in my car trunk."

Bronson recalled walking by Freddie's car, looking in, examining it. He had been so close. "Is he dead or alive?" He held his breath.

"Alive. What do you think I am?"

"Certainly not a saint." He nodded at Hoover, who hauled Freddie up and shoved him toward the parking lot. "Where are the keys?"

Freddie's hand moved toward his pants pocket.

"Freeze," Bronson said. "I'll get them."

Freddie looked at him. "What do you think I have in there? A bomb?"

"You never know." Bronson retrieved the keys and showed them to Freddie.

"The silver one."

As they walked past Hoover's car, they waved at Ellen, and Bronson thought of Clark. Two lonely cars parked next to each other and each had a person in the trunk. The irony didn't escape him.

Freddie opened the trunk of the Impala. Paul cringed, but relaxed when he saw Bronson and Hoover. He flashed them a sheepish smile. Bronson helped him out.

Paul cleared his throat. "Bronson. Hoover. It's good to see you."

"Bronson? Hoover?" Freddie's eyebrows shot up. "Who the hell are you guys?"

"The police," Hoover answered, and Bronson smiled. He liked hearing that phrase.

Bronson turned to Paul. "You all right?"

"Yeah, thanks to you guys."

"Don't thank us yet," Hoover said. "We still haven't decided what to do to you for pulling such a stupid stunt."

Paul shrank. "Sorry."

"Sorry doesn't cut it." Hoover turned to Bronson. "Now what?"

"Now we let Clark out." He walked over to the back of the car, opened the trunk, and helped Clark out. *Déjà vu,* Bronson thought.

Freddie's eyes widened as he watched.

Ellen opened the door and stepped out. She hugged Paul. "I'm glad you're okay, and so are these two jerks, even if they don't admit it."

Paul hugged her back. "Ellen, what are you doing here?"

"It's a long story, but the short end of it is that Carrier is dead. Bronson shot him. It's over. He's really dead this time."

God, I hope so, Bronson thought. Now Paul could go home.

Tears flooded Paul's eyes and he looked away.

The group stood by the cars staring at each other. "Now what?" Ellen asked.

"Do you have an extra pair of handcuffs?" Bronson asked Hoover.

"Got a pair in the car."

"Get 'em. We'll cuff this one—" Bronson pointed at Freddie "—to the park bench, take off, and call the local police."

"That's not how we do things." Hoover threw his arms in the air. "Oh, yeah, I forgot. That's how you do things. I'm going to get creamed on this one."

Bronson frowned. He wouldn't allow his actions to mess up Hoover's career. "Look, I can't let the police catch me. I don't know if I'm still a wanted man or not, and I can't afford to find out just now. I've got to look for Linda and Eric. They're depending on me."

"I know, buddy." Hoover took a deep breath. "Look, why don't you go find a motel somewhere? I'll stay here with Freddie until the cops arrive. I'll join you just as soon as I can."

Bronson nodded. "You'll be okay, by yourself?"

"Who says I'll be by myself? Paul will stay with me."

Bronson nodded, opened the back door of the car, and shoved Clark in.

Ellen cast Hoover a glance that Bronson couldn't interpret. She got in the front passenger seat.

Hoover pulled Bronson to the side. "Bronson, I have to ask. What were you thinking? What would you have done if you reached zero and Freddie hadn't talked?"

"I would've shot the grass right under his feet. That would have set him blabbering."

"And if it didn't?"

"Then I would have shot his foot or his leg."

"And if that still didn't work?"

"What's with you? You sure are pessimistic today." Bronson climbed into Hoover's rental with Clark and Ellen and drove away.

FORTY-FOUR

LIKE ALL THE MOTELS in the area, A Good Night's Rest charged a bit more than they should. Even so, Bronson insisted on two rooms. "As much as I ache, I need my own bed," he said as he slid into the driver's seat after paying. "I can't share. Paul will sleep on the other bed, and I'll lock Clark in the bathroom."

Ellen squinted as though trying to understand what Bronson hadn't verbalized. "What about Mike? Isn't he..." Her mouth dropped open. "You tossed out that remark as casually as yesterday's lunch."

Bronson shrugged. "I don't know about you, but yesterday, I didn't have lunch." He pulled up to the two side-by-side rooms.

"You know exactly what I mean. Where is Mike supposed to sleep?"

"There's no place in my room. That leaves yours." He turned off the engine and reached for the door.

"Oh, no. No way."

"Relax, it's got two beds." He turned to Clark. "You wait here, or would you rather I put you back in the trunk?"

Clark smirked. "You lock the damn car. My hands are cuffed behind me. How can I go anyplace?"

"That's what I like. Be a good boy." Bronson opened the door and got out. "Come on, Ellen. I'll help you get the luggage inside."

"What about yours?"

Bronson stopped halfway to picking up her suitcase.

His luggage was in his car, which he had left parked in Clark's driveway.

Ellen smiled as she watched his reaction. "Come on, I'll drive you to Clark's house so you can pick up your car."

That'd be fine, provided the police hadn't impounded it. Bronson shook his head. "Thanks for the offer, but Hoover and I'll go get it once he returns."

"Once he returns? Won't you be asleep by then?"

"We'll see." He opened the door to her room and led her in.

"You're not planning to go to bed, are you?"

Was he that easy to read? "I have to rescue Linda and Eric."

"But you do plan to wait for Mike, right? You're not going to do this by yourself."

Bronson's cell went off. He checked the caller I.D. "Speakin' of the devil." He showed Ellen the phone, then answered it. "Yo?"

"Things are really messed up." Paul's voice, instead of Hoover's, held confusion. "The police haven't cleared your name yet and now they're accusing Hoover of interfering. I think they're going to hold him. If I don't want trouble, I'm to head back to Dallas right now."

"Didn't any of the cops who showed up at the park see or hear about Marshall's arrest? That should clear Hoover and me."

"I don't know. I don't know what happened. No one said anything. Where are you?"

"At a motel called A Good Night's Rest."

"I'll tell Hoover. Listen, the police are coming to take me to the airport. Gotta go. Good luck."

The line disconnected.

"What's wrong, Bronson?" Ellen's eyes sparkled with worry.

"Hoover may be detained a bit longer. Seems I'm still a fugitive, and he's in trouble for helpin' me."

"I thought..." She threw her arms up.

Bronson handed Ellen the key to her room. "I can't afford to wait. Besides, I'll be a sitting duck here. When Hoover arrives, if he does, have him call me." He set the last of the luggage inside. "Lock the door behind me." He stepped out and waited until he heard the click of the bolt before returning to the car.

He unlocked the car door and got in the driver's seat. He adjusted the rearview mirror until he could see Clark. "You're going to tell me where Eric and Linda are."

"Give me one good reason why I want to do that."

"Because right now you're facing, among others, kidnappin' charges. You don't want to add murder."

Clark looked away. "They won't kill her. They need her to decode the game."

"And once she does, she'll be no use to them. That'll be murder one."

Clark bit his lip. "She's fine. They won't hurt her."

"You keep saying *they*. Who are *they*?"

"I don't know."

Bronson slammed the steering wheel. "I've had a pretty rotten day. If I were you, I'd start talkin'."

"I'm going to rot in jail anyway."

"You'll do jail time, all right, but how much time you do and even which prison you get sent to depends on how much you cooperate. Some prisons are country clubs. Some are hell. I'll guarantee you the worst hell. Think about it, because either way, I'm going to find Linda." Bronson looked at Clark in the rearview mirror. "Where is she?"

Clark squirmed. "I told you about the basement."

"I remember." Bronson turned on the map light and thumbed through his notes. "You said it was good-sized." He waited for Clark to say something. When he didn't, Bronson continued, "You're tellin' me that if I find this basement, I find Linda. So where's this basement?"

"Figure it out."

Bronson felt like strangling the information out of him. "Way I see it, your house is big enough to have a basement, but then the servants would know about it, wouldn't they? No, I don't think it's your basement. That leaves work. That place is huge. That's where you and Mitch worked on the formula. It makes sense. That's where Linda would be."

Clark sighed and nodded. "You can reach the basement from the lab."

Bingo! Finally, a spark of hope. "One more thing. We started talking about Linda and Eric. Somewhere in that conversation, you dropped Eric. Why's that?"

"Linda's in the basement, or at least she was. I've never seen Eric and I don't know what's happened to him. I'm not even sure who Eric is."

Great. Just peachy-cream great.

FORTY-FIVE

"TELL ME ABOUT THE LAB," Bronson said once they were rolling.

"We have security cameras that monitor the entire building."

"Includin' the parkin' lot?"

"Including the parking lot. Two security guards are always on duty. They're supposed to rotate shifts, patrolling the hallways and monitoring the cameras. I'm not supposed to know this, but beginning at midnight they take turns sleeping. One sleeps from twelve to three, the other from three to six."

The digital display on the car's dashboard read 3:16. By the time they'd reach the pharmaceutical research center, one of the security guards should be asleep. Bronson would only have to worry about one guard. "What's their training like?"

"Never asked, but both are older and out of shape—like you."

Sticks and stones might break my bones, but words will never hurt me. The light turned red and Bronson stopped. He wondered why the city didn't change the system to flashing yellow during the night. "Do they carry?"

"Carry?"

Bronson drummed the steering wheel while he waited. He looked all around. Not a car in sight. He gunned it and went. Halfway through the intersection the light changed to green. "Guns. Do they carry guns?"

"I think so." Clark stretched the *I* as though he really didn't know the answer.

"Ever been to the lab at this time of night?"

"Several times. I come and go at all sorts of hours. I buzz the guard, he lets me in. I have to sign the after-hours sign-in sheet."

Another traffic light threatened to slow Bronson down. This time, when it turned yellow, Bronson sped past it. "When you're alone in the lab at night, do the security guards follow your actions?"

Clark shrugged. "Who knows? I never thought about it, but there's a security camera in the lab, if that's what you wanted to know."

Clark had answered every question without hesitating. He seemed to know the system, but Bronson wondered if he was holding any information back. "What else should I know?"

"You'll need to remove these handcuffs."

Bronson's glance drifted to the rearview mirror, where he could see Clark's face. "Why would I want to do that?"

"I can help you. We walk in the front door like I always do. I introduce you as a fellow scientist. We go down to the lab home free. I work at my station, drawing the guard's and the camera's attention. You're free to go down to the basement."

Bronson's gaze returned to the road. It made sense, but it seemed too easy. "What guarantee do I have that you won't run?"

"Where would I go? My house? You know where that is. I have no girlfriend, no real friends, no family outside of my niece and my servants. I can't leave town because my niece needs me. So tell me, Bronson, where can I go that you couldn't find me?"

By now Bronson had reached the edge of town. Soon the streets would lead him to the road that passed the McGory and Stein research center. The idea of not fighting any security guards appealed to him. Walk in, go down to the basement, find Linda, and leave through the back door he recalled from a copy of the floor plans taped to the top of the receptionist's desk. No sweat, no problems.

The city lights dimmed as he left Two Forks behind. He had two choices. One, he could fight the guards, rescue Linda, and keep Clark prisoner. Or two, he could take a chance on Clark running away, but still get Linda out and not fight any guards. If he fought the guards, as tired and as much as he hurt, they might overpower him. Best to take a chance on Clark.

He pulled over, unlocked the car, and helped Clark out. "Turn around." Bronson removed the handcuffs. "Get in." Clark rubbed his wrists and reached for the back door. "The front," Bronson said. "If they're watchin' the parkin' lot when we pull in, it'll look funny if we're supposedly friends and you get out of the back seat."

Clark continued to rub his wrists. He opened the front passenger door and slid in. Bronson got back in the driver's seat, praying he'd made the right decision. "View different from up front?"

"I work here. I drive this road all the time. I don't need to see the scenery. Besides, it's dark. What's there to see?"

Bronson started the engine and pulled out. "Obviously, you're not the one who's holdin' Linda. You're takin' orders from someone. Who?"

"I've got no idea."

Bronson narrowed his eyes, casting him a warning look. "Yeah, I bet."

"I'm serious. I don't know who he is. I call him the Chief because he sits out there somewhere like a big Indian chief and gives orders."

"How do you communicate with the Chief?"

"I have a preprogrammed cell. To reach the Chief, I punch five. Carrier is three and four. I punch four, that means there's trouble. No need to talk to him. If I want to talk—or rather, if I wanted to talk to him, not that I ever did—I punch three. Mitch was two, but his cell was destroyed."

"Let's see yours."

"I don't have it."

"Where is it?"

"Out in the woods somewhere. While you and Carrier fought, I stomped on the cell, hoping to break it. Then I threw it as far as I could into the trees around my house."

"Very convenient."

"I thought so."

Bronson turned into McGory and Stein Drive. "What can you tell me about the Chief? Think he could be McGory or Stein?"

"Maybe. Maybe not. I don't like to point a finger at someone when I'm not really sure."

"How noble of you."

Clark folded his arms. "I'm not really a bad guy, Bronson. I did what I did for my niece, and in spite of everything, I'd do it all over again."

"Then let me rephrase that question. If you were to bet on the Chief's identity, who would you pick? Hypothetically speaking."

"Stein." Clark looked away.

Bronson pulled into the back area of the parking lot and turned off the engine.

Clark pointed ahead of him. "Front entrance is over there. Why did you park way over here?"

"It's closer to the lab's back door. We may have a longer walk to reach the main entrance, but better to walk now than when we have Linda."

Clark nodded.

"Are you ready?"

Again, Clark nodded.

"If you blow this for me, I—"

"No need for threats. I won't interfere with you getting Linda out." He took a deep breath. "Once we're inside, to your right, you'll see some folding doors. You open those and you'll see a closet where we store supplies. Walk into the closet, and to your left, you'll see a wall behind some self-standing shelves. Under the second shelf, there'll be a button. Push it and the door will open. You'll see the stairs. Good luck." Clark opened the door, stepped out, and waited until Bronson joined him.

Together they headed toward the main glass door. Once there, Clark pushed the intercom button. The security guard, a balding man with a big stomach and no gun, waved them in. They entered and headed for the security desk.

"You and your guest will need to sign in," the guard said.

"I'm familiar with the procedure. How's the family, Tom?" Clark picked up a pen and wrote his name.

"Family's fine. Thanks for asking."

Clark handed Bronson the pen. "You'll need to sign in and show Tom your driver's license so he can verify you are who you say you are."

Bronson signed in, retrieved his license, and displayed it. Tom looked at the picture, then at Bronson, and finally at the signature. "Texas, eh? You're a long way from home."

"Well, yeah, you know how it goes. My line of work involves a lot of travelin'."

"And what is it that you do, Mr. Bronson?"

"I'm a scientist. We're here to work on a couple of trouble spots."

"I see." He handed Bronson his driver's license back. "How long do you think you'll be here?"

Clark shrugged. "An hour? An hour and a half, maybe."

"I'll look for you then so you can check out." He sat behind the console, propped his feet up on the desk, and started to watch television. Reruns, from what Bronson could see. Behind him, the system's cameras checked the hallways, various rooms, and the parking lot. Tom paid no attention to them.

Clark led Bronson down the hallway. "You remember what I told you about the basement?"

"Sure do."

"You go there and I'll go to my station. I doubt Tom's watching, but you never know."

As soon as they entered the lab, Bronson scanned the room and spotted the cameras. "If you stand over there and turn your back to the camera, they'll still be able to see you and think you're workin'."

"Why would I want to turn my back to the camera?"

"Because you're going to be handcuffed to that pipe over there."

Clark frowned. "Really, Mr. Bronson, that's not necessary."

"Maybe not for you, but for me."

They headed for the counter. Bronson used Clark's back to block the camera's view as he cuffed him to a pipe that stuck out. He double-checked it to make sure Clark couldn't yank it out. Satisfied, he slowly walked around the room, pretending to be interested in its contents. When he knew he was safely out of camera range, he took a right, spotted the double doors, and opened them.

The walk-in closet was bigger than his living room. He walked to his left and found the self-standing shelves, the only wall that didn't have shelves attached to it. He looked under the second shelf and spotted the button. He pushed it. The wall slid open to show a well-lit area below. Bronson stood at the top. He couldn't see anything but the stairs. He took out his gun and held it at the ready position. He took two steps down and listened.

Nothing.

He descended a couple more stairs and scoped the area. As far as he could tell, the basement held a lot of equipment, but no hostages. "Linda?" He took a couple more steps down and paused.

"Bronson." Linda's voice came from behind the stairs.

He went down the rest of the way, turned toward Linda's voice, and froze.

A giant of a man held a gun to Linda's head.

A chill ran down his spine as he sensed someone standing behind him. Before he could react, he felt a blow to the back of his head. Pain exploded, greater than he'd ever experienced. A gasp escaped his mouth. The warmth of his trickling blood floated him into darkness.

FORTY-SIX

MARSHALL HAD PAPERS SCATTERED on every available area in his small office. He gathered a stack of them piled on a chair and dropped them on the floor. "That's my weakness, you know, paperwork. I hate it."

Hoover leaned against the wall, crossed his arms, and glared at Marshall.

Marshall glanced up and pointed to the chair. "Sit."

Hoover didn't move.

"Oh, I see. You're mad. You don't understand why I haven't been locked up. Well, let me tell you a story. I don't know how you do it in Dallas, but here in Wyoming we have a system that says not-guilty-until-proven-so. Good rule, you should try it."

"Yes, of course. I can see *innocent* written all over you. That's why you pulled that stunt. Your gun was meant to keep us safe."

Marshall half smiled and shrugged. "We have another system here that you Dallas boys need to try. It's called Undercover Cop."

His statement burst inside Hoover's brain like a bomb in a cavernous room, reverberated, and left him stunned. "You're working undercover." His voice came out rough and dry. He cleared his throat. They sure did things differently here.

"We've had a bout of unexplained crimes, so with my supervisor's consent, I've accepted a couple of bribes. So far, I know of three dirty cops, but the ring is bigger, and I'm going for the big fish. I'm slowly penetrating it, and when I have the entire lot, I'm reeling 'em in."

Hoover pursed his lips. "That doesn't explain why you aided Clark."

"Can't prove it yet, but I suspect there's a connection between Clark and the incidents here at the station."

Hoover dropped down to the chair. "Did we blow your cover?"

"Maybe not. I'm having one of my men drive Paul to the airport for appearance's sake. My crew thinks I want Paul out of here so he doesn't open his trap. As soon as he lands in Dallas, I want you to call him and explain why he's got to keep his mouth shut. Think you can do that?"

Hoover nodded.

"As for Bronson, we'll keep him on the wanted list, maybe even intensify our hunt for him, and as for you, I think I'll throw you in a cell for a couple of hours."

Hoover felt his muscles stiffen. He sat up straighter.

"Relax. It'll only be two hours, tops. Then I'll have to release you due to lack of evidence. I'll put you in an isolated cell. I've already had you empty all your pockets and relieved you of your watch and ring. I'll make sure all your belongings are kept together and safe. Work with me on this, will you?"

Feeling like a stone, Hoover nodded. "Bronson needs to know this."

"I'll call him when I can. I'll get his number from your cell."

"Thank you."

"You ready?"

Not really. He stood up.

HOOVER CLASPED HIS HANDS behind his back as he paced in the small motel bedroom. "I can't believe Bronson. He sets it up so that I spend the night with you, then he takes off so I have to spend my time finding him. What goes through that man's head? I've never been able to figure him out."

Ellen sat on the bed, watching her ex, a half smile plastered on her face. "In Bronson's defense, Paul told him you were in jail. He had no way to know you'd be out in two, three hours. How did you get out?"

Marshall had kept his word. An hour and fifteen minutes after he had been thrown in the slammer, Marshall released him. He drove Hoover to Clark's house, where he picked up Bronson's car. "You explain it to Bronson for me," Marshall had said. "I haven't had a chance to call him and I don't think I will. That might arouse suspicion."

Hoover nodded.

Marshall continued, "It really would help my cover if you and Bronson took off. Consider it. Take good care of your selves." He waved goodbye and drove off.

Hoover couldn't tell any of that to Ellen. He wished he could and maybe some day he would. He resumed his pacing as though Ellen hadn't asked anything. "How long ago did you say Bronson left?"

Ellen glanced at the alarm clock. It read 5:25. "A bit over two hours."

"Two hours? Where the hell is he? Why doesn't he answer his cell?"

Ellen looked down. "I don't know." She bit her lip. "I'm worried."

Hoover stopped and looked at her. He sat beside her and wrapped his arm around her. She leaned on him and Hoover wished they could stay like that forever. "You stay here. I'm going to go look for him. Try to get some sleep."

"Mike."

He stood up. "I have to go." He kissed her forehead, memorizing each delicious moment. He fished for the keys in his pocket. "I'm going to the lab. Seems to be the most logical place to begin." He threw her a kiss and walked out.

Hoover reached McGory and Stein Pharmaceutical Research Center in record time. As soon as he pulled into the parking lot, he saw his car at the back. As he approached it, he wondered what so many vehicles were doing there so early in the morning. He reached the car and checked it out. He found nothing incriminating. His heart beat wildly in his chest as he rushed toward the entrance and banged on the door.

The security guard remained seated, his eyes closed. Hoover banged on the door again. The guard woke up. He looked at Hoover, then at his watch, and shook his head *no*.

Hoover retrieved his badge, shoved it against the glass, and pointed to the knob. The security guard frowned but buzzed him in.

Hoover didn't wait to reach the guard's station before speaking. "Is Bronson still here?"

"Who?" The guard looked down at the sign-in sheet.

"Bronson. Harry Bronson. He probably came with Clark."

"They were here, but left more than an hour ago." He pointed to the signatures showing they had checked out.

Hoover looked at the writing. Large, block letters. Anyone—including Bronson—could have done that. "Mind if I check Clark's lab?"

"Do you have a search warrant?"

Hoover leaned forward. "I didn't think I needed one. All I want to do is take a look. You let me in, I won't report you for sleeping on the job."

The guard's eyes widened and he wet his lips. "Sure, no harm in you just checking, but I doubt you'll find anything."

He led Hoover down the hallway and opened the door to the lab. "This is Clark's station, where he and Bronson came.

They were here for maybe half an hour. Then they checked out and left, like it says on the sign-in sheet."

Hoover walked around the room, looked in the trash can, opened the doors to a huge storage closet, and looked at each item on the lab benches. "The car Bronson drove is still in the parking lot."

"Maybe they took Clark's car and left Bronson's here. Bet you anything in a couple of hours Clark will bring him back to get his car."

As logical as that sounded, Hoover had trouble believing it. "Any possibility they're still inside?"

"None whatsoever. They signed out and they can't get back in without me knowing it."

"Did you actually see them sign out?"

"Well, uh, they, uh—"

"You were asleep, weren't you? You don't know who signed Bronson out."

The guard held Hoover's gaze.

"How about surveillance cameras? Would any of them show us what we want?"

"Sure." The guard reached to retrieve the tape. "Damn," he said. "It's gone."

FORTY-SEVEN

BRONSON FELT AS IF AN entire marching-band drum line was practicing in his head. He reached up, massaged his forehead, and struggled to open his eyes and focus. At first, muted colors swirled around him, but gradually, the double images blended into one. He saw a bathtub, a sink, a woman sitting on the floor, her legs pulled tight to her chest, arms wrapped around her legs. Her head rested on her knees.

"L-linn-da."

She snapped her head up. "Bronson! You're awake."

The throbbing pain made him cradle his head in his hands. He tried to sit up, failed, and decided to remain still. "Wh-where are we?"

"In a motel somewhere. They blindfolded me, so I couldn't tell you which motel or where."

Bronson forced himself into a sitting position. He bit his tongue to keep from grimacing as a sharp pain volleyed between his temples. "How long, in the car?"

"I don't know." Linda looked down and shook her head. "They took my watch and my cell away. Maybe two hours. Maybe three. I really don't know."

"I'm sure we're headin' for Minnesota, and if they drove for two or three hours, then we must be close to Custer." Bronson thought of Carol. His arms felt empty. He shook those thoughts aside and concentrated on the bathroom. "Can we open the bathroom door and get out of here?"

Linda shook her head. "It's not that simple. Soon as they

walk out, they move the dresser so it blocks the door. I've tried opening it, but I can't."

Bronson closed his eyes and rubbed his temples. Maybe he could push the door, force the dresser to move. He'd wait for a few minutes while he gathered his strength. His gaze wandered around the various items in the bathroom, but no matter how hard he looked, he couldn't find anything that could help them. The cramped little window wasn't big enough to squeeze through. He pointed to it. "What do you see?"

Linda stood on her tiptoes. "Just more motel. Looks like we're on the second floor. They have this pretty well planned out, don't they?"

"Who are *they?*"

"Two men, both armed. I've never seen them before."

"Can you describe them?"

"Yeah, sure. One wears glasses, has wiry hair and a big nose. The other is much taller, brown eyes, brown hair."

Bronson recalled the man he had seen holding a gun to Linda's head in the lab's basement. "Their build? Big guys?"

"The mousey-looking one is the smaller of the two. The other one doesn't have a football player's body, but he's big."

Bronson felt his eyes close. Struggling, he snapped them open and shook himself. "Muscular?"

"Somewhat, yeah."

Damn. Linda could describe both men, which meant that after she won that game for them, they would kill her. Unable to fight off sleep's embrace any longer, Bronson closed his eyes.

HOOVER SHOULD HAVE BEEN tired, but the adrenaline pulsed through his system and kept him alert. In spite of what Marshall had said, he didn't plan to sit on his ass and wait. If he hurried, he could still catch Stein at home.

A sprawling driveway led to Stein's mansion, a Colonial-style house complete with white columns and colorful flower beds. Hoover rang the doorbell.

A middle-aged lady with a round face answered the door. Hoover flashed her his I.D. badge. "I need to speak to Mr. William Stein."

She opened the door to allow him into the foyer. "Please wait here."

Hoover stepped in. The aroma of frying bacon teased his taste buds. Up until now, he hadn't realized how hungry he felt.

The woman returned. "This way, sir."

He followed her past a living room large enough to hold a Dallas Cowboys practice session and on to the dining room. A mahogany table designed to accommodate twenty guests did nothing to dwarf the room. A distinguished-looking man with solid white hair set the newspaper down, stood up, and offered Hoover his hand. "I'm sorry. I'm afraid my maid didn't catch your name or your title."

"Detective Mike Hoover." They shook hands.

"I've been expecting you." Stein pointed to a seat. "Won't you join me?"

Hoover pulled out a chair and sat down. "You said you've been expecting me. Why's that?"

"If you don't mind, I won't answer anything until my lawyer shows up. I've already called him. He lives a couple of houses down, so he won't be long."

The maid set down a steaming cup of coffee in front of Hoover, which reminded him of Bronson. His hunger went away.

Stein reached for the fruit bowl and helped himself to some orange slices, watermelon, grapes, and sliced canta-loupe. "It's so early in the morning. I doubt that you've had breakfast. I took the liberty of telling my cook to prepare some for you, too."

"Thanks, but no. As soon as you tell me what I need to know, I'll be on my way."

The maid reappeared carrying a tray filled with flavored creams, sugar, and sugar substitutes. Hoover chose Irish cream, passed on the sugar, and thanked her. She nodded *you're welcome* and retreated.

The doorbell rang. "Ah, that must be Roy," Stein said.

The maid set down a plate filled with well-done bacon. Hoover reached for a strip. "There's plenty more," the maid said. "Please help yourself."

She left to answer the door and returned accompanied by a man sporting a military cut and a jogging outfit. He nodded at Stein, then smiled and extended his hand toward Hoover. "I'm Roy Kasdorf. Mind if I see your badge?"

Hoover shook his hand, retrieved his badge, and handed it to Kasdorf. The lawyer's eyebrows came together in puzzlement as he studied the badge. "Dallas? What does Dallas have to do with this?" Kasdorf returned the badge, pulled out a chair, and sat down.

Hoover sat also. "I'll answer that one, then it's my turn to ask the questions."

"Fair enough," Kasdorf said. He looked at Stein, who nodded.

The cook brought in a basket filled with fluffy biscuits and a bowl topped to the rim with scrambled eggs. After she left, Hoover said, "My department has been tracking Benjamin Carrier for quite a while."

Kasdorf and Stein exchanged looks. "Who's Benjamin Carrier?" Kasdorf asked Stein.

Stein shrugged. Both men turned to look at Hoover.

"He's a real bad man. He's already killed several people."

Stein froze halfway to reaching for some bacon. "He's a killer and he's here in our town?"

Kasdorf raised his hands. "I have a feeling we're talking

about two different things. Detective Hoover, why don't you tell us why you're here." He sipped the milk the maid had placed in front of him.

Hoover kept his eyes on Stein, although he knew the lawyer would do most of the talking. "My ex-partner, Harry Bronson, is missing, and I have reason to believe that Mr. Stein can lead me to him."

Stein set his fork down and wiped his mouth with a napkin. "I don't know anybody named Bronson and I certainly don't know where he is. Am I in trouble with the law?"

"That depends on the extent of your involvement."

Stein turned to Kasdorf, a question on his face.

Kasdorf straightened up. "Let me explain Bill's—uh, my client's—involvement, as you so adequately put it." Kasdorf leaned forward and spoke as though addressing a jury instead of two men. "A few days ago, a young man by the name of Eric Randig showed up at Bill's door. He had an incredible tale to tell." He paused for effect. "Seems Eric is the son of our leading scientist who recently fell off a roof and died. Eric claims his father was pushed and that his grandparents were also murdered, all three for the same reason.

"Mitch Randig, our leading researcher, along with his partner, Henry Clark, were working on a formula that will erase and prevent wrinkles forever. According to Eric, Clark got greedy and decided to sell the formula. Bill—Mr. Stein—immediately hired me to protect the company from possible lawsuits and, of course, to make sure the formula stays with McGory and Stein, the rightful owners.

"I keep a private investigator on my payroll. Today, he's supposed to report his findings to me." Kasdorf retrieved his wallet, took out a business card, and handed it to Hoover. "Here's his contact information."

Hoover glanced at the card and pocketed it. "When was the last time you talked to Eric?"

Stein waited until he finished buttering his bread before answering. "Roy and I talked to him at length last night."

Hoover put on a poker face. "Last night?"

"Yes."

"And where exactly did you meet?"

"Here, at my house. In fact, he and his son are still my guests. He's upstairs. The baby is playing outside. One of my maids is watching him. Eric feels safe here. We don't know if Eric really is in danger, but we're playing his game until we hear from Roy's man."

Kasdorf reached for a slice of bacon and broke it in half. "As you can see, Detective Hoover, my client has done nothing wrong. All he's done is protect Eric Randig from possible harm."

"If that's the case, why haven't you gone to the police?"

"But we did. I contacted Captain Marshall." Kasdorf popped a piece of bacon into his mouth. "All three of us agreed it'd be best to keep Eric Randig's whereabouts secret, just in case. Now tell me what all this has to do with your partner's disappearance. Bronson, wasn't it?"

Hoover nodded. "I'd like to talk to Eric."

Stein stood up. "I'll wake him up and have him join us."

Hoover watched Stein go up the stairs and knew he had run headlong into another dead end. No one knew where Bronson was.

FORTY-EIGHT

BRONSON STRUGGLED TO open his eyes, then to focus. He looked around and recognized the bathroom that held them prisoner. Linda's eyes were closed. Her folded arm lay on the toilet's lid, while her head rested on her arm. Bronson stood up and his knees buckled. He grabbed the sink to keep from falling.

Linda stirred, then quickly got to her feet. "Are you okay?"

Bronson waited until the dizziness went away. "I'm fine—maybe a little weak."

"There's some food for you. When they brought me supper, they put the bag in the shower in case you woke up."

Supper? Weren't they way past suppertime? Bronson looked out the window. Still dark. Not much time could have elapsed. "How long was I asleep?"

"One of the guys said you'd been out over sixteen hours. That was maybe an hour ago."

Sixteen hours?

"You worried them. One of them said they were dead meat if anything happened to either one of us. They considered getting help if you didn't wake up in a couple of hours."

Bronson knew why they wanted her alive, but why were they keeping him alive? "That's always good news—bein' needed."

"How's that?"

"It gives us an edge."

"Bronson!" A sharp voice came from the other side of the door. "We know you're awake. We heard you talking."

"I hear you." Bronson scanned the bathroom, noting how the door opened, the location of the shower, sink, and pot. No towel holder.

"Get inside the shower and close the curtain."

Bronson looked at Linda and shrugged. Not seeing any options, he figured he might as well do what they wanted. Maybe when they were together, he could overpower them. He stepped into the shower and saw the bag of food. As he drew the curtain shut, he looked at the curtain holders.

He heard the bathroom door open and considered bolting out, but decided to play it safe. Seconds later, he heard the same voice say, "You're alone now. Use the facilities if you need to, and then come out. The door's unlocked." He heard the door close.

Bronson reached up, unsnapped the brass curtain holder, and pocketed it. Then he slid the curtain open and glanced around. They had Linda. His heart jumped to his throat, but he forced himself to calm down. They needed her alive. He used the bathroom, washed up, retrieved the food bag from the shower floor, and said, "I'm coming out."

"Keep your hands where we can see them."

He opened the door and saw the giant from the lab basement pointing a gun at him. Bronson raised his hands. "I have my food with me." He quickly scanned the room. Double beds separated by a nightstand. Phone on the nightstand. A dresser in front of the beds. Television on top of the dresser. The mousey-looking thug held Linda at gunpoint at the opposite end of the room.

"We've been warned about your tricks, so don't try anything," said the giant. "Jack may not look threatening, but believe me, he's very capable."

"I'm cool." Bronson pointed to his food bag. "Mind if I sit down and eat?"

The giant pointed to the edge of the bed. "Sit down and enjoy your meal. We're under strict orders to feed you and patch you up."

Bronson opened the bag and looked in. "Kind of like fattenin' up before the kill."

"You have no idea how close you are to the truth." The giant flashed Bronson a shark's grin and stuffed his gun in his pants.

Helplessness and dread squeezed Bronson's gut. He bit into his sandwich and glared at their captors.

When Bronson had finished eating, the giant said, "Now listen very carefully. Linda will be fine as long as you do what I say. Do I make myself clear?"

Bronson nodded.

The giant reached into his jacket pocket and retrieved a set of red flex-cuffs. Bronson recognized the type. He'd always liked them because they slipped on easily and seemed almost impossible to get out of. Now he wasn't so sure he liked them after all.

"Turn around and put your hands behind your back."

Bronson did. He felt the snap of the cuffs around his wrists and a tug tightening them.

"We're going for a little trip," the giant said. "If you give me any problems and I'm not back in the room in a reasonable amount of time, Jack will shoot Linda. He won't kill her, but the pain she'll suffer will make her wish she were dead."

"No need to hurt her. I'll go with you."

The giant led Bronson outside and down a stairwell that opened directly onto the parking lot. The darkness of night prevented him from learning anything about the motel's location. The giant stopped in front of a gray Nissan Altima and opened its trunk. "Get in."

Bronson climbed in. His world went even darker when the giant slammed the lid shut.

He tried to sort through the recent events, but his thoughts kept returning to the same question. *Why are they keeping me alive?*

FORTY-NINE

Although Bronson couldn't accurately predict the amount of time he'd spent in the trunk, he estimated it to be somewhere between three and four hours. His joints screamed with pain and there wasn't an inch that didn't feel wretched. Relief swept over him as he felt the car stop. Seconds later, the trunk lid popped open.

As he climbed out, the fresh air hit him like a slap, and he welcomed it. From the looks of things, he was on a well-lit farm. The ranch house, a typical rectangular structure with a two-car garage, stood to his left. A two-story red barn with white trim was to his right. Two four-story high silos flanked the barn. A lone structure displaying a sign that read *Custom Barbeques* hung above its door. Rolling hills completed the setting. Under different circumstances, the peaceful, tranquil scene would have soothed Bronson like a lullaby. Instead, it set his pulse racing.

The car door opened and Linda slid out. Jack followed. Bronson breathed a sigh of relief. At least they were still together. One way or the other, he'd get them out of this mess.

"Quit admiring the scenery and get moving," the giant told Bronson as he poked him in the back.

Much to Bronson's chagrin, the man led him toward the barn, away from the house, away from electricity and a possible phone. Bronson slowed his pace so that Linda and Jack, who were slightly behind them, could catch up. "Are you all right?"

She looked at Bronson through fearful eyes and nodded.

He gave her a reassuring smile. She looked away, and he wished he could promise her safety. He also thought of Carol and prayed she was oblivious. He didn't want her hurting.

As they walked past the Custom Barbeques building, Bronson caught a glimpse of several barbeque pits in various stages of completion. Not too many places specialized in custom barbeques. Perhaps this would give him a hint as to their whereabouts.

A little way past the business stood the barn. It smelled musty and only a single bulb lit its interior, casting eerie shadows. An assortment of tools ranging from rakes to hoes and shovels rested against a wall. The two empty stables were stacked with bales of hay. Wood, in all sizes and shapes, laid haphazardly on the floor to his right.

The giant shoved Bronson toward the first stable. "Take the hay bales and stack them over there." He pointed to the area outside the stable.

"That's kind of hard with these cuffs."

The giant punched Bronson in the stomach. A small whoosh escaped him as the air shot out of his lungs. He staggered forward, regained his balance, and glared at the giant.

"Nobody likes a smart-ass," the giant said.

Bronson remained quiet. He had learned his lesson.

"Turn around."

Bronson pivoted and felt the cuffs eased off. He brought his arms forward and rubbed his wrists. If felt good to be out.

"Get to work."

Bronson glanced at the tools, lingering on the pitchfork. He could accidentally drop it and when he picked it up—

"Just your hands, Wise Guy," the giant said.

Bronson opened the stable gate. Four bales rested on the floor, with three more stacked on top. He heaved as he raised the first bale. It weighed less than he anticipated but more than he could handle in his weakened condition.

By the time he'd removed the top three bales, sweat ran down his face and stained his shirt. He stopped to catch his breath. From the window he could see the beginnings of dawn.

Another day as a hostage. Another day without Carol.

"Get to work."

Bronson bent down and picked up another bale. Once he had removed two of them, he could see the outlines of a trap door. As he raised the last bale, his fears materialized. They were going to be prisoners in a basement on this isolated farm.

Nobody would ever think of looking for them here.

FIFTY

BRONSON RAISED THE TRAP DOOR to reveal a set of plain, wooden steps. The giant twisted Linda's arm behind her, pushing it slowly up toward her shoulder. She let out a yelp. "Step away from there," the giant said. "If you try anything, I'll break her arm." He pushed it up further to show he meant business. Linda let out another cry.

Bronson raised his hands. "No need to frighten her. I'll behave." He stepped away, a feeling of helplessness engulfing him. He watched as Jack descended the stairs. He must have flipped on a switch, as the entire area lit up.

The giant released Linda, grabbed his gun, and pointed it at Bronson. He looked at Linda and said, "You. Down the stairs."

A few seconds later, just about the time Linda should have reached the bottom, she let out a stifled scream. Bronson felt his heart do aerobic loops in his chest, but he forced himself to remain still.

"Ready," Jack said from down below.

"You're next," the giant said.

Once Bronson descended, he realized why Linda had screamed. The entire area had a shine to it that reminded him of a hospital. On the stark white wall facing him hung sets of tools: picks, axes, saws, and various knives, all crusted with dried blood. Before him stood a stainless steel table equipped with hand and foot cuffs. Four steel poles with chains and cuffs hanging from each had been placed at each of the table's corners. Crusted blood covered the floor where clots had flowed to a drain, giving the place the odor of death. Two self-standing iron cells were placed at opposite ends of the room. Each cell contained a plastic bucket and a crumpled bed sheet. Linda had already been locked inside one.

"What do you think of it, Bronson? This is home, sweet home." The giant's eyes sparkled as he spoke.

A chill covered Bronson's body. He ignored it and stared at the giant.

The giant threw back his head and laughed, a growl that sounded menacing. "Too frightened to speak? That's okay. It's better to save your vocal cords so you can use them to scream." He laughed again, sending another chill racing through Bronson. "Go to your room now."

Bronson made a move toward Linda's cell. The giant grabbed his arm and yanked him in the opposite direction. "We were told to keep you separate."

Bronson stepped into the empty cell and heard the clink of the lock.

"Don't know how long you'll be here. It depends," the giant said.

"On what?" Bronson was surprised to hear how dry his voice sounded.

"I'll let you figure that one out. In the meantime, the boss wants me to explain some of these gadgets so you'll know exactly what's going to happen. First of all, Linda's role in this."

Her head snapped up at the mention of her name.

"You're going to watch Bronson die and realize the same thing will happen to you unless you do everything you're told. Now don't get your hopes up, because either way, you'll end up dead. But one way you get a fast, painless death. The other way..." He cocked his head. "Well, you'll see."

He turned to Bronson. "Let me begin the tour." He pointed to the saws, knives, and other odd-looking instruments on the wall. "The boss is very handy with those tools. He uses them to cut your ears off, then your toes, and then your fingers, one at a time. He'll castrate you next. Then, see these gadgets here? They're used to pull your eyeballs out, but normally that's not until the end. He wants you to see what's happening to you. That's why there are mirrors." He pointed to the ceiling.

Bronson looked up at the mirrors and back down at the giant. By now Linda had dropped to the floor, her knees drawn tight up against her. She covered her ears and gently rocked.

"These poles here, your arms and legs are strapped to them. See how they move away from the table?" He pressed a button and the poles slowly shifted position. "Eventually, all this stretching will rip you apart. Then..."

Bronson stared at the giant, but his mind recalled Carol's gentle touch. Her lovely face, her sweet lips. He heard his grandkids' innocent laughter. He recalled his daughters as little girls, giggling, playing. Then as older children who grew into beautiful, rebellious teens, and finally blossomed as women. He held on to the cell bars so tightly, his hands turned white. He released the bars and forced in a deep breath.

"Those are just some of the things the boss wants you to think about while you await his arrival. Sweet, huh?" The giant gave another bloodcurdling laugh. "So tell me, oh Mighty Bronson, have you figured it out?"

Bronson looked him in the eyes. "It's Carrier, isn't it? He's still alive."

The giant smiled.

FIFTY-ONE

BRONSON WATCHED AS THE giant went up the stairs and closed the trap door behind him. Jack sat on the stainless steel table, produced a pornographic magazine from somewhere, and began looking at it.

Linda continued to rock. Bronson went to the back of his cell and flopped down on the floor. Might as well rest. He would need all the strength he could muster.

A NOISE WOKE HIM UP. Bronson bolted to his feet, half hoping this past experience had all been a nightmare, realizing it wasn't. Missing Carol, thinking of Carol, praying she wouldn't know he was in danger so she wouldn't worry. He stepped to the front of the cell and watched the giant descend the stairs.

"I'm driving into town. I'm taking food orders," the giant said.

"I'm cravin' a big juicy steak from Outback or Logan's Roadhouse," Bronson said.

"Don't be an asshole. This is breakfast."

"Pancakes from Village Inn? Or one of those skillet breakfasts from Denny's? And oh yes, a big cup of coffee, three sugars, and lots of cream." He smiled and nodded at the giant and silently cussed him.

The giant threw him a finger and turned to Linda. "And you? What do you want?"

She barely raised her head and shook it. The giant left,

leaving Jack as the bodyguard. Bronson waited for what he thought was five minutes, long enough to make sure the giant had really gone. He wished they hadn't taken his watch away.

"I need to use the bathroom," he said.

Jack looked up from the magazine. "That's what the bucket's for."

"I figured as much," Bronson answered. "But we don't have any toilet paper. Your boss would sure get upset if we both got sick from lack of hygiene."

Jack sat up straighter.

"Come on. What would it hurt? It's just two rolls of toilet paper. One for Linda and one for me." Bronson moved to the back of the cage and sat on the floor, his back against the bars.

Jack frowned, set the magazine down, and left.

As soon as he heard the trap door close, Bronson took the shower curtain ring out of his pocket, unsnapped it, and pulled the ends out. He inserted the end in the cell lock and jiggled it. The lock didn't open. He tried the other end with the same results.

Linda's head came up. She watched him with interest.

Bronson ignored her and continued jiggling. *Come on, come on. You've picked harder locks before. Do it. Do it.* He moved the ring back and forth, sideways, up and down, willing the lock to open.

He stopped, pulled the ring out, took a deep breath, and looked at it. Then he studied the lock.

"Why are you wasting time? Put it back in there. Open the cell." Linda gripped the bars.

A hammer—that's what Bronson needed. If he could just pound the metal ring into an end that resembled a power pick he might succeed. He didn't have a hammer, but his shoes had steel toes. Maybe that would work. He sat on the floor, took off his shoe, and began to pound the ring. Over and over.

After a time, he heard another noise. Someone was opening the trap door.

The speed of Bronson's reactions would have humbled Superman. Within seconds, he pocketed the curtain ring, slipped his shoe back on, and lay on his back. He kicked the cell door with the soles of his feet.

Jack's voice carried down to them as he descended the stairs. "Hey! Hey! What's going on down there?"

Bronson continued to kick, but stopped when he could see Jack. The smaller thug pulled his gun and pointed it at Bronson. "Stop that!"

"Why? I'm only exercising. Have you tried this? It does wonders for your leg muscles." He stood up. "So did you bring the tissue?"

"Get to the back of the cell and sit down. How stupid do you think I am?"

Very, Bronson thought, but kept the comment to himself. Instead, he shrugged, sat down, and watched Jack shove a new roll of toilet tissue through the ten-inch square opening designed to pass small items to the prisoners.

"Go ahead," Jack said.

"Go ahead what?"

Jack leaned against the table and folded his arms. "Go ahead and use the bucket."

Disgust encompassed Bronson as he realized Jack would get his thrills by watching him. Bronson glared at him as he unbuckled his belt. Linda's eyes widened. She turned her back.

BRONSON ESTIMATED THAT two hours had elapsed before the giant arrived carrying two plain white bags. Either they were quite a ways from the closest city or he had run other errands in town. Without a word, the giant shoved one of the white bags through the open area between the bars.

Bronson looked at the bag. No logo on it. Maybe the napkins inside would give him a clue. He peeked in the bag and pulled out a bacon, egg, and cheese sandwich, the type that usually came from a Ma-and-Pa–type restaurant. Bronson preferred that to a fast-food place or a chain restaurant, but it did nothing to tell him where he was.

He reached into the bag for the coffee. At the bottom of the bag, he saw several packets of cream, sugar, ketchup, and mayonnaise. He fixed the coffee and took a sip. It felt good going down.

He took out the two packets of ketchup, realized nobody was watching him, and pocketed them. He spread the mayonnaise on his sandwich and began to eat.

FOR THE NEXT THREE DAYS, Bronson grasped every opportunity to pound the shower curtain ring into shape. He'd hit it with his shoe, and then rub it on the concrete floor to make it thin enough to go into the cell lock. Occasionally, he used the cell bars to shape the end. By the fourth day, he felt ready and eager to try it. His chance came the next day.

As usual, Jack kept watch while the giant did whatever he did. Today, however, the giant lingered for a moment. "Hey, Bronson, I got news for you. Carrier called and guess what? He's feeling much better. He told me to tell you he's eager to start chopping you apart. He'll be here any day—maybe even today." His gloating laugh filled the room and chilled Bronson's bones. "How's that for good news?"

Jack's face brightened. "That's great, Ranger." He looked at the prisoners. "What do you think?"

Bronson felt as if he'd swallowed broken glass. The need

to open the lock filled him with urgency that verged on obsession. He gripped the bars and stared at their captors.

Jack giggled like a fifth-grader as he followed Ranger up the stairs. His mocking laughter echoed in Bronson's brain. As soon as they slammed the trap door shut, Bronson slowly counted to ten. Then he retrieved the U-shaped curtain ring. It now resembled a screw driver on one end and a hook on the other.

Linda stood up. "Hurry, Bronson. Get us out of here."

Bronson slipped the tool he had shaped into the lock and manipulated it, hoping to release the locking mechanism. It made a sound like a ball bearing dropped into a garbage disposal. The clatter seemed to stretch into eternity, but the noise stopped after what was probably just a few seconds. Bronson pushed the door and it opened.

Linda gasped and placed her hand over her mouth as though stifling a scream.

Bronson walked to the far wall, choosing the proper knives, ignoring the crusted blood on them.

"What are you doing? Get me out of here." Linda grasped the bars and shook them.

Bronson chose two butcher knives with blades large enough to do damage but small enough to carry in his jacket pocket. "I'm going to ask you to do somethin' you won't like, but you've got to trust me on this, okay?"

She nodded.

"I'm going to unlock the door, but you're to stay inside."

"No!"

Bronson put his finger to his lips. "Shhh. Listen." He inserted his homemade device into the lock on Linda's cell and jiggled it. "Jack should come back just about any minute now." The door opened. A step closer to freedom, but still miles away. "I'm going to stand behind the stairs and grab him as he comes down. I want you to make noise, create a disturbance, draw attention to yourself, and away from my empty cage. Can you do that?"

Before she could answer, he heard the trap door open. His heart jumped to his throat as he rushed to the area behind the stairs. He wished he'd had enough time to plan his strategy.

FIFTY-TWO

As BRONSON RAN TO HIDE, he heard Linda cry out behind him. "I can't stand it anymore. Get me out of here. Get me out of here!"

He reached the back of the stairs just as Jack came into view. Linda continued to wail.

"Shut up, lady. You're hurting my ears."

Bronson grabbed Jack and placed a knife against his throat. "I can hurt a lot more than your ears. Where's your gun?"

"I—I d-don't have it with me."

Bronson tightened his grip.

"I—I s-swear. I d-don't."

"How about the keys to the cells?"

"I-in my p-pocket."

Bronson signaled for Linda to join them. She approached hesitantly. "Frisk him," Bronson said.

"What?"

"Empty his pockets. All of them." He tightened his squeeze a bit more. "And you, if you move, I'll slice your throat."

Linda emptied the pockets and set the contents on the steel table.

Bronson eyed Jack's wallet. "Take out his driver's license and put it in your pocket."

She did.

"Check his ankles for a gun." Bronson hoped she'd find one. She didn't.

Bronson led Jack to a cell and shoved him in. "Strip down to your shorts."

Jack shook his head. "N-n-no. Wh-what are you going... to do?"

"Just strip. I want to make sure you don't have any concealed weapons."

"I—I d-don't."

"Do it, or I'll do it for you."

Jack removed his clothes. Bronson grabbed them and slammed the cell door shut. "May you rot in prison, and while you're here, you better not do anythin' to warn your buddy."

"I won't make any noise. Ranger is going to be pissed at me."

"My heart is breakin'." Bronson placed the crumpled clothes on the steel table. He handed Linda a knife. She shook her head. "You may need it. Take it."

She frowned but accepted it.

Bronson reached for the keys and pocketed them. "I'm going to need you to do everythin' I tell you. Don't question it, okay?"

She nodded.

"Thanks for your vote of confidence. Are you ready?"

Again she nodded.

Bronson climbed the stairs, Linda close behind him. When he reached the top, he stopped and listened. No sounds. He pushed the trap door open just high enough to peek out. Seeing they were alone, he swung the door further upward, so he could see all around. He climbed out and helped Linda. Without making any noise, he closed the trap door. He looked through a crack in the barn's slats, and immediately moved away. Ranger was leaning against the car, smoking a cigarette. Bronson risked another peek. He saw Ranger look at his watch and down the road, as though expecting someone.

Bronson's heartbeat accelerated. He had to get Linda out, but how could they get past the giant? The only way out meant facing him.

"I'm going out there," Bronson said.

"Are you crazy? Do you want to get yourself killed?"

"I'm hopin' I won't, but no matter what happens while I'm distractin' Ranger, you use that time to get away. Follow the road out, but don't walk on the road or its shoulder. If Carrier is headin' this way, you don't want him to see you."

Linda started to protest. Bronson looked at her, reminding her of her promise not to question him. She nodded, but looked grim. "You can't just walk out there. He'll shoot you and ask questions later."

"I'm sure that's true, but if he thinks I'm already wounded, he might get close enough for me to attack."

"What would make him think you're wounded?"

"These." Bronson pulled the two ketchup packets out of his pocket. He opened them and smeared his shirt with half a packet. Then he had Linda pour the rest of the ketchup on his hands. He plastered them over his shirt around the ribs. "How does this look?"

Her eyes widened. "From a distance you might get away with it."

"Good. That's what I wanted to hear. Pray that I give an award-winning performance."

"I am."

He reached for the door handle.

"Bronson."

He turned.

"Be careful…and thank you."

He winked and nodded once. "Don't forget to hightail out f here while he's busy with me."

She nodded.

"God bless you," Bronson said. He opened the door. Holding his rib cage with both of his ketchup-smeared hands, he staggered out.

FIFTY-THREE

RANGER DROPPED HIS CIGARETTE. Shit! How did Bronson get out? He looked seriously hurt. Ranger imagined Carrier's violent reaction, and froze.

Then he saw Bronson stagger and fall.

If he's dead—Ranger bolted toward Bronson. *That weasel Jack. I'm gonna kill him.* Ranger had told him over and over, "Watch Bronson. He's tricky. Don't fall for anything he does." A few steps from Bronson, he came to a sudden stop, listening to himself. *Don't fall for anything Bronson does.*

He took out his gun, cocked it, and pointed it at Bronson.

LINDA TRIED TO FOLLOW Bronson's instructions. As soon as the giant focused his attention on Bronson, she'd sneak out, head down the road—no, the side of the road, away from everyone's view. She'd find the main road and get help—provided someone would stop. After several days without bathing, she probably smelled like a skunk and looked like a scarecrow.

She watched through the barn slats. Bronson's idea seemed to be working. He staggered out and then fell. The giant rushed to his side—but then stopped and pointed a gun at Bronson.

Linda bit her fist to keep from screaming.

THROUGH SLITTED EYES, Bronson could barely make out Ranger's movements, but he saw enough to drench his hopes. Ranger had stopped, still too far away for Bronson to attack him. He had to narrow the distance. What had gone wrong? His insides tightened, waiting. Anticipating.

Linda threw the barn door open, stepped out screaming, and threw her knife at the giant. Ranger instinctively turned away. The knife fell several yards from its target.

Bronson sprang to his feet, bent down, and rammed him like a charging bull. The mighty shove sent the gun flying through the air and the giant hurtling backward. His head hit the pavement with a loud *thud*.

Ranger's eyes were glazed over, but still he managed to half sit up. He spotted the fallen gun and lunged for it. Bronson pulled the knife from the back of his belt and aimed at Ranger's body.

The knife found its target in Ranger's side, and he screamed. Bronson pulled out the knife and swept the gun toward himself, then grabbed it and pointed it at the giant. "On your feet."

"I'm wounded." Ranger held his side much as Bronson had when he'd staggered out of the barn. Blood leaked from the cut.

"Tough. Get up and head back to the barn."

Ranger glared at Bronson but struggled to his feet. Bronson frisked him. Once satisfied he had no other concealed weapons, he said, "Empty your pockets and drop everything on the ground. Back pockets, too."

"All I have is my wallet, a handkerchief, and a watch."

"Good. Drop them."

"The watch might break."

"No big thing. Where you're going, you won't be needing one."

When he finished, Bronson shoved him toward the barn. As the giant limped past Linda, Bronson said, "Linda, pick up everythin' and bring it to the barn. Get his I.D. and put in your pocket."

Linda nodded and headed toward the items scattered on the ground.

Bronson followed the giant into the barn, opened the trap door, and shoved him down the stairs. Ranger stumbled but regained his balance. Bronson kept well out of striking range as he herded the giant into the prison room.

"It wasn't my fault," Jack said as soon as he saw his partner.

Bronson and the giant ignored him.

"Ranger, you've got to believe me. Ask him!" Jack persisted.

Bronson forced Ranger to strip down to his shorts before locking him in the cell. Then he headed back to the stairs, where he could see Linda at the top. "Please bring everything down here," he said.

"I—I c-can't." She shook her head. "I c-can't g-go b-back here."

Bronson went up, relieved her of the things, went back down, and placed them on the steel table next to Jack's clothes. Then he went back up the stairs and closed the trap door behind him.

"I'm s-sorry," Linda quavered. "I tried to do what you said." She began to sob uncontrollably.

Bronson walked up to her, hesitated a moment, and drew her into his arms. Vaguely he wondered if any hidden surveillance video might find its way to Marshall's desk.

A shuddering spasm racked Linda's body and Bronson held her tighter. "Everythin' is going to be all right." He stroked her hair. "It's almost over."

She raised her head, eyes wet with tears. "You mean it's not over yet?"

Bronson shook his head. "We've got to get out of here."

"Why? Why can't we stay here until the police arrive?"

"Carrier is headin' this way."

Linda gasped and crossed her hands over her chest like a heroine in a silent movie.

Bronson considered his choices. They could go to the house, where there might be a telephone. They could wait there for the police, but if Carrier arrived first, they'd hide and Bronson could take Carrier by surprise. Or they could follow the road, but not knowing where they were or which direction to turn or even how far they'd have to travel, this option appealed less to Bronson.

As he reached for the barn door, he heard tires crunching on gravel. He opened the door a crack and saw Carrier pull in

FIFTY-FOUR

BRONSON CLOSED THE DOOR, took his hand off the handle, and signaled for Linda to remain extra quiet. He walked to the crack in the barn slats and looked out. He saw the garage door go up and Carrier pull the car inside. He got out, walked to the back of the car, opened the trunk, and retrieved something bulky that he swung over his shoulder.

Horror settled in Bronson's gut as he realized that Carrier's burden was a young woman's body. She looked either drugged or dead. The garage door closed, swallowing Carrier, the body, and the car.

"What's going on?" Linda whispered.

Bronson turned to face her. "We can't leave. Carrier has another victim. I'm going to the house. You wait here. If you see Carrier coming, hide. If anythin' happens to me, you know what to do. Down the road, stay hidden."

She nodded. "Please be careful."

"Hey, I've got a gun this time." He gave her a reassuring smile and double-checked the weapon.

She smiled back, but her lips trembled.

"Take care of yourself," Bronson said. He looked out the crack again but detected no movement around the house. He imagined Carrier would be busy with the poor woman he had kidnapped or killed. If so, Bronson could approach the house without alerting Carrier. He wished there were trees to block the view between the house and the barn and to provide some safety, but no such luck.

He took a deep breath, retrieved his gun, held it at the

ready, and opened the door. He kept low, out of a direct line of sight from the house's windows. When he got to the side of the house, he plastered his back against the brick wall next to the window and struggled to catch his breath. He looked down and noticed that the window was open.

He stuck his head around just far enough to catch a glimpse of the living room. A worn-out couch and a plain wooden coffee table occupied most of the area. A bookcase with a TV on top faced the couch. Rectangular, square, oval and round grills lay scattered in several parts of the room.

Bronson moved down to the next open window. A kitchen its countertops piled with dirty dishes and uneaten scraps of food. He looked down the hallway as far as he could see. Again, no sign of Carrier.

He ducked down and went to the next window. Even before he reached it, he heard Carrier's chilling voice. "There you are, all set to go."

He held his breath, then released it when he realized Carrier wasn't talking to him. He moved his head slightly to the right so he could see in. Carrier was tying the unconscious woman to the bed, her arms above her, her legs spread apart. Bronson lowered the gun, ready to shoot Carrier, then stopped. On top of the dresser he saw several butane tanks various sizes and shapes. Some more rested on the armoir even more by the door. One misfired round would blow the house apart. If he meant to shoot Carrier, he'd have to do it close range. Firing through a partially opened window was suicidal.

Carrier continued to talk to his victim as though she were awake. "After I'm through with you here, I'm going to take you to the basement, where I'll introduce you to Bronson. He's going to watch every single thing I do to you. I probably won't start on him until tomorrow so he'll have plenty time to think about what's going to happen to him. So what do you say? Come on, wake up. I'm anxious to get started."

Realizing Carrier probably wouldn't be looking out the window anytime soon, Bronson dashed for the barn. He reached it in record time and was careful not to make any noise when he opened the barn door.

"What's happening?" Linda's anxiety showed in her eyes.

"The woman Carrier's got in there is in trouble. I'm going to have to go inside. Once you see me get in, count slowly to sixty, then scream as loud as you can and keep screamin'. If everything is okay, I'll wave at you from the bedroom window. If three, four minutes elapse and you haven't seen me, get out. Hide. Can you do that?"

Linda's eyes widened with fear, but she nodded. "What do you plan to do?"

"He'll hear you scream and rush out to see what's going on. I'll be waiting for him." Bronson walked over to the woodpile and moved the wood around. He settled for a piece that resembled a baseball bat. He swung it. "This will do."

FIFTY-FIVE

BRONSON ENTERED THE HOUSE, headed toward the bedroom and readied himself.

The first scream he heard didn't come from Linda. It came from behind the closed bedroom door. Bronson prayed the woman was only frightened and not hurt. He wished he could rush in and surprise Carrier, but he knew Carrier wouldn't hesitate to shoot one of the tanks and blow everyone up. Bronson hoped the woman's screams wouldn't muffle Linda's.

"Keep screaming," he heard Carrier say. "I love it."

The woman moaned.

Carrier continued, "Tell me, have you ever had rough sex? You haven't, huh? Then you're in for a real treat. You're about to have some." A small pause followed. Then, "These scissors are very sharp and I'm going to use them to cut your clothes off. You won't be needing them anymore."

Bronson wet his lips as anxiety and anticipation engulfed him. *Come on, Linda, scream. What's taking you so long? Don't let me down.* He decided to wait one more minute, and if Linda didn't come through, he'd barge into the room. He knew he'd be taking a risk doing this. Carrier had scissors in his hands and could kill the woman before Bronson had the chance to shoot him. *Come on, Linda, scream.* He didn't want to be forced to rush Carrier.

"If I were you," Carrier continued from the other side of the door, "I'd stay real still. Wouldn't want to cut you up before I have to."

The woman let out a stifled cry, reminding Bronson of the sound of a trapped animal.

From a distance, he finally heard Linda scream. Relief flowed through his veins as he positioned the wood like a baseball player ready to hit a home run.

Linda screamed again.

"What the…" Carrier said. Bronson imagined him standing by the window, looking out.

The scream came again.

"Damn it! I'll be back for you," Carrier told his hostage.

Bronson heard him rushing toward the door and braced himself.

The door opened and Bronson swung. The impact of wood against flesh and bone sounded like smashing a watermelon.

A grunt of pain escaped Carrier's lips as he fell backward. The scissors dropped from his hand. For a second, he held Bronson's glare, then seemingly pain came with sharp, striking suddenness. His eyes bulged and he spat out blood. "You still…lose." He closed his eyes.

Only firm willpower prevented Bronson from striking again.

"Kill him!" the woman on the bed shouted. "Kill him."

Bronson felt for a pulse. He found one and silently cursed. He checked Carrier for a weapon, but found none. He looked around, retrieved the scissors, and set them and the wood down on top of the dresser. Then he turned to the woman.

She struggled against her bonds, fear in her eyes. Bronson caught a glimpse of himself in the mirror. His unruly hair and unshaven face gave him a threatening appearance. He probably didn't smell too good either. "It's okay," he said. "I'm here to help." He opened his hands and inched toward her. "I'm not going to hurt you. I'm going to cut you loose."

The woman relaxed. "Whoever you are, thank you."

He gave her a small smile. "My name's Harry Bronson and

I'm a retired detective from the Dallas Police Department. Excuse my appearance, but I've also been his hostage. Are you all right? Did he hurt you?"

It took her a few seconds to answer. "I think I'm okay. I'm just so afraid."

Linda screamed again. Bronson went to the window, opened it the rest of the way, and waved at her.

From behind him, he heard the woman say, "I'm Margaret Susans. He offered to buy me a drink, then the next thing I know, I'm tied up in bed. Who is he?"

Bronson reached for the scissors and began to cut her bindings. "His name is Benjamin Carrier. He's a notorious criminal who derives pleasure from killin' people."

Margaret gasped and her eyes filled with tears. "I came so close."

"I know, but it's over now. Soon as I cut you loose, I'm going to restrain him. When he comes to, he probably won' be in any shape to do anything, but I don't like any surprises." He took out his gun and set it on the bed close to his hands.

Margaret gasped.

Bronson ignored her and continued to cut the ropes, but even with the sharp scissors, the process moved slowly Carrier had done a perfect job tying her up.

CARRIER OPENED HIS EYES. Every inch in his body screamed with pain, but death would soon end his misery. He meant t take Bronson with him.

He had placed a gun under the bed and planned to use it t scare the bitch. Rapes were always so much more fun when the bitches were petrified beyond reason. He could see th gun tantalizingly close to him. Pain shot up his body as h inched across the floor toward it. He bit his lip to keep back gasp as he eyed Bronson. The dumb cop hadn't noticed him He was too busy freeing the bitch.

Carrier inched forward some more. Still Bronson wasn't paying attention to him. That fool.

He stretched his arm, wrapped his fingers around the gun, and pulled it out from under the bed.

FIFTY-SIX

A SHOT RANG OUT, IMMEDIATELY followed by another.

Linda's head snapped up as panic tightened her chest. What had gone wrong? She had seen Bronson signaling that everything was all right, but that was before the gunshots shattered the silence. She thought about running toward the house. Maybe Bronson needed help. But what could she do? He had told her to run away. She looked down the road and then back at the house.

She bit her lip.

BRONSON CONTINUED TO CUT Margaret's bindings, but kept constant watch on Carrier in his peripheral vision. He saw him creeping along like a snake, then stopping to assess his situation. When Carrier reached for the weapon, Bronson grabbed his gun. With the speed of a jaguar, he turned and fired at Carrier's head, twice. "Thanks for going for it, sucker."

He turned to Margaret. "Excuse me, ma'am."

Wide-eyed, Margaret nodded.

He pocketed the gun in Carrier's hand before checking for a pulse. This time he found none. Just to make sure, he put his index finger on top of Carrier's upper lip. No flow of air. He found that reassuring.

He went back to the window, hoping Linda would see him before she had too much of a chance to panic. Seconds later she stepped out of the barn. Bronson signaled for her to come inside the house.

His glance drifted from the barn and up toward the sky.

God, he had just killed a man. Not much of a man, but Bronson had set him up and killed him. At this moment, Bronson hated guns and all aspects of police work. He even hated himself. He closed his eyes. *Forgive me.*

He took a deep breath, turned to Margaret, and continued cutting her bonds.

BRONSON FOUND HIS CELL on top of the living room end table. He tried turning it on, but the battery was dead. He walked around the house and found a portable phone attached to the kitchen wall. He picked up the receiver and welcomed the dial tone. The first call went to Hoover.

"Hoover speaking."

What a great sound. Bronson smiled. "Hey, buddy."

"Bronson! Where are you? Are you okay?"

"Long story. The short of it is, I just killed Carrier."

"Whaat?"

"I'll explain, but first, does Carol know?" The pause that followed answered Bronson's question. "Damn."

"Ellen's been staying with her. Carol is a remarkably strong woman. Little Carol is petrified and I think her mother has been trying to stay strong for her sake."

"I want to see them."

"I figured as much. Where are you?"

"I have no idea. On an isolated farm somewhere maybe two or three hours from Custer. There's a separate structure with the sign Custom Designed Barbeques. Can't be too many of them. Maybe that will give you a clue." Bronson walked around opening drawers, looking for a bill or a piece of mail that would tell him where he was. He found a phone charger that might fit his cell. "Am I still wanted by the police?"

"No way. I called the FBI. Pissed off Marshall and Gorman something fierce, but the FBI has full jurisdiction. Carrier crossed at least one state line."

"And speaking of Marshall, I suspect he's dirty." Bronson picked up his cell and plugged in the charger. It fit.

"I know he is. At first, I wasn't sure. He told me he was working undercover."

"And you believed him?"

"I considered the possibility, but when Carrier's body went missing, I started to have suspicions. That's when I called the FBI. They found out that Marshall arranged for medical care."

Bronson set the cell down. "I don't understand why Marshall would willingly help a monster like Carrier."

"He didn't have a choice."

"Everybody has choices."

"Not if you're a policeman and you kill your critically ill wife. In cases like that, someone is bound to find out and either turn you in or blackmail you. Carrier went for the blackmail."

Bronson remained quiet, digesting the information. "That day at Clark's house, why didn't Marshall take the chance to finish Carrier off after I shot him? That would have ended the blackmail."

"Carrier didn't trust anyone. He left clues behind that would incriminate Marshall. Only way to guarantee they didn't become public was to make sure Carrier remained alive. That's the reason you didn't kill Carrier when you shot him at Clark's. He was wearing body armor, and I bet you anything Marshall gave it to him."

"Damn Marshall."

"I'm sure he is. The FBI arrested him and several other so-called police officers," Hoover said. "And now it's your turn. Fill me in."

"Linda and I were held prisoner by two thugs who are currently locked in a basement under the barn. By the way, on of them is wounded—not seriously—but he will need medical assistance."

"I'll make sure an ambulance gets there. Did they hurt you?"

"Nah, you know me. I'm tough."

"Yeah, like grass."

"Exactly, it gets trampled and springs back to life."

Hoover laughed. "Okay, you got me on that one. You deserve that victory."

Bronson smiled and looked at his cell. "My phone is chargin'."

"Good for you."

"Yes, definitely so. It's got a GPS unit."

"I've got you, buddy." Bronson could almost see Hoover's smile. "I'll get someone to track you down. We'll be there ASAP."

Bronson nodded. He could use the time to shower and shave, maybe even rest. "I'll be waitin'."

"How does Carrier fit into all this?"

Bronson filled him in. When he finished, he said, "That accounts for Linda and me, but not Eric."

"Don't worry about that. I found him. He and the baby are okay. But I still don't know who the main power behind the formula-stealing scheme is."

"Definitely not Doc Ponce or Mitch, but we'll take it one step at a time." Bronson flopped down on the couch. He could hear Linda and Margaret murmuring together even though the bedroom door was closed. "Linda needs a break. I'd like to help her and Eric reconcile. Can you bring him with you and drop him off at a local motel?"

"Will do my best," Hoover said, "but there's no guarantee. Is there anything you need?"

"Just for you to hurry."

Bronson hung up and dialed Carol's number. She answered on the first ring. "Harry, is this really you?"

It felt so good to hear her voice, even filled with anxiety. He had done it again. He had worried her. "It sure is, hon. I love you so much."

She began to cry.

FIFTY-SEVEN

IN LESS THAN AN HOUR, an assortment of cars arrived at the farm. A freshly shaved and bathed Bronson, wearing some clean clothes that were a bit too small, stepped out and watched Hoover approach. They stared at each other, then hugged. "Don't you ever scare me like that again," Hoover said.

"If it helps any, I was pretty scared, myself," Bronson said. "Did Eric come?"

Hoover nodded. "I told him why you wanted him to."

"What was his reaction?"

"He feels sorry for her, but that doesn't mean he's going to reconcile."

Bronson shook his head. "At least he came. That's somethin'."

Hoover pointed to a tall, thin man. "I want to introduce you to Schwein, the FBI agent handling the case." They headed toward him. He greeted Bronson with a smile and an extended hand.

Bronson shook it. "Carrier's body is in the back bedroom. Linda Randig and Margaret Susans are in the front. Linda's tryin' to comfort Margaret, who's still very upset. The prisoners are in the basement beneath the barn. There's a trap door inside the stable. Keys are on the steel table inside the basement. One of them has a minor stab wound that will need to be looked at."

Schwein pulled his gun and nodded. "Let's get to work." He signaled for the paramedics to follow him.

BRONSON AND LINDA WATCHED Margaret get in the passenger seat of a waiting car. The driver pulled off. Bronson turned to Linda. "They're takin' her to the hospital for a checkup. They want you to go, too, but I've cleared it with Schwein to make a small stop. Are you ready?"

She nodded. "The sooner I get out of here, the better."

Bronson led her to Schwein's car. "He said I could borrow it as long as I bring it back before he's finished here. We've got maybe two hours."

"Where are we going?" Linda asked once she'd settled inside.

"There's someone you need to talk to." Bronson drove off. Silence filled the ride. Linda couldn't imagine whom she needed to talk to. Probably more police. She didn't care. Her freedom felt so good she didn't bother to ask. She rolled down the window and sucked in fresh air.

Bronson pulled into a motel parking lot and led her up to a room upstairs. When he opened the door and she saw Eric her eyes filled with tears. She turned to stare at Bronson.

"Take your time, ma'am. I'll be out here waitin' for you." He closed the door behind him.

LINDA FACED ERIC. "Hello, son." A gamut of emotions, ranging from relief to anger to resentment to anticipation, flooded over her.

Eric crossed his arms and stared at her.

Linda's mind, like a meandering stream, raised question after question. *Why have you shut me out of your life? Why have you prevented me from seeing my grandson? Six months is a long time. Even a week, sometimes a day, makes a big difference at his age. He probably doesn't even remember me. Why did you keep him from me? What have I done to deserve this?* Aloud she said, "What happened?"

Eric frowned and looked away.

"Eric, talk to me. What have I done?" All the hurt she had bottled up peaked and exploded. Tears streamed down her cheeks. She cried for the loss of her parents, for Mitch's death, for the lost six months, and for all the fright and grief she'd endured in the last few days. She angrily wiped away the tears and turned her back to Eric.

"That would have worked once, but not anymore." Eric's tone spoke of the bitterness inside him.

Linda closed her eyes. She knew a time existed when he would have cared if she cried. He used to love her. He'd wanted her, needed her. Her heart ached for those simpler times. "What happened?" she asked again.

"As though you don't know."

The venom in his tone pierced her heart. *I don't,* she thought and felt too drained to say it aloud. "Tell me."

His eyes glowed like hot coals. "Before Dad—died—he told me."

"Told you what?"

The veins in Eric's temples stood out against his skin. He stepped forward, his shoulders rising, his chest puffing out.

"About the formula."

Linda gasped. "You know."

"Yes, I know." He curled his hands into fists.

"I'm sorry, Eric. But why are you mad at me? You should be angry with your dad."

"He told me why he was doing it, and that was you. He knew if he could no longer provide for you in the fashion you're accustomed to, you'd divorce him."

Linda held her breath. Had Mitch really told him that and Eric believed him? The pain of betrayal came with sharp, striking suddenness. She crossed her arms and took a step backward.

Eric's jaw stiffened and his eyes bored into hers. "How could you? Dad and Grandpa and Grandma are dead because of you and your selfish ways. You killed them." His voice rose an octave. "You killed Dad."

His words hit her like a straight shot just below her heart. She collapsed onto the bed. "And you believed him?" Her mind roared with white noise. He had tried and convicted her, and he hadn't even asked. He had assumed the worst and for that he had punished her.

And Mitch had committed the ultimate betrayal. Why had he lied? To justify the theft? Nothing she could say could ever mend the road that had been paved with lies and deception. Her pain grew and settled inward, like a burrow that had been closed. It would always be present underneath each smile, always behind each tear. She looked at Eric and held his gaze for a long time. Then, silently, she stood up and headed out.

"Mom?" she heard him say.

She closed the door behind her.

FIFTY-EIGHT

BRONSON DIDN'T ARRIVE at The Roost Resort until 7:15 that night. He had bummed a ride with Linda after Bronson, Hoover, and Schwein had found her camper in the storage shed behind the house.

As Linda and Bronson pulled into the campground, Bronson felt as happy as a puppy. His heart swelled with joy as he saw his motor home. It had taken him two days after Schwein and Hoover had arrived at the farm, but he'd finally made it back, safe, alive.

He helped Linda park her rig, this time two spaces down from them. Then he excused himself and dashed for his camper.

Even before he reached it, Carol swung the door open. Bronson stopped to stare at his wife. Her eyes sparkled with love, her extra-wide smile made her face look more round than usual. Bronson had never seen a more beautiful sight than Carol running to greet him. He opened his arms, drew her in, and felt her tremble. She pulled away and said, "Harry Bronson, I could kill you for putting us through hell."

He kissed her lips, and then held her for what seemed to be an eternity. He studied her face, memorizing and loving the little laughter wrinkles at the edge of her eyes. They hugged again, feeling their hearts beat against each other.

He finally looked up and saw Little Carol standing on the camper stairs, watching. Bronson signaled for her to join them.

Each night Mount Rushmore offered a show filled with

patriotic music and lights. They decided the three of them would attend. Afterward, they went to the Purple Pie Place, where Bronson enjoyed pie a la mode and coffee. Carol didn't even complain when he poured in three heaping spoonfuls of sugar.

THE NEXT DAY A KNOCK AT their door interrupted Bronson's family breakfast. Even before Bronson opened the door, he knew it would be Linda and he also knew what she'd say. He wondered what *he* would say. He invited her in and she joined them at the breakfast table.

Linda traced the rim of her juice glass and said, "I know you've gone way out on a limb for me and I have no right to ask you this, but I need this concluded. I have to know who's behind it all."

Carol pushed scrambled eggs around her plate. "My husband isn't a private detective, and he's not a police officer either." Her tone could have melted Alaska's Yentina Glacier.

"I know," Linda said, "but he knows what's going on. Maybe he could guide me. I don't know what to do, where to go." Her gaze shifted from Carol to Bronson. "How about it? I'll be willing to compensate you quite well for your time."

"What good is money if you're not alive to enjoy it?" Carol asked.

Bronson leaned back and pushed his plate away. "The FBI will be doin' their own investigation. You won't be allowed to interfere."

"But there must be something I can do."

"If I were you, I'd try to locate that game, Ella. I think once you find that, it'll answer most of your questions."

"How can I do that?"

"Someone hired Carrier and a couple of thugs to take you to Minnesota. I bet that's where your game is."

"Minnesota is a big state."

"Didn't you tell me that Mitch, prior to his death, became very interested in the computer games your uncle created?" He poured himself a second cup of coffee. Carol glared at him and he shrugged. Things had returned to normal way too fast. He'd behave. He only used two spoonfuls of sugar.

"Oh, God," Linda said, "you don't think Uncle Phillip is in any danger, do you?"

"I think whoever hired Carrier and the thugs is going to be a lot more careful. He's going to go after the game and not the person." He turned to Carol. "Do we have any more sweet rolls?"

She nodded and went to retrieve them. As soon as her back was turned, Bronson reached for the sugar bowl and put one more spoonful of sugar in his coffee.

"Daddy!" Little Carol said.

Bronson put his finger to his lips.

"I'll call Uncle Phillip so I can warn him."

"I wouldn't do that. I'd clear it with the FBI first."

She nodded. "Thanks for the advice. I'll get out of your hair now." She stood up as Carol returned with the sweet rolls, set them down on the table, reached for the sugar bowl, and put it away.

Bronson turned to his daughter. "Thanks loads."

Little Carol smiled.

Less than five minutes later, another knock on their door interrupted them. Bronson opened the door and let Linda in.

She sat on the couch and said, "I'm sorry. I know I shouldn't have, but I couldn't help it. I had to call Uncle Phillip. He was very concerned and distraught when I gave him the news. He has no idea if the game's at his house. He promised to check. Mitch had some games there he enjoyed playing."

"And if he finds it?"

"I'll drive there and pick it up."

Bronson shook his head. "I'd advise you to tell him to turn it over to the police."

"I will, as soon as I play the game. I have to see it. I have to know." Her cell went off. "It's Uncle Phillip." She opened the cell and said, "Uncle Phil?"

Bronson stood up and went to the kitchen where Carol was washing the breakfast dishes. "Hon?"

She looked up at him, her hands covered with soapsuds. "I know." The look in her eyes could have frozen the sun. "You're considering going with her."

"It'll be different this time. Carrier is dead and the FBI will have us wired and under surveillance the entire time. She's a headstrong woman and she's going to find a way to sneak out and go to Minnesota. I can't let her do that alone."

"Then go, but don't ever ask me to make this decision again. I'm not one bit happy about you going."

Bronson placed his hands on her cheeks and kissed her. "I love you."

"Go," she said, "before I change my mind."

FIFTY-NINE

"Now TELL ME EXACTLY what your uncle said," Bronson said. Linda drove and he sat in the passenger seat.

"Right after I called, he searched through the games for Ella. He told me he found it easy enough, but someone else, not knowing what to look for, probably wouldn't have."

Bronson looked at the speedometer needle. It rested somewhere between eighty and eighty-five. He knew Linda wanted to reach her uncle's as soon as possible, but speeding was never the right answer. "Statistics show that when a cop pulls you over for speedin', you'll lose more time than you might have gained from goin' too fast."

Linda shook her head and smiled. "Ever the policeman." She slowed down.

"Sorry. It's embedded in me."

"No need to apologize. That's why I asked you to come. I really appreciate you doing this."

"Strictly my pleasure, ma'am." This was what kept him going each day. He couldn't envision life without police work. "You were sayin' about your uncle?"

"When I told him what had happened, he worried that someone might be watching his house, waiting for us."

"What made him think someone is watchin' his house?" Bronson leaned over and checked the speedometer. It had climbed to almost ninety.

She slowed down again. "He said he didn't think anyone was watching, but he hadn't been looking before. He's concerned about me—us, I guess—and suggested we meet at his Lake City home."

"And Lake City is where?"

"Northwest of the Twin Cities, about an hour and a half drive. It's right on the Mississippi River, by Lake Pepin. The water there stretches for two miles and is twenty-five miles long."

It figures, Bronson thought as he looked out the window and saw yet another lake. The entire state of Minnesota seemed to consist of nothing but water—some small-sized ponds, others good-sized lakes. "What would make him think someone can watch his St. Paul home, but not his Lake City one?"

"He only closed the deal on the Lake City home a couple of days ago. He hasn't told anyone about it. That's why he suggested it. He'll make sure no one follows him there."

"What about a trackin' device?"

"I told him about someone putting one on my car. He drove his car into the garage and checked. He didn't find any."

Satisfied, Bronson leaned his head against the headrest and closed his eyes. He really should tell her to slow down.

THEY SPENT THE NIGHT at the first decent-looking motel they came across. Linda waited until Bronson's light went off, and then added half an hour just to be safe. She opened the attaché case the FBI had provided them with and took out the transmitters they were to wear once they reached Uncle Phillip's house.

Schwein had issued each of them a device, tested them to make sure they worked, and placed them in the case. Linda reached for the first transmitter, a flat box roughly an inch square that they were to tape to their chests. She turned the device over, removed the watch-size battery, and put the box back in its container. She did the same with the other one.

She closed the attaché case, wrapped the batteries in tissue paper, and flushed them down the toilet.

Uncle Phillip had always been so kind to her and had gone out of his way to make sure she and Bronson were safe. She had no intention of bringing the FBI and police crashing in on him for nothing. Besides, if anything went wrong, Bronson would protect her.

"WE'RE ALMOST THERE," Linda said and pulled in at a rest stop. "No offense, but I don't like people touching me, so I've already put on my recorder. I'll help you with yours." She took it out. Bronson raised his shirt and she taped the transmitter to his chest. "There, all set to go."

"Okay, guys," Bronson said. "We're wired and ready to head in. Hope you read us loud and clear."

Linda smiled. The guys wouldn't be anywhere around. By now they should have landed at the small airport at the city's outskirts. From there, they were to set up surveillance around Uncle Phillip's house, except they would be setting up at the opposite end of town. Once, alone with Schwein, she had given him the wrong address. She knew it wouldn't take long for them to figure out what she'd done, but maybe by then she'd have the game in her possession and be heading back to the research lab to return it to its rightful owners.

THE LAKE CITY HOME TURNED OUT to be located, just as Uncle Phillip had said, right across the Mississippi River, not far from the plaque that identified this as the place where Ralph Samuelson invented waterskiing. The house itself must have been constructed in the early 1920s, making it one of the newer homes in the neighborhood. In spite of its age, the place smelled new. The highly polished wood floors brought out the glimmer of the freshly painted egg-colored walls.

Uncle Phillip greeted them out in the driveway and escorted them in. Bronson had expected to see boxes stacked everywhere, but instead he saw a neat, fully furnished home. "I'd rather pay extra and have all the comforts when I walk in. I had a professional designer pick the furniture and equip the house with all it needs, right down to the silverware and pots and pans," Uncle Phillip said. He was tall and distinguished-looking, with impeccable silver hair. He handed each of them a cool glass of wine. Bronson would have preferred coffee.

They sat in the living room near an oversized window that overlooked Lake Pepin. Bronson periodically glanced out, watching each passing car, each pedestrian.

Linda finished her wine quickly and said, "Uncle Phillip, I'm really anxious to look at that game. Would you mind?"

Uncle Phillip frowned and stood up. He set his own glass down. "Very well, dear. I had hoped we could chat a little first. With the string of recent tragedies, I wanted to make sure you're doing well."

"I've learned that when death intervenes, you have to keep going." Linda looked around. "Where's the game?"

"Upstairs, close to the computer. Ready to play it?"

"You want me to play it now?"

"Sure, that way we can print out the formula. The guys at the pharmacy aren't interested in the game, after all." He winked. "Besides, I'm really curious as to what Mitch created." He pointed to the stairs. "Shall we?"

Bronson and Linda followed him.

The upstairs landing opened onto a foyer large enough to accommodate a sizeable computer desk and several bookcases. Uncle Phillip pointed to the two closed doors. "Those are bedrooms. Linda, I put you in this one." He pointed to the right. "It's more feminine. Detective Bronson, this one will be yours." He pointed to the other door. "Are you sure you don't want to take the time to settle in first?"

Linda shook her head. "I'm really anxious."

"I can tell." Uncle Phillip turned on the computer. While he waited for it to boot up, he removed a Thomas Kincaid painting and revealed a safe. He opened it and retrieved the game. He closed the safe door, returned the picture to the wall, and handed the game to his niece. "I believe this is what you're looking for."

Bronson immediately recognized the drawing on the box as the one Manuel had described to him. Linda looked at him and he nodded.

She opened the box and took out the disk. "Let's see what this is all about."

SIXTY

A HANDSOME COUPLE, holding hands, strolled down a street. A gang member stepped out from a building, another from behind a car. Two more came from the alley, more from behind them. Still more approached them from the front.

The couple turned around. They were surrounded. They stood back-to-back, ready to fight. One hoodlum produced a chain and swung it wildly. Another had a knife, others guns. Without any weapons, the couple seemed doomed, but the handsome hero didn't appear alarmed. He turned to his wife and said, "Tell me where you want to go and I'll whisk you away. We could even celebrate our first wedding anniversary there."

A tear glistened in Linda's eye. She and Mitch had gone to Disneyland, acted like kids, acted like lovers. She typed *Disneyland*.

The couple found themselves in a different neighborhood. Their previous success had earned them a small knife. A dog growled...

Bronson's cell went off. He looked at the caller I.D. "It's my wife. Guess I should have called her as soon as I got here. Excuse me." He stood up and flipped the cell open. "Hi, hon. We're here in Lake City. Everything's okay?"

He paused and smiled. "Listen, hon, let me call you right back....Yeah, I love you, too." He disconnected and looked at Linda and Uncle Phillip. "That was Carol. I guess after what happened, she's kind of concerned. Mind if I step outside and call her back? I'd like to take a closer look at the lake across the street anyway. Didn't I see a boat ramp and kids playing in the water?"

"That's a daily occurrence here, weather permitting," Uncle Phillip said. "Go ahead. Make your call and enjoy the view. I'll stay here with Linda in case she needs anything." He turned to his niece. "Is that okay with you?"

Linda nodded. "Of course. Please tell Carol hi for me."

Bronson nodded. "Will do. You need me, call me. I have all-waiting."

"Don't we all?" she said and waved goodbye.

As soon as Bronson stepped out, he noticed the place was thriving with activity. Kids and their dogs ran up and down the sidewalks. Young and old lovers strolled hand-in-hand. Dads and moms had picnics spread out. Several teens played energetic volleyball games.

Bronson whipped out his cell and punched in a speed-dial number. Hoover answered on the first ring. "Yo, honey. I love you, too."

"I always suspected as much." Bronson smiled. "You were sayin'?"

"Before I get into that, everyone over here is pissed off at you. Bronson, what do you think you're doing?"

Bronson searched his mind but came up blank. "I've no idea what you're talkin' about. Care to fill me in?"

"I'm talking about the transmitter. Why aren't either of you wearing them?"

"But I am—we are." He reached under his shirt, took out the device, opened it, and realized someone had removed the battery. Linda. "Shiiit! Battery's gone."

"Bronson—"

"I swear it wasn't me. It had to have been Linda, trying to protect her uncle."

"The address she gave Schwein is bogus. Where are you?"

Bronson looked at the name of the street, gave him the correct address, and scolded himself. He should have known she'd pull a stunt like this.

"I'll tell them and they'll send agents. Make sure nothing goes down before they get there. In the meantime, it look like you're on your own. Is everything okay?"

"Seems to be. Linda's still workin' on that game. Anythin else you need to tell me?"

"I've been checking on McGory and Stein, but mainly o Stein."

"And what did you find?"

"I think McGory is clueless, but Stein, I'm still not to sure about. I know that prior to being arrested, Marsha cleared Stein of any wrongdoing."

Bronson reached the edge of the lake. Children of all ag played in and out of the water. Waves lapped the beach, r minding him of the ocean. "Marshall cleared Stein? Th doesn't sound too promisin'."

"That's why I decided to do my own search."

"And?"

"And Stein is gone."

Bronson watched some kids frolicking in the water. Som one drove a red compact down the street very slowly. Brons strained his neck to keep an eye on the car. "Gone? Where He pivoted, heading back toward the house.

"I don't know, buddy. No one seems to know. Yesterd he walked out of his office, didn't tell his secretary anythin didn't talk to his wife or kids, just disappeared. Thoug maybe I'd better warn you, in case he shows up there une pectedly."

Bronson watched as the driver of the red car made U-turn and again slowly drove by Uncle Phillip's hous

taring at it. "Thanks, I'll be on the lookout." He hastened
is pace.

By now, the driver had parked across the street, his atten-
ion focused on the house.

SIXTY-ONE

As FAR AS BRONSON COULD TELL, the driver never saw him ap
proach. He remained sitting, staring at the house.

Bronson had his gun, but any one of these people coul
become innocent victims. He paused long enough to searc
for a fist-sized rock. He found one with no problem. H
picked it up, put it in his pocket, and approached the ca
from behind the passenger's side. The open front windo
provided easy access to the driver. Bronson leaned again
the car, looking in. "Somethin' I can help you with?" He ke
his right hand close to the rock.

The driver, a black-haired man sporting a scraggly bear
let out a startled gasp as he turned to look at Bronson. "Wh
What?"

"You seemed lost. I was wonderin' if I could help you
Bronson smiled, hoping to set him at ease. Just a friendly d
gooder trying to help out.

"Lost? Me? Oh, no. I was…" His eyes opened wide
"I see. This is your house and you're wondering what I'
doing."

"Somethin' like that."

"I love this house and saw the for-sale sign. I've bee
saving money for a down payment, but now I see the sig
gone. I thought maybe it fell down, or at least I hoped it ha
I parked here to see if it looked like anyone was home. I'
really sorry, mister, and I'm sorry I missed my chance to b
it."

"Keep lookin'. It may come back up for sale in a couple

months. Have a good day." He walked back to the house and let himself in. By the time he looked out the bay window, the driver had gone.

He climbed the stairs and found Linda still engaged in the game. "How's it going?"

She looked up at him and he noticed she had been crying. She said, "This game has taken me through a roller coaster ride of Mitch's and my life together, but I think I'm almost through."

Uncle Phillip sat next to her, keeping record of all of the procedures. He reached out and patted her hand. "You're doing great."

"I bet she is." Bronson shifted his gaze from Uncle Phillip to Linda. "I bet you could use a break just about now. Why don't you go downstairs and fix me a nice, warm cup of coffee?"

IN A WAY, LINDA RESENTED Uncle Phillip sitting next to her, recording all the information, some of it very private stuff. On the other hand, having him next to her helped. She hadn't yet gotten over Mitch's betrayal. Did he know Eric would turn against her? Had he done it on purpose? Why had he done it? All for money? These were questions no one could answer.

She heard the downstairs door open, which meant Bronson had returned. She heard him come up the stairs. She had wanted to be finished by the time he arrived, but realized she had set an impossible deadline.

Bronson must have read her thoughts, as he immediately suggested she take a break and fix him a cup of coffee. That wasn't exactly on her list of things-to-do-in-order-to-relax.

Bronson's cell buzzed. He looked down at it, as if reading a text message, and grinned. "That's Carol."

A sudden, unexpected wave of jealousy washed over

Linda. Bronson had such a warm, loving relationship with h
family. Hers had been reduced to a stupid computer game

Bronson walked over to the window behind the comput
desk and looked out. "About that coffee," he said.

Linda's nerves screamed with resentment. Sometimes l
could be so frustrating. Yet he hadn't really asked much
her. Just a simple cup of coffee. After all he'd done for h(
surely fixing one cup of coffee wouldn't hurt. Not meanir
to, she slammed her hands on the table and pushed the ch:
back so she could get up.

Uncle Phillip reached out and stopped her. His eyes pierc
Bronson's back. "How did you figure it out?" He took ou
gun and pointed it at Linda's head.

SIXTY-TWO

ᴠᴇɴ ʙᴇꜰᴏʀᴇ Uɴᴄʟᴇ Pʜɪʟʟɪᴘ asked the question, Bronson had
ᴇached inside his pants pocket. His right hand wrapped
round the rock.

Uncle Phillip said, "Put your hands up and keep them
here I can see them. I know you have a gun somewhere, so
ᴇep those hands high."

Bronson raised them, keeping both hands closed. His right
ᴀnd clutched the rock.

"Take your gun out and drop it."

Bronson lowered his left hand, using exaggerated move-
ᴇnts to make sure Phillip focused on it. He shifted his grip
ᴀ the rock to get it in perfect throwing position. Then he
ᴇrew it, hitting Phillip in the chest.

Phillip heaved as the air escaped his lungs. Bronson rushed
ᴇm and overpowered him. "See if you can find some rope
ᴀt I can secure him with until the FBI arrives," he told
ɴda. "Then you and I are going to have a long talk about
ᴀat you did."

Linda nodded and headed downstairs.

ɴɢ ᴀꜰᴛᴇʀ ᴛʜᴇ ᴀᴜᴛʜᴏʀɪᴛɪᴇꜱ had gone, Linda and Bronson sat
ᴛhe kitchen table. Linda stared at her coffee while Bron-
ɴ drank his. "I'm really sorry. I didn't think my uncle…"
ᴇ paused and swallowed hard. "Anyway, I'm very sorry."

Bronson glanced at her. He had bawled her out, and now
ᴛ bad for her. She looked so miserable.

"That text message you got, it wasn't from Carol, was it?"

Bronson shook his head.

"Who sent it?" Linda's expression reminded him of an un
wanted orphan.

He emptied his cup and poured another. "I had aske
Hoover to check on the names of the main shareholders
McGory and Stein Pharmaceutical. Hoover texted me th
your uncle held the largest share."

Linda shook her head. "I heard him tell the FBI he plann
to shop the formula around and sell it to the highest bidd
Why do that when he already owned most of the formu
through his shares with McGory and Stein?"

"Greed. If he sold the formula on his own, he'd get a l
more money than the shares would bring." Bronson sipp
his fresh coffee. "I'm sorry about your uncle."

Linda shrugged. "Seems I have a rotten family."

"If it helps any, your uncle asked me to tell you he nev
meant for you to find out that your parents and Mitch we
murdered. He thought you'd be able to understand accide
much easier. Get over the shock faster."

"How could I not find out? Didn't he hire Carrier to k
my parents and Mitch?"

"Not really. He hired Carrier to force Mitch to give him
formula. When Mitch refused, he killed your parents, kno
ing how close your husband was to them. His logic was, '
kill everyone you love until you give me what I want.'"

Linda nodded. "That's when Mitch came up with the ga
thing, right?"

"Precisely. The next time Carrier approached your h
band was that day at your parents' roof. By then, he kn
Mitch had created the game and knew you could just as ea
decipher it. Carrier pushed him off the roof and then cal
your uncle to tell him Mitch was dead. Immediately, Ph
lip told him his job was over. He'd decided to play the l
a-nice-uncle card and invite you to visit him, supposedly

comfort you while you mourned. Once you were with him, he'd find the game, you'd play it, and he'd get the formula."

"What went wrong?"

"Carrier found out how much the formula was worth. He demanded half of the sale money. He took it on himself to terrorize you and lead you to Minnesota. Your uncle had no control over him."

Linda frowned. "He shouldn't have gotten involved with someone like Carrier. How in the world did he even know such a man?"

"Remember, your uncle is a computer geek. Seems he hacked into the NCIC—"

"The what?"

"The National Crime Info Computer. He hacked into that system, got a name of someone he could reach, and that person led him to Carrier. Your uncle's main mistake was not realizing how dangerous Carrier was."

"He's not my uncle." Venom interwoven with contempt spat out. She shrank down in her chair. "At least not anymore. Who would have thought? My favorite uncle, my husband, conspiring. Now one's dead and the other's bound for death row—and my parents, both innocent victims of their greed." Her once sparkling eyes housed a darkness and grief Bronson could barely comprehend. "I'd like to volunteer for the Witness Protection Program." Her finger traced the rim of her coffee cup.

Bronson almost smiled. "People don't volunteer for that. It's more like you're drafted into it. Why would you want to go into Witness Protection, anyway?"

"Everyone I've ever loved has betrayed me. If I went away and started all over again—a new name, a new face—maybe I'd find someone who could love me. Maybe."

"There's always your grandson, Bradley."

"He's a year and a half. So innocent. What does he know? Will he grow up to hate me, too?"

"Do you ever bowl?"

Linda looked up at Bronson, her eyebrows furrowed. "What?"

"The sport, bowling. Ever do that?"

She frowned. "Yeah, a couple of times. What does that have to do with anything?"

"I like bowlin' because to me, it's the perfect sport. It always gives its participants a second chance." He took a sip of coffee and thought about adding a third spoonful of sugar. He decided against it. Carol wouldn't like that. "Before Eric left, he gave me his phone number and told me to give it to you." He handed her a folded piece of paper.

Time ticked away while she stared at it. A small smile found its way to her lips. "Do you think Eric would like to go bowling with me?"

SIXTY-THREE

SIXTEEN MORE MILES, that's all. Just sixteen more miles and he'd reach The Roost Resort.

He spotted a motorcyclist on the shoulder taking something out of his saddlebags. As Bronson drove past him, the cyclist waved. Bronson waved back and kept going. Normally, bikers ignored him. Bronson shrugged and his thoughts turned to Carol.

Tonight she'd be performing onstage and just as he had promised, he'd be there to see the show. He couldn't wait to wrap his arms around her. If he went a little faster, they'd be together sooner. Automatically, he checked the rearview mirror. He saw the motorcyclist approaching at high speed. It figured. Bikers were always reckless, always weaving in and out of traffic.

Bronson slowed down. Let him pass, get away.

Two minutes later, the Harley Davidson zoomed past, but instead of continuing, the driver slowed down and kept even pace with Bronson. He signaled for Bronson to pull over.

Bronson eased off the gas pedal. Now what? The cyclist definitely wasn't a cop. Why was he asking him to pull over? Good thing he hadn't put his gun away. Bronson slowed down, pulled off onto the shoulder, and stopped the car. He watched the motorcyclist dismount and approach him.

He remained in the car, alert, the engine running, his hand ready. The cyclist removed his helmet and Bronson recognized him. The Slug. Jim Babel, Little Carol's soon-to-be ex. Bronson killed the engine, opened the door, got out, and faced him.

"Hello, sir." Jim shook his head sadly. "I know what you think of me. I don't blame you."

"What do you want?"

"I want to treat you to a cup of coffee."

Bronson crossed his arms and stared at him.

"Come on, Mr. Bronson. What would it hurt? You can't possibly turn down a free cup of coffee."

He had a point. "Follow me to the Purple Pie Place."

BRONSON AND JIM SAT in the back room where customers who wanted more than ice cream usually sat. A cup of coffee and a huge slice of warm apple pie awaited Bronson. Jim had a float. "What's all this about?" Bronson asked once the waitress left.

"I messed up." Jim looked at Bronson, his eyes searching for compassion.

"Yeah, no shit." Bronson took a bite of his pie, set the fork down, pushed his food away, and glared at his son-in-law.

Jim looked down. His shoulders were stooped, his head slightly bowed. "All these days without Carol I've been miserable. I've realized how much I love her. She worships you, Mr. Bronson. If you asked her to give me another chance, she'd do it. Please ask her, not for my sake, but for hers. I know I can make her happy. She loves me. She really does. I'm asking—begging—for your help."

Bronson took a sip of coffee and set it down. Somehow today, right now, it didn't taste all that great. "Convince me."

"She's no longer Carol Bronson," Jim continued. "Her name's Carol Babel." He played with the straw in his float, bobbing it up and down. "I really messed up and I'm real sorry. I ignored her. All I wanted to do was ride my bike. We became nothing more than roommates. Then she walked out

'That's okay,' I told myself. I didn't realize then how much I would miss her and how much I love her. We can work this out. I can finally be the kind of husband she deserves. All I need is a second chance. How about it?" Jim's eyes filled with hope and anticipation.

Bronson looked at him and crossed his arms.

"If you do this for me, I promise to spend the rest of my life making her happy. I love her and I know she loves me. I've talked to your wife and she told me Carol's miserable, but even though her mom has begged her to call me, she refuses. She's proud and stubborn—no offense—just like you. No matter how badly she's hurting, she'll kick me out. We're both miserable and you're the only one who can help." He glanced down and lowered his head. "I don't know what else to say."

The silence between the two stretched.

Jim slowly looked up at Bronson, nodded, pushed his float away, and stood up.

"Wait," Bronson said. "Have you ever been bowling?"

* * * * *

REQUEST YOUR FREE BOOKS!

2 FREE NOVELS
PLUS 2 FREE GIFTS!

WORLDWIDE LIBRARY®
Your Partner in Crime

YES! Please send me 2 FREE novels from the Worldwide Library® series and my 2 FREE gifts (gifts are worth about $10). After receiving them, if I don't wish to receive any more books, I can return the shipping statement marked "cancel." If I don't cancel, I will receive 4 brand-new novels every month and be billed just $5.24 per book in the U.S. or $6.24 per book in Canada. That's a saving of at least 34% off the cover price. It's quite a bargain! Shipping and handling is just 50¢ per book in the U.S. and 75¢ per book in Canada.* I understand that accepting the 2 free books and gifts places me under no obligation to buy anything. I can always return a shipment and cancel at any time. Even if I never buy another book, the two free books and gifts are mine to keep forever.

414/424 WDN FEJ3

Name _____ (PLEASE PRINT) _____

Address _____ Apt. #

City _____ State/Prov. _____ Zip/Postal Code

Signature (if under 18, a parent or guardian must sign)

Mail to the **Reader Service:**
IN U.S.A.: P.O. Box 1867, Buffalo, NY 14240-1867
IN CANADA: P.O. Box 609, Fort Erie, Ontario L2A 5X3

Not valid for current subscribers to the Worldwide Library series.

Want to try two free books from another line?
Call 1-800-873-8635 or visit www.ReaderService.com.

* Terms and prices subject to change without notice. Prices do not include applicable taxes. Sales tax applicable in N.Y. Canadian residents will be charged applicable taxes. Offer not valid in Quebec. This offer is limited to one order per household. All orders subject to credit approval. Credit or debit balances in a customer's account(s) may be offset by any other outstanding balance owed by or to the customer. Please allow 4 to 6 weeks for delivery. Offer available while quantities last.

Your Privacy—The Reader Service is committed to protecting your privacy. Our Privacy Policy is available online at www.ReaderService.com or upon request from the Reader Service.

We make a portion of our mailing list available to reputable third parties that offer products we believe may interest you. If you prefer that we not exchange your name with third parties, or if you wish to clarify or modify your communication preferences, please visit us at www.ReaderService.com/consumerchoice or write to us at Reader Service Preference Service, P.O. Box 9062, Buffalo, NY 14269. Include your complete name and address.

WWLI1B

inside and a wide steel structure by two stairways, who are evidently locked in a basement under the barn. By the way, and